Amateurs

Amateurs

a novel

Dylan Hicks

Coffee House Press
Minneapolis
2016

Book design by Rachel Holscher

Coffee House Press books are available to the trade through our primary distributor, Consortium Book Sales & Distribution, cbsd.com or (800) 283-3572. For personal orders, catalogs, or other information, write to info@coffeehousepress.org.

Coffee House Press is a nonprofit literary publishing house. Support from private foundations, corporate giving programs, government programs, and generous individuals helps make the publication of our books possible. We gratefully acknowledge their support in detail in the back of this book.

Library of Congress Cataloging-in-Publication Data
Hicks, Dylan.
Amateurs / Dylan Hicks.
pages ; cm
ISBN 978-1-56689-432-6
I. Title.
PS3608.I2785A43 2016
813'.6—dc23
2015030138

Acknowledgments
Thanks to Anitra Budd, Caroline Casey, Ben Findlay, Chris Fischbach, Amelia Foster, Molly Fuller, Carla Valadez, and all at Coffee House Press. Liz Van Hoose provided exceptionally perceptive, intelligent, and creative editorial direction. This book, I decided, didn't require Herculean research efforts, but I'm grateful to Kurt Froehlich, Jean Mohr, Benjamin Jones, Molly Pfohl Rand, Michael Tortorello, and others for sharing their expertise along the way. Thanks also to the novelist and anagramist Ed Park and to the artist Carolyn Swiszcz. And everything is better because of my wife, Nina Hale, and our son, Jackson.

Printed in the United States of America
23 22 21 20 19 18 17 16   1 2 3 4 5 6 7 8

for Nina and Jackson

Amateurs

Prologue

April 1972

Marion straddled a vinyl-strap patio lounger, absently revising a metaphor about circuit breakers while her mother, Phyliss, trimmed an azalea bush in the Japanesque garden. Phyliss had been working unassisted for several hours (Marion felt a resistible pull to help), and the garden—with its Japanese maple and ornamental pines, its stone lantern and stepping stones, its rock beds, pools, and mossy little bridges—was reviving. Phyliss had majored in art history, and it was sometimes said that she applied that training to the arrangement of her garden and the glass-doored family room that looked out on it. It depressed Marion to think of the largely unused degrees, thwarted ambition, and undertapped potential of her mother's generation of women, potential so undertapped in this case that it was hard for Marion to imagine her mother (bibliophobic, susceptible to insipid prettiness) as a museum curator or a professor of art history, hard even to imagine her as a critic for a lightly circulated daily. But perhaps, in a fairer world, Phyliss still wouldn't have been drawn to such paths.

"I would bottle it," Phyliss said.

"What's that, Ma?" For a moment Marion thought she was being asked to suppress her uncharitable thoughts.

"This is a gorgeous day. I'd like to bottle it."

To hint that a warmer day ought to be bottled, Marion reached for her black crochet poncho, fringed and redolent of smoke, but she didn't otherwise dispute the day's gorgeousness. The willows on the Crennels' two acres were losing their wintry gold, and the elms, red oaks, and birches were budding or about to. A few clouds smeared the cornflower sky. Marion sipped her spiked Dr. Pepper, shaking the highball glass so she could enjoy the sound of ice cubes and rejuvenated carbonation.

Her anger over unused degrees wasn't strictly retroactive. Her own English degree from Northwestern had won her a secretarial position at a literary agency, which in the end was less appealing than the Marshall Field's sales position her mother landed after college; at least Phyliss's gig came with a discount. Marion had initially trusted, despite her professed mistrust of the system, that once dues were paid and her taste and intelligence recognized, she would be given a shot as an agent. Four years on the payroll cast opportunities for advancement in a growingly chimerical light. One Tuesday she didn't come back from lunch.

She heard breeze-blown voices from the fourth hole, then an Oldsmobile Ninety-Eight Regency coming up the snaking driveway. "Here's your father," Phyliss said. He took the stone path to the kidney-shaped patio. Corinne Wrightson trailed behind him in apparently borrowed tennis whites, her encased racket strapped around her chest. She was visiting for a week, home from Berkeley.

"Look who I found," George said.

"I know I'm early," Corinne said. "I thought we could—"

A jet briefly shadowed the patio on its way to O'Hare. When it passed, George turned to Corinne. "Fix you anything? G and T?"

"Jorge, she doesn't want a cocktail before tennis," Phyliss said. The nickname arose from the occasional business George did in Mexico.

George smiled as if he and Corinne were in a secret society of drunken tennists. "Fun to see you girls together again," he said.

Marion and Corinne hadn't been close since they were seventeen, when Marion started to break away from the village of Lammermuir and its namesake country club. It wasn't fair, but for many years Corinne seemed inextricably tied to Marion's earlier self, the neatly dressed, prim yet coquettish, anxiously beauty-obsessed self whose sweaters so magnetized the hearts and paws of local footballers (a history and legacy at the heart of Marion's novel). But these associations were ebbing, and though Corinne had never been a serious movement type, no matter the movement, her subcultural status currently seemed stronger than Marion's. She was living cooperatively, doing something with film, while Marion was living parasitically, doing nothing with literature. In '67, Marion had helped draft a (scuttled) women's resolution at the National Conference for New Politics, shortly after which she became a reserved but allegiant member of the Westside group, Chicago's first women's liberation organization. By now she had lost touch with everyone.

She took the last sip and went to fish her racket out of the mudroom jumble.

The club's six tennis courts were buzzing with the vernal ebullience midwesterners understandably exaggerate. Corinne had learned the two-handed backhand but was still too slack for Marion's drop shots, though Marion guessed it would be unmannerly to demonstrate this more than once. "Let's just hit," Corinne had said at the start, blocking a renewal of their teenage rivalry along with Marion's chances of having much fun. Marion never understood how noncompetitive people so often prevailed at establishing the rules.

Corinne let down her long, center-parted hair as Marion latched the chain-link gate on their way out. They talked about this latest round of bombings, then about Marion's older brother, Chick, now wholesaling baseball caps in Buffalo. It was thoughtful of Corinne to ask about Marion's novel, though Marion wasn't sure she wanted to talk about it.

"I'm nearly finished," Marion said, "which is different than the book being nearly done." Earlier this week, she had started Alix Kates Shulman's *Memoirs of an Ex-Prom Queen* with an uneasiness that built to a crescendo of resignation. Coolly considered, the similarities between her manuscript and Shulman's novel were superficial, perhaps only suggested by the relative paucity of women's art. *Memoirs* was a nonlinear, episodic tour of a life's first half; Marion's manuscript, though long on retrospection, took place over eight days, beginning with a New Left conference, ending with a wedding (though it was meant to be a parody and refraction of the kind of nuptial denouement one finds in Shakespeare or Austen). Shulman's style was straightforward and witty; Marion's, lyrical and sometimes abstract. And so on. Granted, there were thematic links and parallel scenes, but isn't the history of art one of ceaseless variation and telling coincidence? On some level Marion knew that Shulman's book—a feminist novel published by a major house and already finding a hungry readership—should be a spur, not a bridle. What to do was finish the manuscript, get it to an agent, and make her way back to the city. Instead, she felt that her novel had been made redundant, that Shulman had said what Marion wanted to say about beauty and bohemia and body image and sex and power, even though they hadn't said the same things and material like that was inexhaustible. "I just don't feel in a gut way that I need to go on with it," she said to Corinne.

"So take a break. See how you feel in a month."

"Yeah."

"A year."

After crossing a field used mainly for mowing, they reached the road above which their hilltop houses stood. Marion said, "I still have that collage you sent me." It was a weak endorsement to say merely that she hadn't thrown the collage away. Which she hadn't (but: where was it?). She asked if there were more recent collages.

"No. I'm mostly busy with the film collective," Corinne said, and began to talk about the documentaries she made with her three housemates. She and Marion had touched on this the other day, but Marion hadn't asked for details. Now Corinne described the weeks of footage she and her collaborators shot independently and edited into two-hour "polytonal almanacs"—*1970, 1971, 1972* (in progress). Listening, Marion started to see her friend not as a normal wading in the sandier shores of weirdness, but as a relative straight in the rocky thick of it. Marion wasn't sure if these films were often screened for the public, or if they traveled much beyond the Bay Area. Maybe that wasn't of great concern to Corinne. The Wrightsons had more money than the Crennels, and there didn't seem to be viselike pressure on Corinne to work for her keep. "You should come out and be in *1972*," Corinne said. Marion liked the sound of that; so far she'd been in 1972 only remotely.

They passed quietly over the creek and walked up the Crennels' driveway. Ania, the twice-weekly housekeeper, was hefting two sacks into her trunk. She smiled at Marion as she drove away. Many years ago Marion had accused Ania of stealing a locket. Marion stopped at the crest of the driveway, tapping her racket against her calf. "Do you mean it?" she said.

"Of course I do," Corinne said.

"And could we drive?" She pointed to the convertible parked under the basketball hoop.

Corinne took Marion's free hand. "We could drive."

That night in her room—not her childhood room, but a spaceless guest room that George called "el cuartito"—Marion put her manuscript at the bottom of one of the many boxes on hand from the Crennel Paper Board Company. On top of the manuscript she put a pair of too-tight corduroys, three paperbacks, and, as if there were something fragile in the box, a crumpled *Tribune*. A door from el cuartito led to the attic; she walked softly up the dark staircase, not wanting to arouse suspicion (of what she wasn't sure). She pulled on the light. Holding the box at the top of the stairs, she looked for a good spot to stash it, eventually settling on a corner near a complex of retired golf bags and a garment rack protected by a taupe quilted cover. Already in the corner were two identical boxes, one unmarked, one labeled COOKIE TINS, and as she created a new tower with her box at the bottom, she felt a bubbling sense of victory.

Part One

Prenuptial

May 2011

The invitation to Archer's July wedding was beautiful, expensive, and somehow French, its palette of blue and white more reminiscent of Yves Klein than of Tiffany. Karyn at first took the envelope's calligraphy as a sign of fussy ostentation (on the part of the client, that is, not the calligrapher, who's obliged to at least be fussy), but as its imperfections revealed themselves, to the point where you might not even call it calligraphy, her thoughts grew more generous, turned to a leather-topped desk in a sunlit room; an amateur forming a monumental capital in some state of doubleness: intoxicated serenity, maybe, or patient excitement. She handed the envelope to her son. "Look at this writing," she said.

He was eleven and uninterested. "Is it a computer?"

"No, that's just it: it's good but kind of sloppy." She took back the envelope. "I think it's the bride." The sylvan folk music drifting in from the kitchen caught her attention for a few seconds. She was on the verge of what felt at once like the purest of tears and like the class of tears prodded by life-insurance commercials. She compared the address on the envelope with the plainer five-word note on the invitation and didn't say anything for a while. Their meals were often marked by expanses of silence, rarely antagonistic but sometimes sullen, a mood encouraged by the small, woody dining room and its one murky window. The table was the color of rotten apples and half-covered with newspapers, cards for a Tolkienesque fantasy game, and a week of mail, under which there may have been hardened rice. It was one of Karyn's breakfast-as-dinner nights, not unanimously popular. While preparing the food she had taken perverse pleasure in anticipating Maxwell's opposition; she wanted him to suffer, a little, for his choosiness. She loved him fervently but sometimes found herself rooting against him, hoping his occasional pride or sloth would be answered with a chastening defeat. A stern

C plus, say, though his cosseting hippie school didn't give grades. It was hard to square her hopes for his uncurbed success with her lifelong affinity for underdogs.

She watched him conduct a scrambled-egg diaspora on and around his plate. "I can't explain the science of it," she said, "but eggs cool, like, super fast." The construction was meant as a concession to kidspeak, a move at odds with her priggish shunning of baby talk during Maxwell's early years ("Please talk to him in a normal voice, Mom," she would say, a directive that was both resented and ignored). Maxwell pretended to have trouble getting the egg on his fork. "You won't want to eat them cold," she said.

"I don't want to eat them hot."

They laughed.

"I think we should go to this wedding," she said.

Archer was one of Karyn's distant Winnipeg-bred relatives and, absent strong competition, the most glamorous of the scattered Bondarenkos. Having seen a drawing of him in the *New Yorker,* she had a rough sense of what he looked like as an adult (prematurely bald?), but when she pictured him it was as a five-year-old boy, auburn-haired and polo-shirted, crying after a s'more accident, his mother slapping at mosquitoes while rushing to rectify things, marshmallow splotches turning from white to brown to black on a log. Karyn hadn't seen Archer in the flesh since that family reunion in 1982. In his autobiographical novel and assorted other writings she sustained a tepid interest of long standing.

To any other cousin she would have sent polite regrets and bath towels, but this was different. To begin with, there was the allure of wealth; though she had been to at least one wedding of people who were rich by all standards except those of the Western rich, she had never been to a wedding of people who were rich by any standard. And she was on the wide edge of going to Winnipeg anyway. She and Maxwell had been slated to go there the previous summer, but late that July he had decided to play in a youth football league, whose demanding schedule scotched their vacation plans. Perhaps it's too much to say they had plans, since Karyn hadn't booked a hotel, or submitted a PTO request, or even plugged in MINNEAPOLIS TO WINNIPEG on a driving-distance website. She had, at least, rented the Guy Maddin movie *My Winnipeg,* which she admired through some irritation and didn't finish.

Although she liked expatriate novels and could speak Spanish and German, especially if you wanted to speak about hungry cats in big rooms, tourism most appealed to her when the destination was no farther than twelve hours by car, urban, and seldom subjected to discernible incursions of tourists. She and Maxwell had been to Des Moines, Kansas City, Green Bay—all for no special reason and with no itinerary. Winnipeg seemed a logical tick on her indifferent bucket list, the next stop for someone whose faith in her innate eccentricity survived overflowing evidence that her behavior, opinions, and tastes were in truth only slightly out of step with her demographic peers. Here again was a case in point: she considered it whimsical and unexpected to spend one's vacation in Winnipeg, yet half the people she mentioned the idea to had been there themselves, and all but one ("fucking snoozefest") spoke of it warmly. People were going to Winnipeg all the time! One of her colleagues, it turned out, made regular trips to the city with his boyfriend and could name its best galleries, restaurants, and bookstores. Karyn had been happy to hear these names and recommendations, equally happy to forget them as soon as they were spoken. A month later, sitting in her saggy lawn chair while one of the more martial football coaches led an exercise called "butt kickers," she considered, not for the first time, that a benefit of passivity is that there's nothing to undo, not even names to forget or scraps of paper to throw away.

"An old friend of mine makes Winnipeg out to be a bohemian Shangri-la," she told Maxwell nearly a year later.

"What's a Shangri-la?"

"An earthly paradise from a book I haven't read." She didn't much miss her marriage, but she missed having someone around to challenge her half-truths. The "old friend," for instance, was more accurately one of her ex-husband's acquaintances, a hairy-eared flâneur who in the nineties supposedly made a scraggy living recruiting new members into the Columbia Record Club, and who once raved about Winnipeg for several minutes outside a Kinko's. She remembered staring at his ears. It wasn't just that they were hairy, but that he confronted the problem with an electric razor, so that his ears sprouted little flattops. "He also said that Winnipeg is the Chicago of Canada."

"I've never been to the Chicago of America," Maxwell said.

"So."

"So to me the Chicago of Canada is like . . . nothing."

"I love you."

"I love you too."

"But you have been to the Chicago of America," she said, "though I guess it was before you had a full concept of selfhood." Had she and Jason, the ex-husband, known definitively that Maxwell would forget the trip, they might have spent more time looking at art, less time watching fish. She asked Maxwell a few questions about school but learned nothing specific. If she could afford to, she would quit her job and spend the summer with him, though he was getting too old to want that. She often preemptively mourned the passing of his childhood phases: the last time she would understand his math homework without a refresher on operations, the last standing hug in which his head nestled perfectly under her chin, the last time she could climb into bed with him after he was asleep without feeling slightly creepy. She stood up. "I should do some work."

"Oh, okay." He had green eyes, a haircut like a yak's.

She made a subtle show of hesitating. "Do you wanna watch a movie or something? A short one."

After the long action movie and Maxwell's shower, she did her back exercises, took over the bathroom, and swallowed the contents of her pill organizer's Thursday compartment. Instead of hanging up the wet towel Maxwell had left on the floor, she carried it to his bed, laid it on his pillow, and called him back upstairs to bed. She used her fuzzy-socked big toe to turn on her PC tower, its monitor surrounded by tackboards populated with obsolete notes and allegedly inspirational photos. One of the three small bedrooms on the underlit second story of her old house (1911, she'd say confidently when asked, but really she'd forgotten) was a guest room and office that hardly ever lodged guests or facilitated what would normally be recognized as work. It was thinly furnished. Its status as a guest room could be contested on the grounds that it didn't have a proper bed, though an innocently bloodstained futon kept the closet door from closing flushly. Only part of the room's faded balloon-motif wallpaper had been scraped off before a rented steamer was returned at dusk some long-past Sunday; at a later point she and Jason wordlessly concluded that the half-finished job fostered a ruined charm.

As the computer soughed to its vintage speed, she breathed deeply, trying to suck in the calm, flinty mind-set she was after—whenever she wasn't after irruptions of disheveled emotion. She opened the document ("Untitled Play") and scrolled to a stubbornly problematic scene. It had started out as play of a different type. After Jason moved out, she would come to this room late at night to improvise faintly satirical a cappella songs—the most inspired was "Kissing Bug"—and during these retreats she began to imagine herself as a witchy pre-Raphaelite hippie at the romantic center and on the musical periphery of an eccentric Scottish folk group. The group was closely patterned after the Incredible String Band, and at first she didn't bother to change the names of the ISB's joint leaders. She would pretend to play one of her songs for Robin or Mike, usually Robin, and he would demur: the song wasn't ready yet, he would say, wasn't right for the new album, though probably there would still be room for "Kissing Bug." He said the name with a smirk. After their argument and his offstage ramble, a precarious reconciliation.

These fantasies seemed to progress without calculation: Robin took on some of Jason's qualities and was renamed—no, he simply *became*—Callum; Karyn recorded several of her improvisations on her phone and transcribed the best parts into a notebook; at a garage sale, she stumbled on a pair of suede lace-up knee boots and a peasant blouse that smelled, she was sure, like her protagonist, now named Anisette. After Karyn had memorized, effortlessly, much of what was clearly a play, she started typing it up.

Now she fine-tuned Act Three's showcase speech, checked her e-mail, and searched out interviews, reviews, and miscellanea pertaining to *Eminent Canadians,* Archer's debut novel from a few years back. In the interviews he was sometimes charming (to write the book, he told two separate interviewers, he'd "taken pains as well as naps"), sometimes goofily pompous ("I want every sentence to stand as impossibly as a tower of blueberries," he said on the podcast *Dog-Eared,* "and the only means to that end is draconian self-editing"). The reviews were by and large favorable though never ecstatic; a few were cutting (*Bookforum:* "This is one of those novels in which characters are said to 'walk right off the page.' From there, apparently, they amble onto the set of a bad sitcom"). The blurbs, oddly, could also be called mixed. One nasty endorsement praised "a young writer who's just loaded with talent," inviting in-the-know readers to put ellipsis points or a full stop after "loaded." Karyn teleported the book into her e-reader, retweeted a girlfriend's so-so aperçu, and got up to thumb Maxwell's toothbrush for moisture. She could tell from his sighs and rustles that he'd been lying awake for the past hour. "Did you brush your teeth?" she called out. From bed he answered that he thought so. "It would be a very recent memory," she said.

Back in the office or guest room, she used customer-rewards points to book a hotel room in Winnipeg, judged the word *relished* at the start of the Isle of Wight scene to be too breathless, and checked the Facebook wall of a systems consultant who'd spent part of the previous month introducing Karyn's department to the new HRIS. He was home now in Lake Forest, Illinois, where he remained, among other faults, libertarian and married. She resisted looking carefully at his photos but gathered from abashed glimpses that his wife was plain. *Bear'st thou her face in mind? is't long or round?* (She'd played Cleopatra in college.) Karyn was surprised by the wife's plainness, since the consultant was quite good-looking. When considering men at first hand—when she wasn't, that is, in the semi-ironic locker-pinup sphere of waxed Olympic swimmers or Hemsworth-as-Thor—she was ordinarily turned off by physiques denoting even a measured commitment to weightlifting, but the consultant evoked galleries of classical sculptures rather than gyms of grunting bouncers. (Well, kind of.) She lately thought often of how his bicep veins had distended as he hovered over her and held down her wrists, how she'd wanted him to stay like that for longer than would have been comfortable, and at the same time how badly she'd wanted to touch his chest, dotted with cherry angiomas. His orgasmic grunt was short, friendly, and workmanlike, as if he were lifting one end of a couch. Later and without encouragement he rehearsed the case for a flat tax.

After an uncommunicative fortnight of presumed spousal loyalty, he was in the picture again, recklessly liking Karyn's status updates dating back a week. Partly hoping for this very sort of attention, she'd had Maxwell take several photos of her gardening in their backyard, had this morning posted the most flattering one, presenting it as if it were a PSA for growing one's own food and not an exhibit of her fairly well-preserved looks and narcissism. (But surely the person who fears she's succumbing to narcissism isn't a full-blown case.) It really was a remarkable, if not a wholly realistic, photo: her head tilted in the way of a fixated dog without underlining the association; her chin irrefutably single (not wanting Maxwell to shoot from below, she'd made him stand on a birdseed bucket); her black-fingered gardening gloves elusively sexy. Twenty-four likes, close to double those incited by her recent post about neti pots. There were admiring comments too, which after a mood-lifting while started to embarrass her, started to feel well-meaningly condescending, as if the whole procedure were a collectively presented FOXY GRANDMA T-shirt. She wasn't that old, but still.

Though the affair with the consultant was atypical—to deal in numbers, their one afternoon and two nights together represented the lion's share of her nonsolo sexual experience of the past four years—more and more this was how things went during the time between Maxwell's bedtime and her own: the posting and liking and commenting and checking, the distracted revising of her play, the shutting down of her desktop computer, the crawling into bed, the distracted reading of a book, the booting up of her laptop.

Twenty-five likes, the latest from Paul, the systems consultant.

It wasn't, usually, that internet socializing was making her lonelier, but that it was just sustaining enough to discourage socializing off the internet.

A message popped up from Paul: "Hi." Not, so far, a Cyrano of written seduction. Queasily she responded in kind.

She thought she craved conversation of a literary-intellectual bent, but in those rare cases when she was with someone who wanted to talk about books and ideas, she found that the revelation of shared enthusiasms meant less than it once did, that her discourse wasn't as glimmering as her interior monologues augured, that she was sweating to seem sophisticated for one person and constricting herself to seem down-home for another, that her companion's thoughts on the book were fuzzy compared to those in the more accomplished reviews, from which Karyn's own fuzzy thoughts derived. Either there wasn't much to say, or much to say but no spark of affinity and thus little drive to say it.

An ellipsis foreshadowed another IM.

She wasn't nostalgic for the immodest social needs and modest standards of her youth, but she missed the easy birth of new friendships, the seemingly wild luck of three simpatico women housed on a single floor of a small dormitory, whereas now, to find two people whose company seemed more attractive than solitude, she thought she might need a bigger city.

A floater crossed one of her eyeballs, a muscle contracted below her right shoulder blade. The message came through: "They're calling me back to mpls for a few days in June. Looking forward to seeing you." Then, to cover his tracks: "and the rest of the eam." And an addendum: "Typo, meant team."

She decided to rebuff him, then decided it would be better to rebuff him in person.

August 2004

The editor at the *Stickler* seemed to think Sara lived somewhat closer to Manhattan than Buffalo and that her name contained an *h,* but Sara said yes without corrections when he asked her to blog nonremuneratively about the protests surrounding the Republican National Convention. She had done one earlier piece for the website, a fitfully comic essay about kickboxing. On her first day in the city, she felt more than briefly jubilant amid a river of marchers, then galvanized by an Iraq War veteran's speech, his camo blending in not only with the imagined desert but also with his blond hair and suntanned face. That evening she joined a looser, smaller march, falling in with an anarchist funeral band playing "When the Saints Go Marching In." She sloped her head skyward, smiled to announce how serenely she could be alone in a crowd. The man in front of her carried a placard of the famous hooded figure from Abu Ghraib, and when the marcher began to move to the music, the hooded figure bobbed and swayed too, choreographing Sara's shame and weary happiness.

But when she tried to convey that ambivalence in the blog tent, working next to a relentlessly macking Vanderbilt senior with an unfortunate Tintinish haircut, the results seemed forced and unctuous. Her style, too, was wrong, not exactly mandarin but too stiff, her sops to the accidental prose often found on blogs coming off like the outfits John Kerry wore for farm visits: the rolled-up oxford, the work boots diligently scuffed by a campaign aid. As easy jobs went, it was hard. Some of her preferences and aversions militated against reportorial excellence, such as her preference for "soaking things in" rather than taking notes, and her aversion to asking questions of strangers. Normally this was a mild aversion with mild consequences—spending many minutes in the ticket-holder's line before moving quietly to the one for buyers, say—and it only affected her in certain moods. She was fine with people who had an occupational obligation to answer questions, salespeople, for example, except those in stores where she felt outclassed or otherwise prominent, stores where sizes above six were purportedly kept in back. She could remember lots of times when she had confidently asked a stranger a question ("Does this go downtown?" "Is this seat taken?" "Quelle heure est-il?"). She wasn't continuously shy. In fact, her occasional extroversion sometimes retrospectively embarrassed her. The RNC assignment, though, aggravated her reluctance to approach strangers toward agoraphobia, and she spent much of the week in a state of stomach-knotted dread of having to attempt the next interview, mingled with self-reproach for having not seized the previous moment's countless opportunities. She hated to impose on people, and her inexperience and slender credentials made her feel like both an imposer and an imposter.

Knowing she could brave few interviews each day, often fewer than two, she tried to home in on faces combining intelligence and receptivity, qualities that shouldn't be in opposition but started to act that way. Probably when we see what a Victorian novelist might call "an intelligent visage," we're really seeing skepticism, severity, sadness, or the sort of intense tic that mesmerizes Slavoj Žižek fans. Her own face, she feared, was a dumb one; her allergies to dust mites and other microstuff promoted oral respiration. In any case, the homing-in strategy failed. By the second day she had switched to prospecting negatively, eliminating people whose shyness or unfriendliness seemed worth respecting, then those whose opinions, she sensed, would be uselessly naïve, lunatic, banal, incoherent, doctrinaire, or stupid. Through these means she was able to rule out roughly everyone, a winnowing that betrayed reticence more than misanthropy. (Although once, when asked in a job interview if she was a people person, she had detrimentally hesitated.)

During what turned into a lonely, disheartening week outside the RNC, a week in which she ate almost nothing but laxative slices of floppy pizza at odd times of day, she frequently visited the action at Union Square, the site on one afternoon of a long battle between police and protesters for control of a fenced walkway through the park. The cops eventually moved in with riot helmets and shields to keep protesters from partially obstructing the walkway, a show of strength that fully obstructed the walkway. Sara did her best to stay in the thick of things. There were spasmodic waves of moshy movement and at least one instance, she thought, of frottage.

It was in trying to follow a cop's command to get out of the way that she backed into the soft body of Lucas Pope, a fellow fiction writer from the second-tier MFA program Sara had attended from 2001 to 2003. During his MFA candidacy, Lucas had mainly distinguished himself though the prolixity and unrelieved irrelevance of his in-class comments and marginal notes. The closest he came to competence as a writer—a nine-page story about a substance-abusing prison guard, transparently written under the spell of Denis Johnson—might have amounted to something, had he seen fit to make even a quarter of the workshop's more sensibly proposed revisions. His early departure from the program was met with no professorial resistance. After some exclamations, he noticed Sara's blank steno pad. "You're a reporter?"

"In the sense that someone videotaping little Zach's first toddle round the coffee table is a filmmaker," she said. Lucas didn't quite catch her analogy and was candidly disappointed when she repeated it at his request. "But yeah, I could probably be called a reporter," she said, "an exploited one. I was hoping to get a laminated press pass, at the very least a card to slip in the band of my fedora. But I didn't, mostly because I have access to nothing. Well," she added, raising a fist, "nothing but the streets!"

"Except the streets the cops have cordoned off," Lucas said. He nodded at an agitprop thespian sweatily dressed as the Monopoly mascot. For his part, Lucas was wearing Harry Caray glasses, an underproportioned cycling cap, baggy shorts, a LICK BUSH button, and a plaid shirt, short-sleeved and untucked. He looked like a semifamous cartoonist, or like someone who would recognize a semifamous cartoonist. They moved away from the dying conflict.

"That was weird," Sara said. "I've rarely experienced such a convergence of tension and pointlessness, stimulation and boredom."

"You haven't played enough chess or watched enough porn," Lucas said.

"Ha, that might be true. What did Flaubert say about chess? 'Too serious as a game, too pointless as a science'? I think that was it, though now I'm thinking it wasn't something Flaubert said but something he said *other people* said. Stupid people."

"It does sound like something stupid people would say."

She ignored the implications of that.

"Wow, Sara Crennel. Crazy running into you."

"Yeah."

"Serendipity," he said, punning. He seemed to be done with the protest. "It's cool that you're still writing."

"Yeah, sorta. It probably hasn't been long enough to applaud me for persistence." An older woman carrying a Cheney effigy offered a knowing smile reminiscent, a moment's concentration determined, of Sara's late aunt Marion. Still, Sara couldn't bring herself to approach her. She turned back to Lucas. "And you?"

"Still writing? Neh, not really. I have an idea for a screenplay, but . . . no. I'm at Citibank."

"Really?"

"Yeah, in marketing, mostly implementing marketing collateral."

"If I ask what that is, will you keep it short?"

"Signs and brochures, stuff you see in the bank, some white papers. There's a poster of a couple yuppies kind of flirtily painting a room that I was pretty instrumental in."

"Is that the one where they're painting each other's faces, like there's paint on her nose?"

"On her nose? No."

"Maybe I—"

"You're thinking of cake frosting."

"Yeah, I was probably—"

"It'd be kind of wack to purposely brush oil paint on someone's face," he said.

"Yes, okay, I understand," she said. "They'd probably be using latex, but whatever."

After a beat he said, "I'm amped that you were so surprised when I said I work at Citibank." She hadn't been that surprised. "Sometimes I tell people what I do and they don't react much, and I think, Do I *seem* like I work at Citibank?"

"No, you don't seem that way."

"Though they might think I have one of the cooler bank jobs. Security or something."

She saw him checking out a woman in tacky hip-huggers. In school his stories were provocatively libidinous and syntactically carefree.

"Also I have this venture in the works with reusable bags," he said. "Brand Nubagian."

"Brand Nubagian?"

"I don't have all the cheddar together yet, but I've been sensing it forthcoming, feeling things in the works. I know that sounds kind of Joan Quigley, but check it: Two weeks ago I'm flying home for the weekend, right? Settling into my seat, testing the tray-table, adjusting the belt, all that, when this lady asks if I'd switch seats with her. I'm sitting next to her best friend from summer camp or some shit. She's in first class, so I say sure."

"You wouldn't have switched if she'd been in coach?"

"Well, yeah, I would have. So I get promoted to first, and it turns out the guy next to me, 3A, *makes bags.*"

"He sews them?"

"No, his company"—Lucas pulled out a business card from his Velcro-clasp wallet and handed it to her—"is this huge B2B bag-manufacturing operation."

"This doesn't say anything about bags," Sara said.

"That's what they do, though. So now I'm all, *Carpe diem.*"

"Nice."

"Yeah."

"But isn't carpe diem, like, *Live in the moment, don't worry 'bout the future,* more than *Chase your dreams without delay*?"

He seemed to be holding his tongue.

"Not that I'm some shining Latinist," she said, "but I think the nose-to-the-grindstone version is a sort of business-of-America-is-business corruption."

"I'd love making these bags," he said, "so I *would* be living in the moment."

"Where are we going?"

"I don't know. I wouldn't mind looking for a green headband." They were walking south on Broadway. "I want to take the headband thing to that other level. I had this bananas striped one, but I was getting all these *Magnificent Ambersons* comparisons, where I'm going for, like, Slick Watts."

"*Magnificent Ambersons*?"

"I mean *Royal Tenenbaums*."

"You get those mixed up?"

"I confused the names once for real, and now I always pretend to confuse them."

"You don't have any Ativan or Paxil or anything, do you?"

"I've got some cheeb. Not on me."

"I should head back to the blog tent," she said, then didn't. At the Strand she came close to buying a dozen books, but, overwhelmed and underfinanced, left only with a useless tote bag. They stalled on the corner outside the store. "I should go back," she said again.

"I'm so hungry I could eat part of an animal," he said.

On a deli's stuffy upper story they uncovered a pair of complementary facts: that at twenty-six Sara was ashamed to be living with her difficult mother in West Seneca—she usually neglected to clarify that for now she didn't even live in Buffalo proper—and that Lucas's Anglo American girlfriend had recently moved out of his apartment, though this didn't mean, he insisted, that they'd broken up.

Unable to make it back to the blog tent, Sara was constrained to pay twenty dollars to use the internet in her expensively drab hotel. Her midnight dispatch was better, and worse, than the others. She had entered the assignment with a commitment to journalistic ethics, but she figured it would be harmless just this once to invent a few quotes and coax another from Lucas ("I think in a lot of ways the left benefits from a conservative administration . . ."). All night she was sleepless with dreams of metropolitan transformations, giddy, embarrassing dreams that in some slantwise sense came true.

June 2011

Karyn thought of movie couples uncorking their illicit lust in elevators, against hotel walls the moment after tumbling inside the room. Preferable, she guessed, to this heavy-lidded prelude on her couch with Paul the consultant. Perhaps she hadn't anticipated anything cinematically frenetic when she was hunching to put in her diaphragm an hour earlier, but she had at least pictured a carnality onrushing enough to frown on contraceptive pauses, and since it was their last time together, she thought it would be nice to forgo the condom. Paul was complaining now about his new multifocal eyeglasses, how much blurring there was around the edges.

"Maybe progressives offend your conservative sensibilities," she said.

"I wouldn't say *conservative,*" he said, as if her joke required amendment. "I'm a classical liberal."

"Well, they look nice," she said. The contrast between the dark tortoiseshell and his pallid complexion was too stark. "This thing in Jisr al-Shughour or however you say it—over a hundred dead, I heard." The Arab Spring, she thought, might bridge their ideological divide.

He murmured cryptically.

"Assad the next to fall?" *The next to fall.* Please.

"Maybe. Not sure if it'll do much good so long as—" He broke off when a car alarm began pulsing across the street. When it stopped, he steered talk back to his elusive focal points.

She suggested contact lenses.

"I don't believe our eyeballs were designed to take in objects."

She doubted he meant *designed* in an anti-Darwinian way, but he wasn't always legible. "It does take a while to get used to them," she said. "To contacts, I mean. But I was unpopular in high school, so it seemed a worthwhile sacrifice."

"Unpopular with boys?" he said, constricting her meaning. "That's hard to imagine."

"Oh God yes. Awkward. Horrible skin." *Horrible* went overboard, but she wanted to fend off his idealizations. Last time he had looked at her too feverishly.

He faced her. "You think the frames are okay, though?" The phone rang. "Jen says they're too dark."

Her landline's holdouts were mostly strangers—political fundraisers, call-center larcenists, the sandpaper-voiced man who rang once a year asking poignantly for Esther—but she welcomed the interruption. "I'll only get it if it's my kid." The caller ID read GEMMA PITCHFORD. Unable to place the name, she let the call go to voice mail.

When she returned to the couch, Paul said, "But the frames are okay?"

"They're great. Very . . . I was going to say 'distinguished,' but—"

"You don't think they're distinguished?"

"It's just, it's hackneyed to say a middle-aged man looks 'distinguished' in glasses."

"If you say so."

"Sorry, I always do that. I was in this play—I used to be involved in theater—"

"Ah," he said, too enlightened. She thought of herself as an unassuming type who'd been transformed onstage rather than someone drawn to the theater by histrionic disposition.

"Yes," she said, "and I had a part where one of my lines went, 'I'll try to say this so you can understand where . . . my point of view.' She stops herself from saying 'where I'm coming from,' then talks about how she almost said it."

"I know the type."

She laughed. "As do I. When I read that line I knew I was—ha, I was going to say 'born to play the role.'"

It had been her first professional lead, playing Anna in a production of *Burn This* for a peripatetic but well-regarded midsized company. Anna was a dancer transitioning into choreography, and though Karyn struggled to move with convincingly terpsichorean grace, in all other ways she found herself melding with the character. The guy who played Pale, the ramshackle drunk with whom Anna falls in love, was too young for the part, but it didn't matter; he and Karyn had what's called chemistry (the alt-weekly reviewer, pulling a muscle to avoid the cliché, praised "the principals' analeptic symbiosis"). With each performance they grew more intense without, she was sure, overacting. He was gay and exceptionally attractive, and the closed fantasy of offstage eros, she thought, enabled her immersion in the show's sexual energy.

"You gave it up?" Paul said.

"I did. That was pretty much my swan song, actually, spring of '98."

He sighed for Monica Lewinsky, the vaulting Nasdaq, Sosa-McGwire.

The production was momentous personally as well as artistically in that it introduced her to Jason. He was already working for the Minnesota Geological Survey but still moonlighting as a musician, and the director put him in charge of guitar noodles and synth mattresses, dignified in the program as sound design. Karyn and Jason didn't speak to each other during the run, but they exchanged two consequential looks. At the closing party he referenced the where-I'm-coming-from line five minutes before their relationship took a physical turn.

"Speaking of time's winged chariot," Karyn said to Paul. She nodded toward the upstairs bedroom.

"Roger that."

Trying to kindle a more spirited atmosphere, she fell backwards on the bed as if flopping down to make a snow angel.

"I can't believe you called me middle-aged," he said, playfully, as if he wanted to wrestle. When she mentioned the diaphragm, they locked eyes with an excitement possibly tinted with STI anxiety. It passed.

December 2004

Sara's move to New York was hopeful but noncommittal. She had her mother send her a small box of clothes, but she left everything else in West Seneca and told Lucas to think of her as month-to-month. Briefly she worried that he was gunning to make them more than roommates, but soon she saw that he was devoted to the Anglo American, Gemma, whose devotion seemed more controlled. Sara planned to expand her reach as a writer and proofreader, pledged to stay unattached.

It didn't go like that. Her work flattened out, and she spent most of her not quite four months in New York dating an apprentice bike-frame builder from Idaho Falls. Lucas, who had improvidently expensive taste in bikes, had fixed them up during the second week of Sara's residence. The frame builder's name (inauspiciously, she thought) was John Anderson. Lucas advertised him as good-looking, which turned out to be unconventionally true, and a Harvard graduate, which was misleading in that he wasn't ambitious, moneyed, or conspicuously intelligent. Sara suspected his admission had something to do with geographic balance. Coincidentally, she'd written a story set at random in southeastern Idaho, and John's recollections helped her add color to one of its unacclaimed revisions. Still, they weren't a match, John and she. She was about to drop him but instead decided—with six hundred dollars, twice that in credit-card debt, and a trickle of freelance work—to go home for Christmas and sort of not come back. Quickly checkmated but not direly insolvent. Her excitement over learning how not to be the sweating provincial clogging up turnstiles with ineffectual swipes of her MetroCard, over walking to the G past the Polish delis and junky shops of Manhattan Avenue near her Greenpoint walk-up, over knowing there were a dozen interesting things not to do every night—all that excitement had been real but ephemeral. Within a month she felt deracinated and belated, as if she were in that joke about the restaurant no one goes to anymore because it's too crowded. It was true that by tripping into Greenpoint she'd arrived in a neighborhood still only on the cusp of hipsterization, but watching the extension of her begrudged tribe held little appeal. Her bohemian experience would be a Maynard G. Krebs–like simulacrum at a time when the prospects for moderately talented writers without independent resources were grimmer than they'd been since—she didn't have dates and numbers, but a long time, surely. Not that she was underprivileged. She had a grandfather with money, some money, though she didn't feel right asking for any of it, and her dad made a decent salary installing database-management systems for Oracle, though he had three college-bound kids from his second marriage. Her mother had painfully unrealistic dreams of early retirement. So there was safety-net money, not write-your-novel money.

Two nights before her departure, John affably made the haul from Harlem to Lucas and Sara's apartment, where they were to be joined by John's college roommate, just back from a long stay in the Lesser Antilles. The apartment's row of four blippy rooms reminded Sara of a toy caterpillar. It wasn't an altogether charmless place, but neither was it designed for nonamorous cohabitants or for so many bicycles. She hated walking through Lucas's bedroom in the middle of the night to go to the bathroom, not to mention all bathroom situations in which her noises weren't entirely private. Lucas was in many ways a good roommate—cleanly despite his hoarding impulses, glad to pay a bigger share of the rent in return for the better room—but he didn't always respect her work time. He would interrupt her writing and proofing with shouted reports of celebrity arrests, step into her room—granted, she didn't keep the door closed—to show her some dubious new acquisition: a baseball cap signed by J Dilla, a roll of nonpareil handlebar tape. Sometimes during these visits he would massage her shoulders, making note of her supposedly tangible tension, partly produced by the unsolicited massage itself.

Gemma, at least, rarely stayed overnight or even visited her former apartment, but she was there now with the others in Lucas's bedroom, its futon couched to reference a living room, two vinyl-and-chrome chairs imported from the kitchen, shoeboxes stacked profusely against the walls. (Lucas was a pioneer of sneaker speculation; he'd recently sold a pair of vintage Adidas for more than four hundred dollars.) The plan was to go to an inauthentic Mexican restaurant—secretly Sara's favorite kind, though at this restaurant there'd been an unpleasant episode with a slug—then proceed to a Williamsburg gallery where tinily meticulous dioramas were being displayed next to magnifying glasses. "Will we have to wait in line to use the magnifying glasses?" Sara asked.

"I suppose we don't know what to look forward to in terms of attendance," Gemma said.

Sara had hoped that she and Gemma would become pals, but despite herself she had stymied more than nurtured the possibility. Really she hadn't made any female friends since moving to New York, though everywhere she turned there was someone whose friendship she might have sought out in high school or at UB. Maybe it was like the summer she worked at Kone King: after a while the ice cream not only stopped being tempting but grew slightly repellent. She missed

Emily, her best friend from Buffalo, though the distance between them had grown more than locational. Emily married shortly after college and had in recent years swerved deeper and deeper into neo-traditionalism. She now attended church services of some kind in a former Office Max, spent many after-work hours on avowedly punk-rock needlepoint.

Mostly to Gemma, Sara said, "Because stuff like that makes me feel bullied. And then when I get my chance to use the magnifying glass, I'll have to look with philistine brevity or else irritate the people behind me."

"I doubt they'll be put out," John said. His voice was unusually deep, a true bass that would have been frightening had it been more energetic. Hearing him in a group setting could call to mind recordings by the Oak Ridge Boys.

A comfortable silence. There was something sedative about John; he was dull, one could argue, but more than that he was calming. He was one of those impressionist posters sometimes tacked to ceilings above surgical tables. Sara didn't feel completely calm around him—especially now that she was poised to abandon him—but she felt calmer around him than she did around most people. He was an equanimous, accepting man: accepting of people, accepting of failure. He was twenty-eight but had the drawly air of a graying widower soliloquizing while rearranging the toolshed after church. "I reckon that'll do for now," she could imagine him saying as he clapped dust off his hands. His settled tone was deceptive, though, or at least premature. He had once told Sara that in the end he would become a programmer, accountant, or analyst, and she guessed he was capable of all those things, but the prediction reminded her of boys slinking away from playground fistfights ("I'd clobber you if I wanted to!"). In a real fistfight he would probably have an edge; he was a Viking mesomorph who moved with an upright fearlessness in contrast to his general diffidence. In addition to building bike frames, he worked part-time at a men's clothing store on the Upper East Side, and as a result he was often flagrantly overdressed, this time in his three-piece suit of brown, chalk-stripe flannel. The suit had recently earned him a full-body shot in Bill Cunningham's On the Street.

Gemma, refusing to pursue the argument about the magnifying glasses, turned to John. "Is your friend as a rule a punctual man?"

"He can run late," John said. He had pulled out a mandolin from his weekend bag and was arpeggiating what he believed to be a G-major chord.

"People from hot climates have a reputation for tardiness," Sara said, "but do people from cold climates have a reputation for punctuality?" John opened his mouth to respond, but she went on: "I suppose that's obvious. I suppose people from temperate and cold countries that aren't part of the former Soviet Union set the criteria by which those from hot climates are condemned."

"Archer's from Canada," John explained.

"I believe that's racist," Gemma said.

"Being Canadian?" Sara said with what she hoped was a subtly parodic British lilt.

"No, the correlation between southerly climates and laziness."

"I didn't say laziness, I said tardiness."

"It is racist," Lucas said.

"Or xenophobic," Gemma said.

"Depends on how you feel about time," John said. If she stayed with him, empty remarks like that would become a source of wincing regret.

"That's so," Gemma said charitably. Her top had an enterprising V-neckline and silver rivets on its sleeves. England was Europe's most buxom nation, according to a book Sara had skimmed in a London bookshop on her one overseas trip. The book was by an unfunny French humorist who preferred small breasts.

"Germans have a reputation for being on time," John said, not seeing that the conversation needed to change course. He put down the mandolin and looked at Sara: "Does it get very cold there?" And yet she liked the admiring, unmasculine way he sought and advertised her knowledge, which didn't significantly extend to German temperatures.

"Cold but not Canada cold," she said.

"I've been thinking—"

"In the mountains, maybe."

"I've been thinking about what you said about lugged frames," Lucas said to John. "Maybe for my next bike I'd be more interested in that than the, er . . ."

"Fillet brazed? You'd definitely open up some sweet design options, but you'd want . . ."

Sara stopped paying close attention. She courted a look of sororal boredom from Gemma but got nothing. Stylish, milky-skinned, dimpled, Gemma was attractive—probably not in danger of being accosted by reputable modeling scouts, but attractive, notably more so than Lucas. It made Sara wonder if Lucas was more attractive than he looked, like that quip about Wagner's music ("better than it sounds"). A sexual virtuoso, he could be, if such people existed outside books and songs by men who, as her aunt Marion once put it, thought women were violins. And yet: since there were obvious differences in sexual ability, generosity, invention, and knowledge, it was reasonable to think virtuosi existed and were distributed across the sexes, though not so far among Sara's seven or eight partners, ten or eleven if one didn't require penetration, a less heteronormative but perhaps unduly inflationary standard. Maybe there was something about her that failed to recognize or inspire virtuosity. Or failed to desire it; in songs and books, sexual virtuosity usually had to do with superendurance, which sounded painful. John wasn't the worst, but, in life as in bed (and it was really just a mattress), he was too tentative, too puppyish, too much the follower. She wasn't into heartbreakers, but she was on the lookout for traits more exciting than loyalty.

"... still fairly green when it comes to making custom lugs," John was saying, "but I'm working on some now—for none other than Archer, matter o' fact." This last phrase was delivered with a suspicion of affectionate irony; it seemed that John was trying to assert a native right to elide the *f* in *of*, but simultaneously conceding that the right had been surrendered or was controversial to begin with. He was proud o' his rustic roots, talked more about the relatives he had in and around Zellwood, Florida, than those he had in suburban Denver. His Floridian grandmother, he said, used phrases like "belly girt" and once warned him not to get above his raisin'. "I'll send you some photos when the bike's done," he told Lucas.

"Yeah, I'd love to peep it."

Gemma sighed in a sort of iamb.

"What's he do for work, then, your friend?" Lucas asked John.

"Archer?" It was clear that John didn't care for this line of inquiry. "I don't think he's working a steady job at the moment."

"According to John," Sara said, "he's a man of means."

John gave her a peeved look to suggest she'd disclosed a guarded secret, though one of the first things he'd told her about Archer was that he had a lot of money. The word he used was "shitload." Once, as part of an ambitious bike trip, John had visited the house where Archer spent most of his childhood. Archer's parents, he said, owned matching Range Rovers, paintings by Gerhard Richter, a vacation home in Dominica, and a professional hockey team.

"A man of means," Lucas echoed.

Gemma turned to Lucas. "You should suss out his interest in rare and vintage trainers."

"So where's all the cheddar from?"

"Oh, I don't rightly know," John said. "His parents are in business."

"Dr. Knox," Sara said.

Lucas squinted, looked up: "Dr. Knox . . ."

"Rhymes with *cocks,*" she said. "They make dildos." In a comic whisper she added, "Archer's family makes dildos."

John said, "Not just dildos," while Gemma said, "Of course, Dr. Knox! When the doctor knocks, open up."

"Fuck outta here," Lucas said. "That can't be their slogan."

"I just dreamed it up," Gemma said. "I told you I should be in advertising."

"You *are* in advertising," Sara said.

"Yes, but I don't write the adverts."

"Anyway," John said. "Archer's not uptight about it or anything, but don't bring it up when he's here."

"Okay, okay."

"We'll just hint at it incessantly," Gemma said.

"I'm sure he's heard it all," John said. "In school they called him—not to his face, but—what's the word that means, like, *heir,* but it's not *heir.*"

"Heiress," Lucas said. "It's like a girl heir."

"Scion?" Sara said.

"Scion," John said. "They called him the Dildo Scion."

The buzzer buzzed.

June 2011

"Hi, Karyn, this is Gemma Pitchford, Archer's fiancée."

"Oh, hi, yeah, it's—I believe you called a few days ago."

"Yes, and didn't leave a message. I hope in time you'll be able to forgive me."

For a moment Karyn suspected a prank call from a friend, but her friends, Facebook aside, were scarce, no longer given to prankishness, and unfamiliar with Gemma Pitchford. Also the accent seemed genuinely English, not that Karyn had a refined ear for such things. "Well, congratulations on your engagement."

"Thank you. Rather out of the blue of me to call, I realize, or it would have been had you picked up the first time, but I have an odd little proposal to run by you. You see I'm quite sure you and your son—who sounded charming on the phone, by the way—"

("Hullo," he'd said flatly, and "I'll get her.")

"—quite sure the pair of you make up two-thirds of the wedding's Minnesota contingent."

"Oh."

"I don't excel at maths, but these calculations I'm certain are correct." After a flitting pause, Gemma provided the questionably called-for laugh herself. "I have a friend, you see, Lucas Pope, who also lives in Minneapolis. I mentioned your name to him, but it seems you two are unacquainted."

"It's a reasonably good-sized metro area."

"He's having nasty car trouble. And ongoing financial trouble. Constant calls from creditors; now even his mother is dunning him. Really he's quite clever, but he was made redundant some two years ago and has been unable to find suitable employment since. You're familiar with the discouraged?"

"I don't keep up on music."

"No, no, it's the people excluded from unemployment figures because they've stopped looking."

"Oh, right, yes," Karyn said.

"Lucas has joined their ranks." A moment of mute sympathy. "There was an ill-starred entrepreneurial endeavor as well. The greater exigency from my vantage is that he says his car trouble will keep him away from our wedding. He can't afford to hire a car and obviously can't afford to fly. So," she sighed, "I'm wondering if you might consider car sharing with him to Winnipeg."

"Give him a ride, you mean?"

"He was trying to convince me to bring him in as the DJ, but I fear that's not quite the fix. It's how we met, actually: he the wedding DJ, I the too, too intoxicated dancer. Brilliant music, but there was something wrong, a balky needle or something with the calibration of the tonearms—I can't claim a consummate understanding of the technicalities, but the records kept skipping." She imitated the sound. "I suppose I could pay his way, but I've already established a dangerous precedent of charity."

"Yeah, I—"

"It's vital to me that Lucas attend the wedding. Naturally at this stage I'm inclined to believe this will be my *only* wedding, and just as naturally I want to be amidst the people I care most about—as well as interesting new people such as yourself! I'll confess to you now that there was a time I fancied Lucas almost intensely"—Karyn weighed how and whether one should modify *intensely*—"and saw myself walking the aisle towards *him,* though in the end we couldn't make a go of it."

Gemma seemed to expect an answer to a question Karyn had lost sight of. "I guess I was looking forward to a road trip with just my son," Karyn said after a moment. "Sometimes it's hard to get kids to talk, you know, but a lot can come out on a long drive."

"Vomit, for instance," Gemma said.

A hesitant laugh from Karyn.

"I only say so because I'm susceptible to carsickness, motion sickness of all stripes, really. I recently became dizzy while riding an extremely aged and sweet-tempered horse."

"Hmm."

"On even terrain."

"That must be frustrating," Karyn said.

"The horse was called Sleepy."

"Still, I think it'd be nice for Maxwell and me to be alone."

"But you practically would be alone."

"Well, we'd be with your friend."

"Let me ask you something, Karyn:"—like someone selling a dishwasher, Karyn thought—"When you share a taxi with a friend, do you think, Oh, we had better include the driver in every aspect of our conversation, we certainly wouldn't want him to feel left out, or do you proceed essentially as if you were alone?"

"If anything I'd be *more* likely to chat with the cabby if I had a friend to act as a buffer."

"Lucas would be mortified if he knew I was asking you this favor. Mortified. He's not a freeloader or an idler at heart."

"It's not that I have any objection to him," Karyn said, "except that he's a stranger."

"Yes, well, perhaps it would be better, then, for the two of you to meet in advance."

"Wait, is this whole thing—"

Gemma interrupted, "Sorry, one moment." Now to someone else: "Oh, how thrilling!" To Karyn: "*Publishers Weekly* has given Archer's new book a starred review. What do you think of the title, Karyn, *The Second Stranger*? It's too late for changes, so do say you approve."

"*The Second Stranger,*" Karyn said thoughtfully. "What was I supposed to say again?"

"That you like it."

"I like it."

"It's quite an unusual book, much more so than the first. Archer's been joking that it should be called *The Second, Stranger.* With a comma, you see."

"Ah."

"Oh my, listen to this: 'Not since Norman Rush's *Mating* has a male novelist rendered a female narrator with such authenticity and brio.' The reviewer is doubtless male," Gemma put in sotto voce. "But it truly is a striking piece of ventriloquism."

"I can't wait to read it."

"Can you not wait? Because people said that to Archer about his first book, that they could not wait to read it; but often they would say so when the book had been out for many, many months and they had already—well, just then!—admitted to knowledge of its existence. In a word, they *were* waiting, and proving they could do so quite contentedly."

"I see your point."

"I suppose those people are better than the ones who play at having read the book when they so obviously haven't, which is what I tend to do with writers other than Archer—who doesn't care a whit about any of this, I should say. I'm more sensitive about these things than he."

"Well, I'm eager to read the book," Karyn said.

Gemma called out again to Archer: "May we send your delightful cousin an ARC?" It wasn't clear if she had waited for an answer when she said, "I'm sending you an advance review copy."

"Oh, you don't have to—"

"But I'm sorry, I cut you off. You were about to say . . ."

"I'm not sure I remember."

"In connection with Lucas."

"Oh, it was—it was just that this call was starting to sound like a matchmaking ploy."

"Mmm, I can see that, now you mention it," Gemma said. "But if it were a matchmaking ploy, I suspect I would have downplayed Lucas's expanding indigence and would not now raise the issue of his appalling clothes."

"Maybe—"

"Or the fact that he spends much of his time at a computer looking at pictures of women dressed like Jessica Rabbit."

"Maybe you think I'm into mothering sad cases," Karyn said.

"I don't get that sense at all. On the contrary, frankly."

They listened to the phone static for a few seconds, then Karyn said, "Do you just mean redheads in sexy dresses, or do you mean women deliberately trying to look like Jessica Rabbit?"

"Oh, very deliberately, Karyn. It's a whole community."

They laughed.

"Just to be clear," Karyn said, "I'm kind of seeing someone." She wasn't *seeing* Paul the consultant, of course. He was now plotting a dirty weekend in Wisconsin, but Karyn wasn't egging him on.

"You misunderstand me," Gemma said. "I have no ideas in that direction. I only suggested you two meet in advance because I see that you're right, it would be uncomfortable to make the trip as strangers."

"Yeah, I'm not sure."

"But you'll think about it?"

"I can't imagine my thoughts will change."

"I'll call you back," Gemma said, and hung up without saying goodbye.

December 2004

"Laqueur's central point is that what he calls 'modern masturbation,' in other words, masturbation as a medical and social crisis, arose synchronously with the Enlightenment—"

Sara missed a few of Archer's words while sliding a knife under a dab of misplaced guacamole. Lucas, who "hadn't eaten all day" (she'd seen him eat breakfast), was hogging the thick, limey chips, Archer the conversation. Sara, too, had come to like the sound of her own voice—droll, she hoped, and in a cultured midrange (squeaky at matriculation, she had worked to drop her pitch by a quarter octave over her freshman year), but she didn't need to hear it all the time. Archer's was a tall, stocky voice, though he was of average height and slightly built. For the past hour or so Sara had been trying to figure out if he was an asshole. He didn't seem aloof, exactly, but he could be disdainful, which to her was worse. When she mentioned how much she had enjoyed *Eternal Sunshine of the Spotless Mind,* he flicked his wrist as if executing a Ping-Pong winner—"overrated"—and added that one of the supporting actors was "an absolute fucking tool," insinuating that the appraisal was derived from real-world experience. When Sara asked for elaboration, he scrupled as if he'd been transported by palanquin to the high road. It was a new variety of name-dropping for Sara (or a new variety of name-withholding), different from the sort practiced by John, who constantly, artlessly, and with genuine enthusiasm brought up his two semifamous college friends, the minor tech entrepreneur and the one in the floundering sitcom.

". . . perversion of Enlightenment ideals," Archer was saying. "Instead of aggregate self-interest serving the greater good, self-pleasure serving only itself; instead of quiet reflection, solipsism; instead of . . ."

A long pause. Sara, Lucas, and Gemma looked at Archer. John picked napkin lint off his suit.

"It was about imagination. Sorry. I was quoting from my essay and drew a blank." His first show of humility.

"I thought you were quoting this Laqueur," Sara said.

"Well, yeah, quoting my paraphrase of Laqueur." He then spoke at half speed, as if the sentence were returning to him word by word on a baggage carousel. "It went like, 'Not imagination applied to great social and artistic puzzles, but . . .'"

"Fantasy run amok in an intemperance of secret violations," Sara said, feeling a frisson when Archer responded with a stream of decaying *yeahs* like the dying of a lawn mower engine.

"I told you she was crazy smart," John said.

"Really, it's off," she said, not wanting John's embarrassing use of the third person to go unchecked. "*Amok* is too recent a loan word to apply to a discussion of the Enlightenment."

"We have to use period language when speaking of the past?" Archer said.

"One would need to be quite polyglot," Gemma said.

"Yes, all right, point taken," Sara said. She hadn't been challenged like this in a while. "But I'd rather summarize an old idea in language neither blithely anachronistic nor strainingly antique."

Unconvinced silence from Archer and Gemma. "What Laqueur shows," Archer resumed, "is that the 'problem' of masturbation developed with the Enlightenment, as I was saying, because it was a perversion of Enlightenment ideals. Before that it was sometimes ridiculed as the domain of losers and satyrs or whatever, and some Protestants thought of it as a monastic vice, and here and there it was, you know, censored." Did he mean *censured*? She might have misheard him. "But generally people didn't think of it as such a big deal."

"What about Onan?" Sara said as the food arrived.

"But if you actually read the story, Onan wasn't even beating off."

There was no grosser term.

Archer went on, "Onan's older brother did something to displease the Lord and was killed, right?"

"I don't really know the Bible," Sara said. It was one of the few major books she didn't mind confessing ignorance of.

"Well, that's what happened. So it was Onan's duty to marry his brother's widow, Tam-something—"

"Tammy?" Lucas said. Earlier, while Archer held court on an invasive fish species that was "plundering" the Caribbean, Lucas had indiscreetly rolled his eyes.

"Tamar, maybe," Archer said. "So whenever Onan fucks Tamar—or whenever, I should say, Onan *knows* Tamar, his sister-in-law-cum-wife—no pun intended."

"Nice," John said. He was ignoring his food, busy again with the napkin lint. Once, when visiting him at work, Sara had been baffled by how long it took him to incorporate a small influx of necktie inventory into a display organized by color and pattern. The ties bordered a round wooden table, and he would hold them up to the light for what seemed like cryogenic minutes, looking for the perfect progression of shade. His deliberation intimated the craftsmanship associated with watchmaking or cabinetwork; but he was just dawdling.

"It's not what *cum* means, though," Sara said. Archer had pronounced the word not to rhyme with *womb* or *loom,* but like the vulgar variant of *come.* She was happy to let that part slide; a word's more defensible pronunciation isn't always the right one.

Gemma said, "Isn't it just 'wi—'"

"It's about duality or simultaneity," Sara rushed in. "Like if you lived in your car, it'd be your Honda-cum-home. Or if you were a flea living on the skin of a collie, it'd be your Lassie-cum-home."

Lucas was the joke's lone supporter, laughing dorkily between bites. He was eating as if his burrito had said something unkind about his mother.

"So it's like *slash,*" Archer said.

Sara wasn't proud of her know-all streak, particularly when one of her elucidations or corrections contained its own mistake. (A week after this dinner, for instance, she consulted five dictionaries and found disparities about when *amok* was introduced from Malay into English, apparently by way of Portuguese, while she herself concluded that her argument about anachronism was pretty much groundless.) In the teeth of arrogance, however, pedantry seemed a lesser crime than meekness. "*Slash* usually connotes either-or," she said.

"You should send Sara your essay," John said. "She's a professional editor."

"Proofreader."

"The piece isn't that far along yet," Archer said, which may have been true, though he said it as if the weight of his borrowed ideas would overwhelm all errors and infelicities.

"Do you write, then, for a living?" Lucas said.

"No, for now it's more of an avocation than a vocation," Archer said.

"So what's your vocation?"

Lucas could be such a jerk, but Sara admired him for it. It had so far been an odd, tense meal, and she kept switching sides, just as she had as a kid during sports broadcasts in which neither the Bills nor the Sabres were playing. "You have to pick a team," her dad would say, and she would answer, "I just want it to be close."

"I do some consulting," Archer said vaguely, "some work in the art market. It's a patchwork of self-employment."

"Hey, I wonder if you know anyone who'd want to invest in this company I'm starting," Lucas said. "Sturdy vinyl grocery bags."

"That's the name?" Archer said wearily.

"No, the name's Brand Nubagian."

"The first name was better," Archer said.

"They're to come in all sorts of bright colors and designs," Gemma pitched.

"It's an opportunity," Lucas said. "The reusable bag thing is moving way beyond self-righteous hippies in bad shoes."

"Soon even the smartly shod will be self-righteous about their tiny sacrifices and adjustments," Sara said.

"Eminently machine washable," Lucas said. "In cold."

"I doubt investors will care what temperature you wash the bags in," Archer said. He looked back at Sara, changing his expression from bemusement to something hard to interpret. "So Onan always pulls out," he said, "spills his seed, because he doesn't like the idea of giving it in some magical way to his dead brother." Sara didn't understand why Archer felt the skeevy need to look at her during this part of his lecture, or why he wouldn't let the subject be changed. People were always misreading the clearly marked maps of conversation. In fairness, she had drawn him out on his essay (of course he would never send it to her). Once prompted, though, he had proceeded as if he were sitting down for a half-hour interview with Leonard Lopate. "God kills him for failing to honor the rules of levigate marriage," he said. She silently reiterated the new-to-her word; later that night, she saw that he'd meant *levirate,* with an *r.* "Only way later was Onan's coitus interruptus conflated with masturbation."

"But don't you think," John started to say, then faltered. "Don't you think that when he pulls out he jerks it a little to come?"

"Charming," Gemma said.

"I actually think it's a good point," Lucas said.

Archer: "Genesis is, um . . ."

"Silent on that particular question?" Sara filled in. John could say the dumbest things, but now she was contemplating the matter, picturing Onan by some dusty pillared house, bearded, she guessed, like John, whose beard bothered her face but felt good on her thighs. It was unusual but possible, she could testify, for a grown man to come without much direct genital stimulation, for instance—

"Yes, completely silent," Archer said, interrupting Sara's thought and finally moving the discussion in another direction, away from himself but not explicitly toward anyone else. He wasn't a great asker of questions. Sara—big on civility, insecure about her current status—disapproved of this but liked not having to answer the customary questions. As a confident man with a putatively Croesan net worth, he was probably used to being the center of attention, even if he wasn't someone you'd necessarily notice on the subway, or for that matter on an airport shuttle bus with many available seats. His strongest feature, if something below the chin can be called a feature, was his very pronounced Adam's apple, almost ugly, though again, not to such a Tom Pettyish extreme that you'd necessarily notice it. He was jowly and his hairline was receding, but unlike most of his young-and-balding peers, Lucas for one, he wasn't keeping his hair cropped, was in fact showing what she hoped was an inadvertent comb-over. His face, in contrast, was wide and innocent, a Boy

Scout's face; looking at him could yield the sort of chronometric confusion one might get before a neo-Gothic building. Maybe a tendency to arouse such confusion united Archer and John? Archer could have found more interesting companions than John, Sara thought, though maybe Archer didn't want interesting companions; maybe John put him at ease like he nearly did with Sara, or maybe Archer saw John—legitimately working class: his father a pipe-fitter, his mother a part-time church secretary, his brother reportedly the kind of guy who blows marijuana smoke into the mouths of dogs—as a sartorially assimilationist exotic. The check arrived.

Gemma and Lucas had been getting more tactile over the past hour and decided to return early to the apartment, while Sara, John, and Archer shared a cab to the art gallery. John paid the fare and tipped with what Archer implied was a yokel's munificence. Archer laughed about the tip as they slalomed through the millers and smokers outside the gallery, John accepting the teasing as if it held only affection. Archer's full smile was strange and gummy, like an angry horse, and that ugliness probably made his teasing seem crueler than he meant it to be. "It's no crime to send a taxi driver back to Queens with a few extra dollars," she said, but by that time the men were filing into the gallery, and either they didn't hear her or chose to ignore her.

Inside, everything was crowded and cute, like the squeezed rightward letters on a grade-schooler's title page. She watched Archer and the others drift away from her, or maybe she drifted away from them. She had expected Archer to be handsomer, having envisioned the playboy aristocrat of half-remembered movies. She gave some credence to the terrible idea that the rich are better looking than the middle and lower classes. The exceptions were countless, of course; most members of the lower- and underclasses wouldn't get the chance to rise no matter how spectacular their beauty, and plastic surgery's frequent deformation of elderly elites was a great leveler, though obviously not an inheritable one. Maybe Archer wasn't as rich as John said. There was nothing immoderately swanky about his appearance. He wore jeans that had blued the tops of his canvas sneakers, a button-down shirt the color of avocado flesh, and a parka that he stashed in a corner of the gallery, unconcerned about theft. She watched his loose-limbed movements through the crowd, watched him greet someone with a shoulder-level handshake, low-key but affected, like they were fellow messy-haired indie rappers, their music as white and uneven as salt stains. Archer's shirt, she noticed again as she pressed into his widening circle (in which John looked ludicrous in his Ronald Reagan getup), was much too big, definitely not tailored, unless, paying a premium to ward off foppish perfection, he had asked his tailor to duplicate a shirt bought hastily off the rack from a store catering to gutty businessmen. The jeans were Levi's, though they did seem to be one of the upmarket selvedge reissues. On the right leg there were two bleach drips that might have pushed someone altogether money-blithe toward a new pair. The stains also advertised that from time to time Archer handled bottles of bleach, that he took pride and pleasure in doing things for himself. Near the end of their stay at the gallery (Archer bought two of the dioramas, the same two Sara found most bewitching), she examined the back of his head, staring at it from a distance, the crowd now thinning in sympathy with Archer's hair, and she wondered if, like a thrifty and suicidal boyfriend she'd had briefly in college, he even served as his own barber.

She didn't really like him but was thirsty for his approval, the approval he wouldn't give that "fucking tool" of an actor. She wanted to finish the evening with Archer and John in some quiet bar where she could show that, in addition to being sharp and glib, she could be soft and contemplative. After social outings she often had fantasies of laconism, wishing she had maintained a mysterious but not detached silence interrupted infrequently by blinks of gnomic wit and koanlike wisdom. And often she *was* quiet and shy, especially at parties, but rarely in small groups or around people who interested her. She wanted to interest them too, after all, and she didn't have the reputation, beauty, wealth, or power to do so without talking. Maybe once in a while she could arouse curiosity with the sphinxian wonder of her interiority, but more often she would just be thought boring, burdensome, and pudgy, if she was thought of at all. People are sympathetic to the shy, sometimes, but they resent them for making others do all the work. Then again, someone like Archer might welcome any boon to his conversational hegemony.

Saying goodbye, Archer touched John's back with a force harder than a pat, softer than a slap. Then he hugged Sara gingerly, caressing her back for a few seconds. "It was great to meet you," he said, wrinkling his forehead, making eye contact, putting the words in a consequential minor key, like he was telling a child not to forget her mittens. In theory she didn't like that either, but something about it felt good, to be looked at with such passionate intensity, the right phrase, she thought, though one yoked to Yeats's famous line about what the worst are full of. His eyes were brown and prettier than the rest of his face, and it surprised her to realize that one of the things she was feeling was lust.

That feeling haunted her on her last night in New York, lying guiltily in her little bedroom, listening to John's de trop words of love and dedication. She didn't think of Archer while she and John made love, not much, but he returned in force to her thoughts immediately afterwards. She waited five minutes to ask, "So how much money specifically do you think Archer has?"

"Oh, I don't know," John said into the semidarkness. "A shitload." (Again with that.) "In college he got a major allowance. Like, major. I don't know how much, but it seemed . . ."

"Inexhaustible?"

"Near about. It was tricky at first, 'cause he always wanted to go out to restaurants and concerts and that, or like go to New York for the weekend. And I didn't have too awful much money. Then midway through freshman year he called his parents. It was cool because he was talking to his mom on the phone, but he was also talking to me—I mean, I was in the room and he was looking at me, and he told her how he'd lucked out with his suitemate, the Idaho one, not the other guy, but that I was broke, and could she maybe send something extra for me."

"All so the two of you could pursue recreational opportunities on a more equal footing?"

"Yeah, I guess. Just to narrow the gap. I don't like to feel beholden and all, but, you know, it was really nice of him."

"Sure, very," Sara said. From Lucas's room someone sang in a melancholy falsetto over squelchy dance beats. "Though I suppose you could argue that it was a somewhat wanting act of noblesse oblige, in that if his allowance was really so inexhaustible, he could have given up some of his own money without noticeable deprivation."

"Well, maybe, but—"

"Petitioning his parents for an extra allotment was just a way to seem thoughtful and openhanded without making any sacrifice whatsoever."

"That's pretty harsh. His own money was his parents' money too, so I don't really see the difference. Someday his parents will die—I don't like to say that, 'cause they're really nice—but someday they will, and he'll inherit a bit less money because he gave some to me. Or *they* did."

She drowsily pretended agreement, though she wasn't tired, and they both lay together for another quietly wakeful two hours. Then, as if a day passed outside of memory, she was back in her single bed in West Seneca.

June 2011

Standing in the gym's jump-ball circle, the camp director reached what Karyn hoped was the peroration of his speech about adversity, teamwork, and much of his own childhood. Too grudgingly respectful to take out her phone, Karyn instead inspected the remains of Maxwell's lunch: the sandwich bitten daintily into the shape of Arkansas, the browning apple slices, the wrapper for one of the invariably stale youth-market energy bars she often bought for the last time. She shifted her weight, tried to obscure the pain in her back by focusing on the pain in her knee. Some days she wished she could just be a consciousness floating on cotton balls; other days she wished she could be on codeine. In the car she said, "So how was that?"

"Good," Maxwell said, meaning the opposite. Questioned further, he explained that he didn't like his group; the better players were imperious ball hogs, the lesser ones distractible doormats. "This one kid yells 'Brick!' every time I get the ball, even though I hardly ever shoot and only one of my misses was a brick miss."

"He says it just to you?"

"I don't know."

She never knew how to advise his responses to minor bullying. A certain cheek-turning sangfroid seemed wise, but she didn't want him to grow into a knot of stanched resentment. At a different day camp, she had complained when a sexist little homophobe said Maxwell's shoes were in a "sissy color," but her intervention, she feared, had succeeded only in making the taunting subtler. "I'll mention it to the coach," she said now as they drove into the garage, the side mirror bumping against an unfinished credenza from Jason's bout with woodworking. "Maybe robotics camp will be better."

"Maybe."

The landline was ringing when she turned the back door's deadbolt. In her work voice: "This is Karyn."

"Gemma Pitchford, but you know that."

"I just got in. Can I call you back in an hour?"

"Bated breath."

While the meat grayed for hamburger mac 'n' peas, she ran up to change (drawstring shorts, Miranda Lambert baseball shirt, toe socks), poured a glass of wine from the seventeen- rather than the twelve-dollar bottle, and set up her laptop on the kitchen island, resolved to an efficiency she rarely applied to her nonprofessional life. First she would cut it off categorically with Paul the consultant, who at this moment, conceivably, was reserving a B and B on Lake Winnebago and wondering if he had after all married too young. She tried to formulate a discreet cipher: *I think we should keep the system offline,* something like that, though of course discussing the HRIS on Facebook would in itself be—

It seemed, however, that he had already unfriended and—she ran a few more tests—blocked her. Beeswax versus an unsinging siren.

She took a moment.

She dumped the peas and pasta into a strainer, mixed them in a plastic bowl with the meat and the packet of powdered cheese, called Maxwell away from the collaborative computer game he was playing over Skype, and closed her laptop screen. She called him again.

"Two minutes."

Seven minutes later, he took the stool next to hers and raced through his first half-dozen bites. Karyn was almost finished. "How'd your game go?" she said.

"We could've won but Galen rage-quit."

"Oh."

Some silence.

"If a genie gave you a million dollars," he said, "would you wear the same Hammer pants every day for a year?"

"How do you know about Hammer pants?"

"Everyone does."

That point didn't seem worth arguing. "I've *paid* to wear dumber things than Hammer pants," she said.

"So you would? It's every day," he stressed. "To work, to church."

"We don't go to church."

"But if we did. Or like to that wedding."

"How would you feel about a guy driving with us to that wedding?"

"What guy?"

"I'm not exactly sure—I mean, not a hitchhiker or anything; I know his name."

He shrugged. "And you can't wash 'em."

"The Hammer pants?"

"Yeah, 'cause then what are you wearing?"

She sipped her wine. "I'd do it for fifty thou. Less if I knew I wouldn't lose my job."

"What if they had swastikas on them?"

"Do I get the money ahead of time?"

"No, after."

"So I couldn't just stay inside like a Nazi invalid." She thought for a moment. "No, not worth it."

"A billion?"

"Then it would be wrong not to take the money," she said. "I could help a lot of people."

"Yeah, like me. You could help me buy stuff."

"Better to disgrace myself for the greater good. Utilitarianism. Not that disgrace has to enter the—"

His chair honked when he stood up. "Did you know there were swastikas before Hitler?"

"Yes."

"You could say they were those kind of swastikas."

"Put your bowl directly in the dishwasher, please."

She pushed her own bowl aside and opened her screen. Googling Lucas Pope led her to a website, its design clearly guided by thrift, for a badly named line of reusable vinyl bags. The last of the site's three blog posts was two years old and underpainted with frustration. She didn't find much else: he, or another Lucas Pope, was quoted in a competently written, poorly reported piece from 2004's Republican National Convention, and his name turned up on a few old alt-weekly calendar items for DJ gigs in and around Philadelphia. She clicked back to Facebook and paused over his five-day-old friend request. To her mind, accepting his request was the same as agreeing to drive him to Winnipeg, the same as demoting Maxwell to third wheel. Having a child ride shotgun when there was an adult in back would be an affront even to her progressive ideas about natural power.

Buying time, she did yet another search on Archer. A few new items emerged: a picture of him looking stylishly rumpled at a fundraiser for refugees, a skiing piece for *Outside* magazine in which he courageously used the word *schussboomer* in the first sentence, and, on the third page of results, an essay from a journal Karyn knew by reputation to be fashionable. It began:

> In college I took a fiction workshop from a prominent visiting novelist whose marginal notes were sometimes incisive, sometimes obliquely pictographic. He wasn't like those famously egomaniacal, belittling writing instructors who rip up manuscripts in front of the class. He was soft-spoken, warm, and encouraging. Much of his encouragement must have been disingenuous, but he provided clues—pauses, equivocal inflections, ambiguous adjectives—by which one could gauge his sincerity. I reasoned at the time that he was sincere when praising my work, insincere when praising almost everyone else's. For one of the early classes I submitted a story written in the form of a family Christmas letter and heavily indebted to Donald Barthelme, my literary polestar of several weeks. One of my classmates, a hiccupping Arizonan whose story I considered precious and backdated, though I hadn't said so, accused my story of being "masturbatory." Later in the semester, another of my stories was summed up in the same way, this time by a student whose work I jealously admired.

The criticism is scarcely unusual and has been leveled at work of infinitely greater value than my collegiate "fictions," as I was then calling them. Byron, for instance, used the metaphor to excoriate Keats, as Thomas W. Laqueur reminds us in *Solitary Sex: A Cultural History of Masturbation.* The artist is most readily linked with the onanist when his or her work is fantastic, silly, rebarbative, abstruse, or ostentatiously intellectual (rhymes with "hen-peck'd you all," as Byron himself reminds us; I note this perhaps to admit that I'm especially stung by and defensive around the criticisms of women). But any imaginative artist is open to the attack, since the campaign against masturbation has been in part a campaign against imagination, or against the wrong breed of imagination, not merely the concupiscent sort but the indulgent, daydreaming sort that is seen to serve no public good. (The self-indulgent writer is the masturbatory writer snubbed by more polite critics.) Often the campaign is fought not in the name of disciplined purity but of disciplined cooperation. If one wants to make love and one's partner instead chooses what William Gass called "handmade sex," one is angry. Likewise, the reader undelighted by a story that seems to have been oodles of fun to write (or, short of that, a story rooted in antisocial pleasure) might feel a kinship with the housekeeper—alas, I'm thinking of a specific one—compelled to handle tissues, wadded and dusty, under a forgetful teenager's bed.

In my case, though, the criticism was subtextually pointed. I went to an elite university where wealth was relatively common, but just the same many knew me as a student of exceptional means, and further knew that my wealth flowed to some extent from my stepfather having founded a company that was for several decades the world's leading manufacturer of sex toys. I had courtiers and detractors. In both camps there were people who found my inheritance amusing; in the latter camp, I inferred, there were people who associated my presence at the school, where I was an undistinguished history major and budding alcoholic, with a pulling of strings sufficient for the most Napoleonic of puppet-theater battle scenes (and it's true that my parents, particularly my stepfather, Cole Neblett '66, were major donors, though I'll add that Cole was the first in his family to go to college and that, some three decades after making his fortune, he still delights in playing Trimalchio). I'm close to certain that my second critic, the talented writer and teacher's favorite, knew something of my family. She was a homely spurter of nonsensical arguments, but I was attracted to the challenge of her unmasked antipathy toward me. For the record, in the early part of my college career I was spending not from an inheritance under my control but from a liberal allowance, and when I did succeed to a full independence, the money came mostly from a trust established by my maternal grandmother. Her father, among other things, developed a kind of borosilicate glass widely used for lab instruments and kitchenware. Nor has Dr. Knox (toys and marital aids) been my stepfather's most successful enterprise. But there's rarely any percentage in making these points, explaining, in other words, that my (considerable) sex-toy money is just a drop in the bucket. Besides, the mere phrase *borosilicate glass* seems to have soporific effects. I've accordingly grown accustomed to being thought of as the Dildo Scion and variations thereof.

All this has made me predisposed to . . .

Karyn reached the firewall. She would have paid to read on, but her credit cards were several feet away, and she was late in returning Gemma's call. She accepted Lucas's friend request without further rumination and reached for the phone.

"Ms. Bondarenko," Gemma answered.

"All right, have him call me."

January 2005

Bad form to alter a colleague's work, but the more John examined the mannequin, the less he liked the foulard pocket square that Ray or Clee (probably Ray) had puffed out in the mocha herringbone jacket. For starters, the Quadrangle model was cut trim; properly fitted and tailored, it would never accommodate a bulging puff. Sure, you could finesse that on a mannequin, but you were leading the customer astray, just as you were when you sold a 42 Quad to an obvious 40. Basically spits on the whole point of the design! Just sell him a Walbrook in the right size!

He studied the mannequin some more, reached back to tighten one of the pins. He could fold the square—not so meddlesome—but its relationship to the tie would still be a mite too on the nose. Decent guy, Ray, but kind of Garanimals.

After picking out a subtly patterned linen handkerchief, he surreptitiously made the swap. Archer's greeting startled him while he was smoothing out the breast. "Ah hell, sorry," John said. "I thought you were Ray."

"Who's Ray?"

"Or Clee. But don't sweat it." John motioned Archer to one of the store's tufted leather club chairs. "New swatches came in last week. I picked out a high-twist blue that'd be great for you." Archer sat down, started flipping unobservantly through the fabric samples. "The one I have in mind's right in front," John said.

Archer held up the card. "Seems just like my current suit."

"Well, but it's a much lighter shade." John's Moleskin contained many comprehensive and maybe only subtly differentiated lists of his dream wardrobe. It killed him that Archer wore the same blue suit year-round to weddings, funerals, and charity functions, the same one he'd worn for graduation.

"Yeah, I don't see the difference," Archer said.

"In sunlight you would."

"I'm not gonna wear it to the beach."

"Even in artificial light, though, if we did a side by side." John had been an authority on style and grooming long before he had the testifying closet, and in college he had sometimes played the valet. Archer arrived in Cambridge just barely able to tie a four-in-hand and with no knowledge of the half Windsor, a more complementary knot for his widish face. Surprising ignorance, it seemed to John, or, as Archer joked, "Engels-level class treachery." John laughed at that, not quite getting it, then stood behind Archer in front of the cloudy mirror John had hung in their suite's common room, guiding Archer's long-fingered hands through the steps of three essential knots. "Lighter weight too," John said now. "Nine seriously airy ounces. We could have this made just in time for spring."

Archer brushed threads off his jeans.

"I noticed last time that your current suit's getting awful shiny at the elbows," John said.

"Lends character."

"That comes from dry-cleaning and pressing it overoften. Really a suit shouldn't need more than a natural-bristle clothes brush like the one I gave you and occasional sessions in a steamy bathroom. Resort to the cleaners—I still like Jeeves on Madison—only if the suit's been dirtied beyond the hopes of at-home spot-cleaning."

"Got it."

"Which I can help you with, man. Just come over sometime; I'll run you through it."

Archer decided to hold off on the suit, left instead with a cashmere robe for his stepfather. He was a great one for unoccasioned gifts. Over the years he had given John a pair of vintage cuff links, a monogrammed flask, a mandolin (a challenge for John's fat fingers, but still). On his way out of the store, Archer proposed a jogging date for the unspecified future. It seemed to John—not always, but it sometimes seemed to John that Archer was trying to maintain their friendship in the most efficient way possible, often building plans around mundane things he was going to do anyway. But then, maybe that two-birds-one-stone approach had always held sway; maybe in the past Archer would have gone from restaurant to gallery to bar to party whether John was with him or not. It hadn't felt that way, though; it had felt as if the barhopping and what all were secondary to their togetherness, even if it was agreed—established, you could say, by Archer—that they would abandon each other on the arrival of what Archer called "sex-type potentialities."

Not heaps of those arrived for John, who had little aptitude for bar chat and assumed that all lack-love sex started with dishonesty and led to heartbreak. Mostly he and Archer stuck together, talked about movies and Archer's travels and their mutual friends; sometimes they touched on spiritual matters in a chill way that made John feel deeply understood. These days, a jog's spare, panting conversation met their needs, or Archer's, and even when they had more to say, the extra words only stressed what was missing. Or worse, what had never been there, like with the italicized words in the King James Bible: what often seems like random emphasis is actually the translators' honesty, their way of pointing out clarifying or grammatically necessary words not found in the Hebrew or Greek.

On their respective housing applications, John and Archer had reported an interest in music, French, and late but quiet hours, presenting themselves as more placid and artsy than they would prove to be, and in fact John's interest in music didn't run much deeper than Archer's commitment to French. Funny how they'd been matched so impeccably through misrepresentation, though the Freshman Dean's Office would have had other interests, class mingling maybe chief among them. John, though never a dynamo, grew less retiring than he'd been at home, partly owing to the boost of Archer's quick acceptance, the unbelievable fact that someone like Archer enjoyed his company. Their suite's third resident, an intimidatingly focused mathematician, may even have seen Archer and John as out-and-out partiers, though that was wide of the truth.

Back at his apartment, John took off his tie by undoing the knot rather than brutally pulling and stretching the thing, inserted cedar shoe trees into his bench-made wingtips, and brushed his suit while a kitchen timer rattled for three minutes. Based on past experience, Archer would eventually call to make good on the proposed jog, but it would take a while. Better, sometimes, to remind him. He wrote CALL A on his wall calendar, then inserted an arrow to move the call date ahead a few days, lest an exact two weeks seem too planned.

May 2011

"That you, Ania?"

Sara took the stone path from the driveway to the patio, rounding her shoulders apologetically as she entered George's field of vision. "No, Grandpa, it's Sara."

"Of course it is," he said, perhaps guessing her visit was forgotten rather than unexpected.

"Sorry to just turn up on your doorstep like a foundling," she said. Her father, Chick, had insisted on the surprise element. "I had some business in Chicago; then my phone died."

"These phones!"

She sat down on the chaise longue. The Japanese garden had fallen into somewhat embarrassed circumstances, but the patio was in good shape, the nearby hedges trimmed, the grass mowed. "Beautiful day," she said loudly.

"I can hear you."

Only planning to stay for a few days, she needed to gather as much info on George's lucidity as she could without getting full-on interrogational. "Isn't Ania dead, Grandpa?"

"Yes, that's right." A brief hush. "I suppose I've taken to calling her daughter by that name."

"Would it help to write down—"

"She doesn't correct me but sometimes flinches." He took a sip of what looked to be bourbon. He was wearing an open cardigan over a gas-blotted guayabera, formerly his yard-work shirt. "Fix you anything?"

"No, thank you, I'm fine."

"Marion loved Dr. Pepper. She'd add rum and think we didn't notice."

"That sounds like her," Sara said, not sure if it did. "Feeling all right since your fall?"

"Fine, fine."

Squirrels shook an oak branch.

"These chairs look good," she said. She patted the meshed vinyl between her legs.

"John refurbished them."

"Ah."

"It took several years."

"Where is he, anyway?"

"I don't know."

"At his other job?"

"Yes."

"And what do you make of—"

"Well." George put his hands on his knees and stood up. "Nap time." Gesturing toward the trees, he added, "Though with these damn birds you can't get a lick of sleep." He made his hand into a beak.

"I might catch a few winks myself. Think I'm coming down with something."

"Mi casa . . ."

This was the second time in five years that Sara had been asked to run reconnaissance on her grandfather, as well as the second time in five years that she had visited him. She had promised to join what remained of the family for Thanksgiving '09 but had bailed at the last minute, citing a freelance deadline, the imminence of which was significantly exaggerated. She thought the excuse would seem more plausible if she told her dad that she had procrastinated on the assignment, that she had already asked for two extensions, that the editor was on the cusp of dismissing her as a deadbeat. (Why, she later asked herself, were her lies so self-incriminating?) She wasn't racked with guilt over her grandfilial neglect, but it needled her now as she snooped around George's abandoned office and sporting den, its walls decorated with dusty-nosed African hunting trophies, its closet equipped with superannuated tennis gear, a teal vaporizer, an armory of redundant windbreakers. She lay down on the daybed and resumed reading an oppressively acclaimed novel in which so far there were two incorrect subjunctives. Despite the ambient chirping, George was snoring in the bedroom across the hall.

Chick had requested and funded both visits, the funding unnecessary but accepted without protest. The first trip, around Christmas of '06, sought to determine whether George could go on living independently in the house he and Phyliss had bought sixty years earlier; the second sought to determine whether he could go on living under the suspect care of John Anderson. Chick had recently passed through Lammermuir and had ideas of his own, but he was looking for a second opinion, or he wanted to poke the embers of Sara's loyalty. "You won't want to see him next in his coffin," he had said over the phone, though as a rule the Crennels were cremated.

Loath as she was to admit it, Sara's inspection so far told of John's professionalism. The house was clean and in many spots obsessively ordered; the kitchen was stocked with healthful food; a promising menu was taped to the fridge. George was grouchier than in his younger days and no longer consistently rapier, but for a man born before the establishment of the League of Nations, he was in good health. He didn't seem hobbled by his recent fall. Still, Sara resented John's weaselly presence here. He had horned in on the caretaker-factotum search back in '07; then, like Dick Cheney, he'd nominated himself to Chick (busy and suggestible) as the fittest candidate. He was the main reason she had reneged on that Thanksgiving.

Chick didn't think John should still hold an outside job, selling navy blazers and orange polo shirts part-time at some mall, but Sara was glad now to have a few quiet hours before she had to face him. She blew her nose, dropped the tissue on the floor. The last time she'd lain on this daybed was the night after her grandmother's funeral, only a few weeks after Sara's sixteenth birthday. The dominant notes during dinner had seemed to Sara deficiently reflective, everyone talking and asking about the usual things: hockey and Newt Gingrich and O. J. and what classes one was taking, what plans one had for college. Over dessert, the oldest extant cousin casually applied a slur to Carol Moseley Braun and wasn't properly rebuked. Sara retreated to George's den shortly thereafter. Fifteen minutes later, Aunt Marion was leaning against the doorjamb. "Mind if we hide out together?" she asked.

"Yeah—I mean, no." She closed her book. She'd brought two on the trip: *Foucault for Beginners,* one of several illustrated précis from a series she'd been collecting for about a year; and the Mary Gaitskill book she was about to finish.

"Don't mind Grace," Marion said. "She's a pig, but it's too late."

"She's nice, usually." The Crennels weren't without their divisions, which sometimes led to all-out enmity and estrangement. Sara had noticed her father and Steve, Grace's son, roll their eyes at each other during Marion's eulogy. The gesture was true to form but disappointing, even considering the eulogy's shortcomings, its weird braid of sanctimony, local history, and score settling. Marion, typically a no-show at family events, was often spoken of in joking terms, and Sara could never tell to what degree hostility outbalanced affection in this ridicule, or if the hostility was mostly that of the bully or mostly that of the castoff. Sara had only met Marion four times aside from unremembered baby meetings, but she idolized her as the cool Crennel, the one with ties to avant-garde film and Subaru loads of yellowing radical bona fides. For much of the seventies and eighties Marion had been a social worker in Berkeley. Now she and her partner ran a catering business.

Marion stepped into the room, sat sideways on an easy chair, and lit a cigarette. "Looks like I'll have my first and last smoke in the same room," she said. They were in Marion's former bedroom, Sara was reminded. Marion described how it had been furnished in the fifties and early sixties: the squat bookshelf, the peach vanity, the Japanese tissue-box cover. Then she asked about the Gaitskill book. Few took an interest in Sara's reading, except sometimes to argue that she was doing it too much or at unsuitable times. "When I read her," Sara said, "it makes me want to write, to write for people, I mean, because I want to make someone else feel how I feel when I read her." Marion smiled—not condescendingly—and said she'd felt the same way when she discovered Doris Lessing. It didn't seem that Marion was saying she'd felt the same way because youthful feelings pass like batons from one generation to the next, but rather that they, Marion and Sara, were really alike, akin in spirit as much as in blood. Marion had even written a novel, she said, or most of one, but had never shown it to anyone, not even to Corinne. "Wow," Sara said. "But," Marion advised, "you shouldn't be so clandestine." A few days later, with a receptive, sophisticated reader in mind, Sara started working harder than ever on her writing. For her that meant slowly and sedulously, and by the time she had two presentable pieces, Marion was sick. Sending her the stories no longer seemed appropriate, or rather the stories no longer seemed appropriate, too trivial for a dying woman's time.

Now she heard John entering through the mudroom. They met in the kitchen. His beard was fuller than before and ended in a curling point.

"Whoa!" he said.

"Sorry to ambush you—I'm not ambushing you. My dad asked me to pop in."

"He did? He was just here, not two months ago."

"He worries, is all," she said.

"This about that fall? Like I said, it wasn't bad. Missed his hip altogether. I just reckoned you should know—Hey, George."

Her grandfather was coming down the long hallway in a different cardigan, past Chick's old bedroom and its blanched baseball pennants, past the so-called front door on the side of the house, past the second bathroom and el cuartito, finally to the kitchen. "Sare Bear take you unawares?" he said.

"The more the merrier," John said.

George glanced toward the fridge and touched his stomach. "Tengo hambre, Juan."

For dinner John served rosemary chicken, brown rice, and a quinoa salad brightened by cubed cucumbers and gibbous watermelon.

"No bread?" George said.

"There's rice, Grandpa."

"Is rice bread now?"

"And quinoa," Sara said. "If anything, there's an excess of grains."

Unfazed, John got up to close the sliding glass doors that looked out on the patio and garden. On his way back to the table, he touched Sara's shoulder. "Nice cashmere."

"It's a blend."

He sat down, reached over to feel the sleeve, knitted his brow. "Can't be a blend."

"John."

"I'd trust Beau Brummell on this one," George said.

"How's the editing and whatnot going?" John asked.

"I'm still making a living. Lucky in this market."

"Yeah, Archer says it's a squeeze."

"Early in the season for watermelon," George said.

"I can't wait for Archer's new one," John said. "He posted a rave review from *Circus* the other day."

"*Kirkus.*" A slip—Sara's: she was trying to grow out of these pointless corrections. Also, it wasn't a rave.

"That's the one," John said.

"Was he 'humbled'?"

"Don't recall him saying anything along those lines. You'll be at the wedding, right?"

She sensed that he already knew for certain she would be there. If only he were less pathetic, she could feel better about finding him insufferable. "Yes," she said.

"This is the wedding I told you about, George." John's tone was artificially upbeat.

"That Greek's wedding?"

"Greek? No, he's Ukrainian. Half Ukrainian."

"Early in the season for watermelon. Not too bad, though."

"Kristen Hanson will be staying here while I'm away."

"Fine."

"After dinner," John said to Sara, "maybe you'd want to take a peek up in the attic at some of your grandma's old clothes. Some great pieces up there."

"She had a wonderful eye," George said.

"There's a tweed skirt suit with a Givenchy sort of look."

"I went through that stuff years ago, John. Most of it doesn't fit me."

"If there's something you like, it'd be no trouble for me to let it out 'fore you leave."

"No thank you."

"There's a mess of cool stuff up there, not just clothes."

He made two more attempts to lure Sara up to the attic, as if he were desperate to reveal—the thought amused her—his new line of laboriously handcrafted bondage apparatuses, though when they'd been together he had never pushed to transgress beyond reverse cowgirl.

The next morning, he organized a "World Series of Parcheesi," for which Sara tried, reluctantly, to match some of his enthusiasm. George found none of it contagious and seemed to be making deliberately self-destructive moves. "You sure about that one, George?" John said at one point.

George looked at his Bulova. "Very."

By midafternoon Sara had switched to an earlier flight home. She didn't know what to report to her father but was beginning to suspect that George was safer in John's vicinity than John was in hers.

February 2005

A few weeks after Archer stopped into the store but did not order a made-to-measure suit, John called to pin down those jogging plans and was instead invited to Archer's SoHo condo for Saturday brunch. When John arrived, Archer was sifting through the filing cabinets in his main room's office partition, filling plastic tubs with old bills, bank statements, and investment reports that someone else would later shred. Brunch was just a bag of bagels. "There a cutting board?" John asked from the kitchen.

"By the microwave."

John brought Archer a bagel, carrying a kitchen stool with his other hand. The stool's seat was made out of an old disco LP. "So how'd that essay turn out?"

"It's the best thing I've done," Archer answered. "I'm setting it aside so I can see it fresh in a few weeks."

"Smart." The seat was about as comfortable as an old disco LP. "Let me know if you want Sara's contact info. She's a whiz at editing."

"Yeah, not really my style, but thanks."

John couldn't say what "style" referred to there, but he didn't think it was a cut on Sara. After that night at the gallery and all, Archer had made a point of saying she was cool.

"She back living with Rodney Road Bike?"

"With Lucas? No." Lucas's latest bike, despite some snafus with the seat tube-bottom bracket weld, was John's best and lightest to date, not much more than nineteen pounds when kitted up with two full water bottles. "He's actually a decent guy," John said.

"He's a putz."

"But no, Sara—'member I told you how she's staying home for a spell in Buffalo, mapping out a novel or something?"

"Right."

"We were trying the long-distance thing, but . . ."

"Tricky," Archer said. He sounded like he had a pencil in his mouth.

After a few beats, John said, "One of the hardest things these past months has just been—just not seeing her."

"Well, yeah. *To miss,* I think, is the standard verb."

"But I mean *looking* at her. I just really want to see her. I know she's not beautiful in the usual way—"

"She's great looking."

"You think so? Yeah, 'cause I see her and it's like I'm *struck* or *smote* or—those Bible words." In fact, the first time John had seen Sara—she was walking tentatively through Balthazar toward the shepherd's-check sports coat he'd promised to wear—he had actually gasped as he started to take in her doll-like brown eyes, her slightly open mouth, her porcine nose, how her bangs curved like a cluster of parentheses above her dark eyebrows, only one of which showed over her crooked Velma glasses. Maybe he'd hoped she would hear the gasp, though she couldn't have (gasp too soft, restaurant too loud), and maybe he was unconsciously mimicking the dumbstruck procedures of ladies' men in bad reruns—but no, he hated that kind of thinking, that phony tough-mindedness that was really just fear. His reaction had been true, instinctive, and not only about her looks. Later, the memory helped convince him that Sara was *the one,* and that his love for her could withstand severe droughts of reciprocity. "Tell you the truth, I was thinking of moving there."

Archer raised his head. "To Buffalo?"

"I'm not going to."

Archer looked down again at a glossy corporate packet. "Buffalo's where you move *from.*"

"Or just someplace different. Sam says Detroit's cool."

"But he's another putz. You need to get better at putz recognition. I'm joking but not. Jesus, why do they send me this crap? Anyway, who's gonna buy thirteen-hundred-dollar suits and custom bike frames in Detroit?"

"Auto executives." John would never say this to Archer, but he thought it was sad to be from a country that didn't manufacture its own cars.

Archer chucked a few more sheets into one of the bins. "Well, you could do anything you set your mind to, right?"

"Doubtful."

"I don't really mean *anything.* I always thought—I know it's not your scene, but I always thought you'd wind up on Wall Street or at Accenture or something like that."

John had once thought something like that too. Through junior high he'd been an unexceptional student, strong in math but not the type to rouse lavish praise. Back then he was mainly known, and only to a few, as an uncommonly patient builder, first of Lego and papier-mâché mises en scène for his *Star Wars* figurines, then of model aircraft, and he devoted many more painstaking, steady-handed hours to those pursuits than he did to his homework. If the model didn't work out, he would destroy it. Eight years younger than his burnout brother, he absorbed early on the immersive pleasures of solitary play, and from the day he was born to the day he and his parents walked in on Archer slouchily thrumming his Martin D-28 in Lionel Hall, he made only one good friend, a prankish but good-souled Jack Mormon named Frank, who moved away suddenly at the start of high school. Soon after that, John started spending more time on his schoolwork. It wasn't a resolution; it was something he slipped into for comfort, like how people start doing a lot of cleaning or cooking after a divorce. He had a feel for math—maybe nothing prodigious or, as he eventually confirmed, world class, but a feel, and in the middle of ninth grade he was promoted from Algebra 1 to Geometry. He caught up quickly, started to draw energy from bisection, proofs, and summing angles in polygons; when by trig they moved on to solving differential equations using Taylor series expansion, he experienced a kind of high while working through the problems, became taken with the idea that math existed independent of human thought, that it was discovered rather than invented. Mathematical Platonism, this was called. He liked how important that sounded, liked even more the thought that math existed beyond human thought not just in the way other planets existed before we saw and named them, but because it was divine, that it was created by God, or *was* God. Even the most repetitive plug-and-chug, then, could be a form of communion, a means of being supremely in the moment while partaking of something beyond the world.

To Archer he said, "But I don't think it matters so much what you do." He tried to give this philosophical sally an exploratory air, like when you're testing out whether it's safe to say something mean about a shared acquaintance.

Archer reached to put an envelope in his to-read tray.

"Whether it's math or building bikes or picking a sweet shirt-and-tie combo or studying an outside lineman's toes: is he poised for the pass or for the run? It's just about concentration, zeroing in, letting the experience take over. Like in school with Heidegger and that hammer or whatever."

"I feel that sometimes when I'm writing."

"Exactly, yeah." John felt bad that his examples had been so self-centered. "Of course."

"So if it doesn't matter what you do," Archer said, "it doesn't matter where you do it. No need to skulk off to Detroit. But listen, I should bounce. I'm supposed to visit this guy's studio in"—he looked at his watch—"shit, three and a half minutes."

"Oh."

"You can walk with me if you want."

June 2011

In the front yard of Karyn Bondarenko's house a Seussian shrub hung over a Little Free Library stocked with mass-market thrillers, kids' VHS tapes, and a decades-old investment guide. When Lucas carried his last remaining bike one-handed onto Karyn's dumpsite of a porch, she greeted him cautiously, perhaps with second thoughts. She was wearing a black tech shirt and densely branded bike shorts. In an hour and a half, she said after apologizing for the "ridiculous" shorts, she and her son were cycling over to a friend's house to return a violin. She seemed eager to stress that this familiarizing brunch wouldn't seep into the afternoon. Lucas couldn't be sure, but she seemed to glance admiringly at his bike, a pearl-white racer with JOHN ANDERSON stickered on the down tube. A tyro job, if one knew what to look for, but generally one didn't. The last Lucas had heard, John was out of that business, working as a houseboy for Sara Crennel's grandfather in some tassel-loafer suburb.

Might this brunch be called a date? Lucas, wobbly after a bad run on OkCupid, didn't quite see it that way, but he had put some thought, possibly inapparent, into what he'd wear. Karyn's apology for the shorts indicated that she'd thought about it too, which, as far as the occasion justified semiotic speculation, seemed like a good sign, even if she'd settled on dressing for the day's next activity in clothes she disliked. Tight clothes, however. He followed her through a dark hallway to the kitchen, explaining that although he'd long dismissed bike shorts as a yuppie affectation, in recent years he'd conceded that they really were more comfortable for long rides. He was chattering.

Karyn lit a burner under a teakettle. It was a sunny day, and soon the kettle was exhaling steam shadows on the white stove's backsplash. She poured a bowl of bubbly beaten eggs into a pan and turned around to face Lucas while tapping a splintering wooden spoon on her leg. She had severely bleached blond hair, shortish and pulled away from her high, rounded forehead. There was an undercolor of brown roots and some gray at the temples.

"Mine pill, though," Lucas said. "They pill at the crotch. Yours don't seem to be doing that."

She responded briefly in a brow-furrowing timbre.

"It might be a gendered hazard," he said.

"I'm seeing some pilling on the thighs," she said, "if you really want to discuss this."

"Yeah-no, it's funny—not funny, really, but . . . I first started wearing spandie—I don't know if Gemma told you, but I've been unemployed for a minute."

"She mentioned it."

"Yeah. So after I lost my job I bought a pair of the shorts and was biking like forty miles a day, losing all this weight—I found a lot of it last winter—and I'd look down at myself while riding, and I was so amped about the weight and about generally—I was gonna say generally pulling my shit together, but that's wrong 'cause in a lot of ways I was falling apart. But, I don't know"—he stressed and pitched up *know*—"I'd get kind of turned on looking down at my legs, at what seemed like new muscles, hairs poking through the spandex. I'm not sure why I'm telling you this. I'm not . . . I don't think I have strong narcissistic leanings."

"Are you sure? You might want to take a good look at yourself before deciding that definitively." They traded variations on the joke. "But I understand what you're saying."

"Yeah?" It wasn't clear if she planned to elaborate.

"I've looked in the mirror and been aroused." She poured orange juice while she talked and didn't look at him. "I've been disgusted too, but I've been aroused, once or twice, when I focused on some part of my body and ignored my face."

"But you—"

"I'm not trawling for face compliments," she said. "If I think about it, I suppose I've looked at my face and imagined leaning in for a kiss, even as an adult, but that—it wasn't arousal." At least tonally there was a bespectacled primness to these intimacies that made them more exciting. (Karyn didn't wear glasses, but Lucas could imagine chunky, rectangular frames slipping down her nose.) "I was only saying that I've had to abstract my body to find it arousing."

"Right"—he pointed at her in a showbiz gesture of agreement—"on the bike it was like you're saying, like my legs were *abstracted* from my body. Though that doesn't make sense since what was so cool was how, I don't know, incarnate I felt. Later I got self-conscious again about the shorts. Now I probably wouldn't stop for coffee in them or anything."

"Or wear them for brunch," she said.

"They're unpardonably incorrect brunch attire." His attempt at an across-the-pond accent foundered somewhere around Bermuda. Karyn hmm'd, amusedly, he hoped. She seemed able to acknowledge that something was sort of funny without laughing, as you might when watching an episode of *Mike & Molly* on an airplane. Another possibility was that she didn't find Lucas even sort of funny, and her smile was an attenuated version of sociable laughter. "Gemma says you're a lawyer?" he said.

"No, that's the other Karyn-with-a-*y* Bondarenko, a public defender from Pittsburgh. Weird, I usually show up higher than she does on Google."

"Search is localized, though. Maybe you're only winning in the Twin Cities."

"Damn, I never thought of that." The Twin Cities Karyn Bondarenko explained that she was an employee-benefits specialist for a large retailer.

"So, talking to insurance people and stuff?" he said.

"I'm on the phone with vendors a fair amount, yeah. It's a lot of, you know, helping someone go on short-term disability, sorting out compliance issues with the FMLA."

"That's the Salvadoran guerilla outfit?"

"Family and Medical Leave Act."

"I took a Latin American history class in college."

"Wanna give me a hand with these?" She held out two plates.

It was a small dining room with one turbid window and a built-in cabinet, behind whose glass doors there was little but aging phone books and a monster doll handmade, Lucas learned, by a neighborhood artist with only one name. "I gave it to Maxwell for Christmas," she said. "It was the year of my divorce, and I hadn't really figured out presents, even though I'd been given a list and shopping could hardly be more convenient for me."

"And you must get a discount, right?"

"Yes." Pause. "I got it for him on Christmas Eve at this ultragroovy gift shop where I kept buying totally wrong things just so I'd have something." She interrupted herself to call Maxwell downstairs. In a quiet voice and while listening for her son's footsteps she said, "He was sweet, tried to be grateful. But it was dismal."

"Fuck."

"That same year his dad bought him a Wii."

Shortly after Maxwell came to the table, Lucas asked about the fantasy game responsible for the dissemination of so many cards and dice throughout the first floor. Several minutes later he wished the boy were slightly more afflicted with the mumbling taciturnity that often marked prepubescent responses to strange adults. Alongside the eggs there were fat slices of wheat toast, microwaved vegetarian bacon, hard smiles of cantaloupe, and very good coffee. "Oh, that's cool," Lucas said to Maxwell about a particular card's complicated properties.

"Well, no, that's bad," he said, his face showing a mix of frustration and embarrassment.

"No, yes, bad. It's confusing for me," Lucas said with a surge of affection for Maxwell, though he didn't see himself as the type who had to bruise someone's feelings to fall for them.

"I'm sorry," Karyn said, "Gemma didn't tell me what kind of work you've done."

"I'm a public defender from Pittsburgh. No, I—well, I was working in banks. For a while in New York. Implementing marketing collateral, if that sounds like English to you."

"Sure."

"Then my dad got sick, so I came back to Mipliss to be closer to my folks, and without really trying to I got another bank job. Then the recession hit and . . . yeah. Now I'm in a *What Color Is Your Parachute?* phase."

Maxwell nonverbally asked his mother to elucidate the reference.

"It's a book for people trying to get jobs as parachutists," she said. The sound of her voice had lightened now, though there was still something attractively serrated about it.

Lucas: "The metaphor is . . . do you remember?"

"It's, if you can work out what color your metaphorical parachute is . . . no, I can't remember." She turned to Maxwell. "But it's about matching a career to your talents and interests. Like for you, your ideal career probably isn't to be a concert violinist, since you don't seem to be interested in playing the violin."

"I'm interested."

"Not in practicing."

"I would be if I didn't suck so bad."

"That's . . . I don't even—"

"I feel you, though," Lucas said, holding a piece of half-eaten bacon like a stumpy pointer. "It's like, people are always trying to make ice cream or pop or whatever at home, and that shi—that stuff is never as good as store-bought."

"I'm not sure I see the connection," Karyn said.

"Just that not every labor is justified."

She laughed, a slightly mocking laugh, he feared. Already pegged as a bumbler. "You might want to strike school counselor from your list of career prospects," she said.

"Yeah, no, you should definitely stick with the violin," he said to Maxwell. "You could be the next, uh, Itzhak Perlman."

"Or Nero," she said.

He had so far asked two questions about her job. His goal in situations like this was five; he sometimes pictured hash marks in his head. "So are employees constantly asking you the same things about, like, their 401(k)s?"

"Well, when I was a rep, they were, but now I'm not so much on the frontline."

"You're more management now?" he said.

"Not management, just the second line. The reps will come to me if they can't figure something out, and I deal with employees when something gets escalated."

"Like what?" (𝍸)

"Stuff no one pays attention to till there's a problem at the pharmacy. Or someone dies and I have to deal with the family about life insurance." She forked the last of her eggs on a corner of toast. "It's nice of you to take an interest," she said, "but it kind of bores me to talk about work."

"Oh, sure, it's—"

"I don't mean to sound crabby."

"S'all good." He adjusted his posture to relieve the pressure from his jeans. For a few weeks he'd been wearing the pair with the thirty-six-inch waist instead of the thirty-sevens in hopes that the discomfort would be motivating. Maxwell began noisily rolling one of his many-faceted dice on the table.

"To tell the truth," Karyn said, "I sometimes miss talking about work. One of the things about being married is—well, this isn't always true, is it?—but hopefully you're with someone who wants to hear the details of your dumb day. Like the exciting thing this month is that there's a new guy who's a pig in the kitchen."

"He makes sexist remarks and stuff?" Lucas said, not really confused.

"He leaves food in the sink, crumbs on the table. I sent out a group e-mail but nothing's changed."

"This kid at robotics camp leaves food everywhere," Maxwell said. "He hides it."

"Maybe he's hungry," Lucas said.

"I seriously don't think he's hungry," Maxwell said.

"Are you saying he's fat?" Lucas said.

"No."

"It's something hungry people do," Lucas said. "Hide food."

"He has mental health," Maxwell said.

Lucas asked for clarification.

"He told me, 'I have mental health, FYI,' and then ran away."

"He means mental-health problems," Karyn said.

"Yeah, 'cause mental health is a good thing," Lucas said. "Or neutral."

"May I be excused?"

After Maxwell finished his clomping ascent of the stairs, Lucas figured it was time to say "great kid" or something to that effect. Instead he said, "I have mental health, FYI."

"Yeah, me too," Karyn said.

"Not serious, though. Like I'm off all the meds."

Without sarcasm: "Good for you. My boss went off her Celexa a few months ago, and I really hope she goes back on."

"She talks to you about that stuff?"

"God no, it's just information I have access to."

"Oh, right."

"Something of a perk," she said.

"For me—probably for your boss it was the wrong move—but for me, I didn't like how the pills were flattening and maybe controlling me. Or the thought that I'd let doctors and pharmaceutical marketers convince me that I had a medical condition, as opposed to just being sad sometimes in the regular way."

"Or sad sometimes because we live in a depressing society."

"And the pills are just getting us to accept a situation that's more fucked up than we are sick." It was a less articulate version of something he'd read.

"Well put," she said.

"I felt trapped, you know, 'cause when I told my therapist I was feeling good and wanted to go off the meds, she said, 'If it ain't broke, don't fix it.'"

"Therapists should stick to the clichés of their field," Karyn said.

"I mean, she didn't literally say that. Then a few years later when I explained that I was still on the meds but depressed, she advised me to up the dosage or switch to a different drug. I couldn't stand to be part of that anymore."

"They seem to help me."

"Plus I lost my insurance."

Karyn laughed again, this time a snorty, Bugs Bunny laugh. Lines fanned from her eyes like plumage. Lucas was trying to make out how old she was. A good seven to nine years older than he was, he guessed. But beautiful, beautiful in the way his wife would be beautiful if he were seven to nine years older and long married, married so happily that his wife would be more beautiful to him than ever, and when they went out together he would be proud of her beauty, which would contain and erase all the ways she'd looked before. He pictured holding her hand at a funeral.

She said, "It's not what I wanted."

"What isn't?"

"A lot of things, but you were asking about my job, and I'm sorry I shot you down back there when you were just being nice."

"No worries."

"It's a good job and I'm lucky to have it, but it's not what I wanted," she said. "I used to like how concrete it was, how there was an answer for everything, and if the answer was no, then it was no. Outside of work, most of the questions I'm interested in are unanswerable. That makes me sound so metaphysical." She scraped something off the table with her fingernail. "But maybe I prefer uncertainty and ambiguity to certainty and clarity. Keats's negative capability, which I'm probably calling on just to dignify my ignorance. Sometimes the whole world's a mystery to me."

"Word."

"Even the simplest mechanical operations." She picked up her last scrap of toast. "How a toaster works."

"A toaster?"

"But there are other, more complicated appliances." She filled her lips with air but didn't sigh. "Back in the Mesolithic I thought about going to law school."

"Inevitably," he said.

"Maybe I should have. Then I could be an unsatisfied lawyer."

"Hey, there's still time to pursue all sorts of unsatisfying second careers."

She pressed her fingers into her cheekbone. Throughout the morning she'd been touching her face, even while preparing the food. "There's a German word," she said, "Torschlusspanik, 'gate-closing panic.' You see that the unending possibilities you imagined when you were young weren't in fact unending. You freak out."

"Midlife crisis, you mean?"

She shrugged. "I suppose that's all I mean. Trying to skirt cliché through borrowed idioms must be a symptom of midlife crisis."

"If it ain't broke . . ."

Through the window a chickadee called in two notes like a rusty swing set.

"Sorry," she said. "I feel weird."

"I'm enjoying it—I mean, not enjoying your feeling weird."

Another nasal laugh. "When I was younger I thought I'd do something more creative and intellectual, or something demonstrably beneficial, something for social justice. So many things have pissed me off in my lifetime—welfare reform, the War on Drugs, the erosion of reproductive rights, the government's fucking anemic response to climate change—and I've done so little in response; I mean, talk about anemia: a few rallies, a few contributions, sporadic volunteerism. In fact I've often felt obligated to vote for people who've enacted or enforced the very policies I disdain! That's a real failure on my part, and every time I read something that fires me up to change, to really do something, I put things off a few days till I have more time. Then weeks become months, years."

"Most of us have failed in that way."

She dimpled the left corner of her mouth. "Anyway, I saw myself doing something that used more of my skills, not that I'm always sure what those skills are."

"Yeah, that's my Achilles—Achilles heel probably isn't right, but—as a kid I was led to believe I was exceptional. Not like off-the-hook exceptional, but, you know."

"I think that's what they say to most kids," she said.

"Do they, though?"

"No, you're right. I should say it more. Maxwell, you're exceptional." He was out of earshot.

"So I've carried that around for the longest, this idea that I'd do something noteworthy."

"That you *would*?" she said. "Like it was destiny?"

"Or that I could."

"I'm sure *that's* true."

"I'm not. And now I think my desire to be exceptional, like be a famous DJ or a great artist or an entrepreneur, I think it's the same as my desire to be tall."

"You're not *short,*" she said. "Yeats was around forty when he started writing most of his greatest poems."

"Was he? That's good to know."

"Not that his earlier work is unpopular or without interest."

"He wrote plays too, right?"

"Yeah," she said. "I haven't read those."

"I had an idea once for a screenplay," he said. "More an idea *about* a screenplay than an idea for one. *Three Times Courtney,* starring Lauren Ambrose and Mekhi Phifer."

"You got as far as casting?"

"I had some names in mind. I was thinking: commercial but fairly low budget, and about working-class people. I have this thing about romantic comedies—not a thing, really, I just like them. So I thought I could write one."

"And did you?"

"Part of one, yeah. I probably spent too much time trying to get the formatting down. I don't know how much you know about screenwriting, but it's very precise: the formatting, the structure, everything. Like your climax is s'posed to happen on a specific page."

"Ugh."

"Well, it's just about mastering form."

"I see these action movies with Maxwell, and my interest always decreases as the action accelerates."

"But that's about, you know, combat fatigue, the tedium of CGI heroics and destruction, where everything is possible so nothing matters; it's not about story templates. Probably the movies you like climax on the prescribed page too."

"Which page is it?"

"I can't remember. My script was so boring, I never got to that page. If it was boring me, it was bound to bore everyone else, right?"

"Sorry, I wasn't listening."

"Though a minute ago you said you were bored talking about your job, but I wasn't bored listening to you. My problem, I decided, was that I like romantic comedies, I'll surrender to them, but part of me still feels superior to even the cleverest, craftiest ones. Like I know I'm incapable of writing something Deep and Significant, but still I think I'm too good to write something frothy and formulaic and bighearted that would make people happy."

"I bet a lot of frothy screenplays are written through those same anxieties."

"But I think for things to really work, you have to be, just, pro-froth," he said. "Besides, it's not like Hollywood's clamoring for proletarian romcoms by unknown midwestern screenwriters."

She seemed to concur.

"No, you're supposed to say, 'You won't know 'less you try!'"

"No, I think you were right to throw in the towel," she said. "Not every labor is justified."

"A great philosopher once said."

"More coffee?"

"I'm good." He looked into the living room, wondered if they might sit awhile on the couch.

"So, I haven't spelled this out," she said, "but yes, you're welcome to join us on the road to Winnipeg."

"Thank you."

"*The Road to Winnipeg,* one of the less beloved Hope-Crosby pictures."

"Criminally underrated."

"Should be an interesting weekend," she said. "To be honest, I don't really know Archer."

"I'm not sure how knowable he is."

"Huh. He's so open in his writing," she said. She asked if Lucas had read any of his work.

"I've gotten a feel for it. I read one of his essays. It was about jerking off."

"I read that one too, part of it, and the one about Arkansas Bob. And I just finished his first novel."

"That's the amateur-Canadian-art-thieves thing?"

"Yeah. It's good. Light, but charming."

"A friend of mine was kind of working for him," he said.

"Yeah? Working for him how?"

"She was his research assistant, I'm pretty sure, and she proofread his manuscripts." Lucas would struggle mightily to feel sympathy for Archer, but if he were to, it would be over having to suffer Sara's proofreading. It had taken him several years to forgive her uninsightful and infuriatingly pedantic notes to his MFA stories ("if distilled in the United States, use 'whiskey'; if in Scotland, 'whisky'"). To Karyn he said, "Maybe she's still doing it. We mostly lost touch. But she's like a walking *Chicago Manual of Style,* and supposedly he's a bad grammarian, or dyslexic or something."

"Really? He seems so elegant."

"You don't think dyslexic people can be elegant?"

"I didn't mean that, I—"

"I'm joking. I should probably read more of him."

"Gemma sent me an advance of the new one," she said. "You could borrow it when I'm done."

Without getting ahead of himself, he noted that borrowing a book usually involved two meetings.

"Oh, and I'm wondering what your thoughts are on the rehearsal dinner," she said.

"I'm thoughtless about the rehearsal dinner."

"It's just, it's a lot of socializing in one weekend. I might need a month in a hermitage to recover. I'm thinking of telling them I have to work on Friday morning, that we can't make it to Winnipeg till after the rehearsal dinner starts."

With a facetious shudder: "You would lie to your *own cousin*?"

"I would," she said, kind of sexily. "Maybe blow off Sunday brunch too."

"At least for brunch we could just throw on our bike shorts," he said. She smiled. "But hey, that's fine." He liked the chance to be conspiratorial so soon. "As much as I want to see Gemma, I was pretty happy to decline the invitation. I mean"—he caught Karyn's eye—"I'm looking forward to it now, but . . . I'm not at a place in my life where I enjoy making small talk, having to tell people my job is selling sneakers on eBay and participating in psychological studies, which I've only done twice."

"A lot of people are unemployed," Karyn said.

"I know, a ton. But it's more than that." A more general sense that he was three touchdowns behind at halftime. And he didn't relish watching Gemma marry Archer. He wasn't still hung up on her, not meaningfully, but the guy was a tool. How could she not see it?

They talked more about the economy, about hydrofracking, Winnipeg ("a bohemian Shangri-la," according to an old friend of Karyn's). Things flowed smoothly, and when Lucas listened to his voice, it sounded like his actual voice, like he was just pushing air through his lungs and vibrating his larynx and moving his tongue around and doing whatever else people do when talking, rather than doing all those things with slightly unnatural variations, as he would have when talking to a stranger at a rehearsal dinner. He wanted to stay longer, but Maxwell came downstairs with his borrowed violin at noon, almost as if he'd been instructed to reemerge at precisely that time.

March 2005

only if you have time ......
FROM Archer Bondarenko
TO Sara Crennel

Sara,

I really enjoyed meeting you the other month, my only complaint being that just as I did you had to shuffle off to Buffalo. (What's that from, anyway?) Saw John the other day, & heard you guys were taking a break. He had nothing but good things to say about you, case you were guessing to the contray. Actually, he was the one that reminded/urged me to sned you that essay I mentioned at the restaurant. (I just googled shuffle off to Buffalo, did you?) N.b.: the essay's still drafty in spots, not developed in toto yet w/r/t ideation, but I *think* its getting close. Anyway, if you have time maybe take a look. I'd love to hear your feedback unless it's negative. No biggie if you're slammed, & holla next time your back in the city.

Yrs,
Archer

Parts of the essay were indeed "drafty," and those were its most refined parts. The rest was rather more like notes toward an essay—at times *exactly* like notes toward an essay ("Something here about Roth?" "Consider story of aunt's panties tho prob too much"). Despite the e-mail's semiliteracy and disclaimers, Sara wondered if Archer had intended to send, or sned, such a nubbin-like thing, or if he had attached an earlier document by mistake. If he'd sent the wrong doc, it would seem condescending of Sara to treat inchoate jottings as if they were ready for scrutiny, though to broach the subject even in the most delicate terms would probably give offense; Archer might in fact find delicate terms more offensive than blunt ones.

She was pretty good at spotting bad writers in advance of direct exposure to their writing. In writing workshops she would listen to certain comments and before-class chat and think, When this guy submits his story, it'll be awful. And her prejudice would be vindicated. She held her own work in similarly low esteem—perhaps she didn't think her work was *awful,* but neither did she think it was profound, original, or in any way necessary, and maybe some of her workshop peers, seeing that her insecurity and amour propre were interlaced, tried to discount her opinions in bulk, as if self-doubt canceled critical acumen. (Surely self-doubt is just the inward nadir of critical acumen, and somewhere she'd read that when contempt of others rises to contempt of self, it becomes philosophy.) Archer was an odd case in that, from what she had seen that night in New York, he was quick and articulate—not in proportion to his pride, but verbally fluid nonetheless, as well as prestigiously educated and tasteful (he'd been right to buy those beautiful dioramas); and though none of that guaranteed that he'd be a good writer, all of it gave ground to expect that he'd be better than he apparently was. He needed an amanuensis more than a word processor; even voice-recognition software would have helped.

His essay did, she allowed, contain some good phrases and sturdy sentences, but very often it was slipshod, graceless, and surprisingly pocked with grammatical and orthographical mistakes. Transitions were absent or strained; the erudition seemed feigned. Even furbished, the piece would be too long and eggheady for a newspaper or magazine, too short and superficial for a journal. She could better picture it converted badly into HTML on some dinky website, stray number signs, question marks, & ampersands filling in for apostrophes, smart quotes, and diacritics and making the piece seem Tourettically dotted with cartoon profanity, all of it underscored by one spammy comment from Estonian identity thieves.

She stared at her laptop till the screen went charcoal, uncertain how to respond to the e-mail, much less how to respond to the essay. On these late-winter afternoons, her mother's dining room was quieter than you might predict of a room in an old, uncarpeted house, especially one containing robustly mechanical means of dispensing water to cats. At times in her life Sara had longed for such quiet. Now it was just depressing. She walked upstairs to her mother's bedroom—dust motes floating over an ironing board piled with damp towels, jackets from Chico's, a leopard-print vest—and turned on a telenovela, having previously been inspirited by how the voices at a distance sounded like gossip-worthy neighbors. She watched a long scene in which a man drove somewhere ardently. Returning downstairs to her workspace at the dining room table, she raised the dimmer on the chandelier, but the room remained chromatically compressed: floors the color of wheat, walls pale yellow, popcorn ceiling spottily browned like old cauliflower.

The moment seemed ripe for a meditative walk, though all routes everywhere deterred pedestrians. Under the pretense of responding to an automated call about one of her mother's prescriptions, she put on heavy socks, boots, and her grandmother's circa-1969 coat, snug but wearable. The vintage orange leather would furnish safety advantages during the walk's daredevil stretch on the shoulder of Mineral Springs Road. Before setting out, she chipped ice on the porch, pausing once to say hello to the neighbor kids, who were homeschooled and got a lot of recess. An unpretentious suburb southeast of Buffalo, West Seneca wasn't the dreariest or most suffocating place in the world but also not a place Sara had expected to return to at length. When her parents bought the house in 1980, they were trying for a second kid and wanted something the family could grow into. There were fertility problems, however, trailed by marital problems, so the house was first somewhat too big for three, then notably too big for two or one. It had a brown brick façade, black shutters, cream vinyl siding on its front gable and its side- and rear-facing walls. The old and cheaply constructed jungle gym out back, sometimes used by the homeschoolers, was a litigation hazard. Sara wasn't sentimental about the touchstones of her childhood and wished her mother's plans to buy a modest condo in the city would pick up speed.

The blocks to the north of hers didn't rate sidewalks, so she had to walk on the edge of the street, around and past the cars and trucks and down-and-out snowmen. As she walked she wondered again about John and Archer's friendship, whether it might have been built on a base of shared mediocrity. Perhaps, in a storied microcosm of privilege and achievement, they had each recognized in the other a fellow second-rater. A mean thought, but, if true, maybe part of a continual pattern; possibly they saw in her the same also-ran qualities, were drawn to her narrow vision, her middling state-school credentials, her extra pounds and dumpy clothes. Or, to use the president's solecism, she misunderestimated them. She allowed that she wasn't qualified to judge, and in certain cases didn't value, intelligence or ability in business, math, science, and other professional and academic areas outside the humanities, and accordingly that John, who'd been a math "concentrator" in college, must be intellectually talented in ways beyond Sara's ken and underexposed by his conversation. Not extraordinarily talented, but talented, though she was remembering now as she said hello to the mailwoman that he had switched majors, presumably to something easier. Archer wasn't without talent; Sara guessed he would find success in one pursuit or another. There was little financial risk in failure, for one thing, ample scope for the see-what-sticks approach. Wise to cultivate his friendship. Still, both of them, John and Archer, seemed unworthy of their degrees, and the thought nettled her perpetually underlying resentment to the surface.

She started to fantasize again about returning to the dawn of her teens, becoming an industrious middle-class comer, marching wanly into the meritocracy with pink eraser swarf on the heel of her right hand, savoring her mother's tears at the welcoming letter from the University of Chicago, or Wellesley, or Swarthmore, or Yale, earning Harold Bloom's rumbly praise for her paper on Dryden (whom in her actual life she hadn't read), landing an internship at Farrar, Straus and Giroux, then passing quickly through one or more of publishing's largely distaff realms—proofreading, publicity, editorial assistance—to more lucrative and visible triumphs. She'd been Yale material, she now believed, in every respect except most of those important to admissions officers. At West Seneca High she was an erratic, disaffected, indisputably lazy student who shunned extracurriculars, volunteerism, and SAT preparation. (Yet still she managed a nearly perfect score on the verbal, or so she had told John and one other person, applying a lenient standard of near-perfection.)

An SUV honked at her on Mineral Springs as she passed the tumbledown used-car lot with its cheerless streamers and crooked GO SABRES sign. She couldn't live much longer in a world without sidewalks.

For someone still at an age of expected and in some cases feasible fresh starts, Sara dreamed all too often of getting a do-over, reliving her childhood either to reverse pivotal mistakes or simply to take diligent notes on her surroundings, boxes and boxes of lyrically persnickety notes that would let her write about the past with Vermeer-like precision. Of course, she could take diligent notes on her surroundings now and attempt to write about the present with Vermeer-like precision, but that seemed tedious and optimistic. She knew she should be enjoying the bright suspense of relative youth, falling asleep to visions of odds-bucking artistic success instead of staying awake with pangs of premature regret, the sort of regret that aligned her with those who announce in museums that they or their droopy-chinned children could have, under unexplained circumstances, executed major works of abstract expressionism. Nevertheless, she couldn't shake the feeling that she was cleverer than her accomplishments indicated, that she had to do something grand to requite her past mistakes.

Back home in slippers, she left her mother's pills on the kitchen counter and revived her laptop. After reading Archer's essay a second time, she concluded that it wasn't irredeemably bad. It was meagerly promising. After a third reading she decided it *epitomized* unmet potential. It stumbled now, yes, but she saw how elegantly it meandered even into its most egregious flaws. If it wasn't as deeply self-critical as the best personal essays tend to be, it was without question forthright and self-aware—no, the self-awareness was with question, but there were strong signs of it. The content, improbably for a piece about masturbation, was as inviting as the composition was repellent.

And what it invited her to do—something she vexingly couldn't do as a proofreader—was rewrite, with a free and heavy hand that after ten days' work reduced Archer's draft to the faintest pentimento. She dilated the piece by nine pages. She gave Archer experiences he hadn't had, such as her own. When his unaccompanied sex acts seemed pedestrian, she added a squirmy detail. (About his invented and borrowed experiences he was fearlessly, disarmingly frank.) She worked in Andy Warhol, Lynda Benglis, James Joyce,

Jim Morrison, Georges Bataille, George Grosz, Philip Roth, Lord Byron, Cyndi Lauper, and the auntly underwear. She tried to make reasonable arguments, but where convenient she embraced a brand of sophistry that could, in a pinch, pass as satire. Over those ten days she was driven to write from the moment she woke up, feeling as instantly eager and alert as a nine-year-old on Christmas morning. After many months in which the urge to write tugged most forcefully when the act was impracticable, this was restoration, proof that she could still work the stalwart hours of a resident physician or trucker, still lose herself in the challenge of a sentence and go on composing in her head while she showered, made coffee, or microwaved a frozen entrée from the line her mother favored, the box showing a middle-aged woman eating alone, proclaiming in jaunty emerald script, JUST ME.

Even the light through the dining room window shone more brightly—spring coming on, but the shift seemed more symbolic than seasonal. Never before had writing been so much fun, and, in a troubling concurrence, never before had the results been so wanting in integrity. Or maybe that was wrong; maybe the reworked essay's integrity surpassed that of all her previous work. It was fraudulent, both as far as the facts went and "w/r/t ideation," but it boasted a certain soundness, a certain . . . it was all kind of vague . . . *inevitability* that usually eluded her, along with the obscure prizes and adjunct teaching posts the stars of her MFA program had gone on to receive. Of course, she hadn't been a star in her program, and hadn't bloomed outside of it. She had published next to nothing: a piece of flash fiction on a website whose name gave her bio an unwelcome antic air; the kickboxing piece and RNC reports for the *Stickler;* and a smattering of hackwork, most recently an unbylined guide to Niagara-region hiking trails, most of which she hadn't technically visited. She routinely applied for grants and fellowships that she unfailingly failed to win.

She had entertained dozens of first responses to Archer's e-mail, settling on temporizing concision ("I'll try to look at it"). Only on her third day with the piece did she really consider how he might react to her work. He hadn't specified what he wanted from her, but surely it wasn't an expansionist Gordon Lish, a class-confused Henry Higgins, or a ghostwriter. Acknowledging the likely futility of her efforts gave them a prodding taste of danger. The risks were probably no greater than a pissy e-mail from a man she would never see again, but that was enough to taunt her rebellious streak. Since Archer wouldn't want to do anything with the revised essay except delete it, and she couldn't do anything with it except save it, the pages reached a level of art for art's sake that her publication-craving stories only pretended to. On that count, she reasoned, the essay's integrity did surpass that of all her previous work, and it was with humming satisfaction that she sent it off to Archer at 3:48 a.m., having set her alarm for 3:45 in order to buttress her e-mail's apologetic explanation that she was desperately tired and probably manic and that his brilliant draft had carried her away.

June 2011

"I won't keep you, Karyn," Gemma said. "I'm sure you're extraordinarily busy."

"I wouldn't go that far."

"I just wanted to express my gratitude. We're delighted—Archer less so than I—that Lucas will be in attendance at the wedding, thanks to you."

"It's my pleasure."

"An exquisite solution, this," Gemma said, as if the solution had been Karyn's idea. "And let me add, with no matchmaking colorations intended—I know how tetchy you can be on that front—let me just add that Lucas very much enjoyed meeting you. I haven't heard him in such high spirits for millennia, and I'm inclined, Karyn, to credit his reanimation to your hospitality. He has even resumed his job hunt in earnest."

Karyn didn't know how to respond to this likably preposterous woman. She thought she should tamp down whatever romantic subplots Lucas and/or Gemma might be conceiving, though she didn't want to tamp them down conclusively. Lucas had drifted into her mind often enough since their brunch, and it was refreshing to entertain such thoughts without the moral qualms that shadowed her fling with the consultant. Certainly conversation with Lucas had poured more smoothly than it had with Paul or the two divorcés from last summer's brief return to online dating. To Gemma she said, "He seems like a nice guy."

"I would chance even higher praise, but rest easy that the admiration is mutual. Lucas was all but rhapsodic about you and Maximilian. I gather he has begun production on a mixtape for the drive—again, I speak without motive."

"The lady doth protest too much," Karyn said.

"Ha, so like you, Karyn. Archer tells me you tread the boards."

It wasn't exactly an insider's quotation. "Not for years," Karyn said, moderately surprised that Gemma could use "tread the boards" without detectable irony, more surprised that Archer knew of her acting career. "It was just a few roles here and there."

"A footnote of the footlights!"

Perhaps too accurate.

"Well," Karyn said.

"Yes, I'll let you run off."

"Oh, and thank you for the book. It's outstanding." And it *was,* so far, a marked advancement from the perfectly fine debut.

"A marvel, isn't it? From day one I was, as I like to say, aquiver for an Archer—please credit me if you have occasion to repeat that wordplay—but his gifts continue to astound me."

Karyn was again at a loss. "An exciting time," she said.

"Yes. Well, safe travels, Karyn. Till Winnipeg!"

May 2005

When Archer's response finally arrived, it bore no signs of umbrage and no mention of the six-week delay. Sara's work, he wrote ambiguously, was "extraordinary." He hoped they could meet in person to revise the essay further. He would be happy to come to Buffalo, or, if she preferred, he would pay for her ticket to New York and put her up in a hotel.

He lived on the fourth floor of a brand-new condominium with a view of the Hudson. It was on Greenwich Street in the nominally disputed neighborhood variously called Hudson Square, West SoHo, or the South Village (real estate agents were keen to gerrymander it into SoHo). Until a few years ago, Archer told Sara as he handed her a glass of sparkling water, there'd been a garbage center just down the street. For a moment this seemed to summarize Archer: someone proud to live near a defunct garbage center. She drank her water nervously as he gave her a partial tour. The apartment didn't seem to belong to a young man, at least not to any of the young men Sara knew, most of whom aspired in one way or another to hobohemia. The design was postmodern with a bricolage motif; there were many objects fashioned from cute, unlikely materials: stainless-steel dining chairs whose seats and backs were wavy beds of spoons, a desk lamp shaded by sewn-together sweater zippers, a jumbly chair made of old chairs. In a few cases Archer attributed the articles to their creators—the chair was by so-and-so, the clock by such-and-such. He had a talent for pronouncing foreign names respectfully, perhaps even accurately, but without a jarring change in his accent, so that the names seemed at once exotic and anglicized. There was no TV in sight, but he had an audiophile's stereo system that Sara guessed cost about as much as you might make hanging drywall for two and a half years. The plinthlike turntable was spinning a record on which gnomes, it seemed, were forming a drum circle. A line of unpainted cement columns, an electric guitar, and a barely perceptible smell of burnt rice caucused for vestigial grit, but all in all the apartment was surprisingly clean and orderly, to an extent that Sara doubted could be wholly ascribed to professional help. Surprising because Archer's appearance was untucked, his manuscript downright slobby. Midafternoon sun pervaded the large, open living room, where there were correspondingly large and vibrant paintings by John Currin and Kehinde Wiley; a panorama of Henry Darger's Vivian girls in mixed poses of pastel victory and strangled distress; a hanging shark by the tire sculptor Yong Ho Ji; a photo of a street preacher by one of Archer's friends; and three small, storybookish drawings by Marcel Dzama, a Winnipeg native whom Archer spoke of with a tincture of idolatry. People were depicted in all but the shark piece, Sara noticed, and she wondered if that signaled loneliness. She admired the Dzamas up close, not sure how admirable they were. There were three art history classes on her college transcript, but she didn't trust her judgment of work not yet historicized. "I like how there's no background," she said. Archer reached for her glass, lightly touching her fingers, and asked if he could get her another water. She felt she had drunk the first one too quickly.

The first days after sending him the reimagined essay, she had checked her e-mail even more excessively than usual, feeling, each time her mail page loaded, a turbulence in her stomach made up equally of excitement and dread. After a few more days this gave way to the gastric calm of unalloyed disappointment. She had congratulated herself for putting in all that time with a blind eye to reward, but she hadn't imagined being ignored by her one certain reader (and as the weeks went on, she realized that her eye had always been squinting at reward). Briefly she chalked up Archer's nonresponse to restraint, then to cowardice and arrogance. Finally she blamed herself for going overboard on his piece, not knowing when to quit, falling prey to the same brakeless perversity that had driven her as a girl to keep painting and painting until she was looking down at an eight-by-eleven study of trampled goose shit. She had hoped that editing Archer would lead to a rehabilitation of her own writing, but in the weeks following her work on the essay, work that had already taken on an added glow of inspiration that she was careful not to dim by consulting the essay itself, she accomplished very little: she proofread a numbingly circumstantiated book about the racehorse Phar Lap, she updated her résumé, and she listlessly revised one of her doomed short stories. Her freelance services, never in hotcakey demand, were less sought after than ever, her main proofreading client having returned, supposedly, to doing the work in-house, while another reported that a novel assigned to Sara's finishing pen had gone to press with several errors, including a cringingly Texan spelling of Jane Austen's surname and a homophonic mishap in which a character was allowed to buy fancy linen stationary. The editor was reservedly forgiving about the mistakes, but the news was a blow to Sara, who if anything considered herself too scrupulous, too much the proofreader and too little the artist. Perhaps she was too little of both. She thought of her still-shaky grasp on the past-participial forms of *wake, awake,* and *awaken,* the scores of unencouraging rejections she'd amassed, often from online journals whose content pointed to editorial standards of rampantly open-armed unselectivity. Her fear that she would go to the grave as a marginalis of the publishing industry was being replaced with the fear that she wouldn't even succeed at that. She was biding her swollen time. It wasn't surprising to discover, one recent Monday morning, that her sole obligations for the week were an eye exam and a loose promise to help her mother make a chandelier out of milk jugs. So it was with considerable gratitude that she received Archer's response letter that same morning, up to her elbows in rinsed-out plastic.

He returned from his Inspector Gadget kitchen, handed her the refreshed glass of water, and sat near her on a blue-gray sectional sofa, low to the ground and uncomfortable. He softened the music by remote control, making several adjustments until the volume was just right. They each had a copy of the manuscript. "So I really like what you did," he said.

"Thanks." The word came out croakily. "I took pains as well as naps."

"My stepdad's a big believer in the power nap."

"Actually, I didn't nap at all while working on your essay," she said, "or even sleep much. But lately I've been overnapping. I used to say that napping was crucial to my writing process, but now I think writing is crucial to my napping process."

He chuckled. "At first when I saw what you'd done, I thought it was a bit much."

"Yeah."

"But I'm into it now. It's like you have a psychic sense of"—a boyish hesitation—"I think this is the piece I would have written if I were a real writer."

"You're a good writer. It just needed—"

"Yeah, I mean, I still think some of the best stuff here is from my original draft. But I know I'm not a serious writer, I know I'm a dabbler." She tried to use silence and her shoulders to both contradict this and endorse its clear-sightedness. "I guess that's one of life's tasks," he said, "discovering your limitations, trying to stretch them while also learning to accept them."

"Yes," she said. Perhaps, that night in December, she had imputed more arrogance to him than he really possessed. Maybe groups brought out his worst.

"Have you wanted to be a writer since you were a kid?" he asked.

"No. I wanted to be a vet. And you?"

"Hockey player."

"Were you any good?"

"At wanting to be a hockey player?"

"At being one."

"Pretty good. I got a lot of my growing out of the way early, so for a few years I was big for my age, believe it or not." He dropped his eyes, apologizing for his slight frame. "And I thought I had a leg up, since my parents have some connections in sports."

That seemed a rather demure way to put it. She smiled.

"Well, they own the Manitoba Moose. But the Moose aren't an NHL team, so—"

"Archer, I'm from Buffalo."

"So you know hockey."

Not well, actually.

"Needless to say, my nepotistic advantages wouldn't have extended to the rink."

"Just out of curiosity," she said, "have you ever met Bobby Hull?"

"Yes!"

"He's one of my dad's heroes."

"Mine too. More water?"

"I'm fine."

"Girls, for the most part—would you say girls tend to have more realistic dreams than boys? Little girls and boys, I mean."

"There are very few professional ballerinas," she said.

"True, but I remember in elementary school how we had to write an essay on what we wanted to be as grown-ups, and most of the boys wanted to be athletes or rock stars or the prime minister, where the girls wanted to be things they could actually become—teachers, say, or vets."

"Again, there'd be an alarming surplus of veterinarians if every animal lover followed through on her childhood ambitions," Sara said. "Maybe more of those girls wanted to be pop stars and fashion models and the prime minister, but they thought they'd be laughed at for saying so, or they already thought they weren't good enough. And of course they didn't have as many role models as their male counterparts."

"Sure, sure," he said. "You don't need to run through the whole syllabus. And I think it's good you didn't become a vet. I liked that piece you had in *Kinetic Pepper Mill*."

"Oh, thanks. That's kind of old."

"Anyway, I think we could get the essay published. A friend of mine helped start this cool literary journal. No guarantees, obviously. He's not a good friend, and to be honest he turned down something I wrote last year. He's a fuckwad, in a way. But he'd look at it."

"When you say *we* could get it published, what do you mean?"

"I mean I could get it published." He had his hands on the back of his head and was drumming with his thumbs. "But I want to pay you for your work."

"You don't have to do that. You didn't hire me; you just asked me to look at something as a friend."

"Were we friends? I mean, I hope we become friends, better friends," he said. "The point is, now I want to submit the essay for publication, and it's almost as much your work as it is mine."

Almost!

"I'd like to pay you eight thousand dollars for it."

"Eight thousand dollars?"

"Yes."

She conquered a smile, not wanting to look transparently venal. She was humbled by the instant knowledge that she would take the money. That humbling, she supposed, was intrinsic to patronage, though this wasn't quite patronage.

"That's more or less two dollars a word," he said, "which I understand is the going rate at the top glossies."

"I hear Norman Mailer gets four dollars a word when he writes for *Parade,*" she said.

"But I think it's a fair—"

"Kidding! Really it's way too much. No offense, but I don't think this is bound for a top glossy."

"Well, obviously. Quite probably my friend won't even take it at his nonpaying literary journal. But you should be compensated for your work."

"That's always been my contention," she said, trying for breeziness. She felt hypotensive, as if she'd stood up suddenly after watching seven hours of televised billiards in a solarium. "Not about my work on your essay," she added. "In general."

"I know what you're saying. I agree."

She pointed at the stereo. "Is this Devendra Banhart?"

"No, it's the Incredible String Band, but I'm pretty sure Devendra was influenced by the ISB."

"Don't you think you should use the active voice there: the ISB influenced Devendra?"

He looked at her warily.

"Kidding again."

"Ah, that's good, you got me," he said, touching her arm. "That's good. They're my favorite band. They were doing some reunion shows in the UK a few years back, and I even followed them around for a while."

"Yeah? Do you people have a special name, like Deadheads do?" It was a relief to talk about something other than money.

"Not that I know of," he said. "I think you can just add *head* to any band name or abbreviation."

"An unwieldy solution, though, for fans of Talking Heads, or Radiohead, or Edith Head."

"Who's Edith Head again? Is that the porn star?"

"God, you guys aren't even properly furtive about your porn anymore. No, she was a famous costumer."

"She made costumes for pornos?"

She laughed. "She did do the costumes for *She Done Him Wrong:* Mae West, Cary Grant, very hot." She liked articulating the movie's hotness in Archer's presence.

"This is my favorite part," he said as the singer lullabied over two arthritically changing chords. "Kind of an acquired taste, I guess, but they're, I don't know, so pure in their eccentricities, so . . . I wish I could describe how I feel about them." He looked at her hopefully, perhaps expecting her to fire off that elusive description.

She listened out of politeness. Now the singer was warbling in unison with a sitar. "Well," she said when the song ended, "if you want to pay me eight thousand dollars, I'd probably only demur one more time."

"I could give you half now."

"Oh, I couldn't," she said.

He walked over to an escritoire in the adjoining office, sectioned off by a screen of what looked to be a bamboo-based composite, and pulled out a checkbook from a pigeonhole. "Is it Crennel with two *n*'s?" he asked. She said yes, and he reached over the sofa to hand her the check. Its dimensions exceeded the currency-sized norm.

"Sorry," she said, "but this says 'Crellen.'"

"What? Jesus." He wrote another check and returned to his place on the couch. Now he was leaning back more, for a few seconds trying to rest his feet on a coffee table that had been placed deliberately beyond the reach of all but the very long-legged. "Of course there's still more work to do. A lot of what's here"—he tapped the manuscript with his pen—"isn't . . . how to put it? . . . It's not true."

"But what is truth?"

"Though some of the made-up stuff is remarkably close."

She pushed her hair back. "Goethe said something about *Elective Affinities,* that it didn't contain a line that hadn't been experienced, but no line the *way* it had been experienced."

"That's cool. The key, I think, will be nailing down which of the false claims are, like, artistically indispensable, then which of those could be disproven. A few tweaks here and there and I'd say we're golden, but we'll want to be careful. Oh, I should have you sign a nondisclosure." As it turned out, he already had one prepared. "And if the essay does get accepted, I'd want you to respond to all editorially directed changes. Posing as me."

"I'll try to write in a deeper voice."

He ignored her admittedly lame joke. "I opened a new e-mail account for writing stuff," he said, writing down the address. "The password is *sarcher.*"

"That's a terrible password."

"It combines our names."

"I see what it's doing, but it's totally insecure."

"Sara, we're all inse-curr." He said this like Kanye West. "On that subject, uh, this part you have about me being—where is it?—'especially stung by and defensive regarding the criticisms of women'?"

"Yeah."

"I really don't think that's me at all."

"It could be argued that your objection proves the point."

"Maybe, but—"

"We're trying to create an essayistic persona, right? Maybe you're not like that in real life, but you are for the purposes of this essay. I think your essayistic persona—"

"Are you gonna say 'essayistic persona' a lot?"

"Are you gonna contractually prohibit me from doing so?"

"Probably not."

"I think your essayistic persona should be nakedly forthright, uncompromising, unconcerned with what other people might think."

"Wow, wouldn't that be cool, huh?"

She couldn't tell if he was being sarcastic.

"Also"—he flipped to page four—"I think male masturbation *is* more maligned today than female masturbation, you know, the male masturbator seen as abject, comic, lonely; the female, healthy, liberated, self-sufficient."

"Frustrated that she can't get off with her boyfriend," Sara said. "Anyway, male masturbation per se isn't ridiculed and maligned so much as its trappings: the porn and the blowup dolls and the crusty tube socks or whatever. And maybe female masturbation is portrayed differently *by men* because it arouses them. They can't imagine that girls and women attach far more remnant shame to it than boys and men do. You see that cluelessness in, say, the pie bit versus the flute bit in *American Pie*."

He nodded. "Let's get that in the essay, the *American Pie* thing."

"It's not really a thing," she said. "More like provisional blah-blah-blah, to be honest."

"You shouldn't."

"Shouldn't what?"

"Be honest. Maybe watch the movie again and cook something up."

She wrote a note to herself.

"I remember reading in *Playboy* that men rape themselves when masturbating," he said, "when they should be making love to themselves. I tried switching to my left hand, but . . ."

She let him soak for a moment in quiet.

"But first things first," he said. He didn't have sleeves to roll up—he was wearing khakis with frayed hems and a Che-like T-shirt featuring a drawing of the Métis leader Louis Riel—but he transitioned into more systematic work by moving closer to Sara and fluttering his pen over the essay's opening sentence.

It was thrilling to look so closely with another person at something she'd written, away from the shibboleths and nitwit observations she'd endured in writing workshops, and as they moved through the pages she got happier and calmer. He knew how to reject an idea, not too bluntly but without lots of time-wasting gingerliness, and he endorsed his favorite revisions with theatrical flair, in one instance shouting his approval and rubbing his hands together like a melodrama's villainous landlord. She typed up some of the notes on her laptop while he made a competent Thai curry. He asked about her writing while they ate, seemed really to be listening (though he didn't ask to read any of her stuff). As they were clearing the dishes, he asked if she would "care to take a postprandial constitutional." She got over her annoyance at the phrasing and enjoyed the shoulder-brushing walk. They worked late into the evening, late enough for her to consider dozing off on his hard sofa, a consideration that included a mayfly thought of him patting her blanketed arm or performing some other tucking-in procedure. In the end she mustered the strength to leave. Feeling flush, she took a taxi.

She bought a drink, a fifteen-dollar drink, at the hotel lounge. She thought about the wardrobe overhaul her windfall would facilitate, but she knew she would spend the money reasonably (damage deposit, bed, credit-card payment, sofa). She rotated on her barstool to face the crowd, made a show of waiting for someone, checking the time on her phone, scanning the room with an impatient brow. A woman near her kept tugging at the back of her miniskirt while her boyfriend talked loudly to someone else. The lounge was burbling with anodyne dance music, peppered with preciously designed chess sets, filled with people Sara probably wouldn't like, but at least for the moment contempt and superiority had slipped from her thoughts like subscription cards from drugstore *Elles*. The music continued in the elevator up to her room, and she swayed her shoulders and smiled at herself in the reflective gold doors.

In bed she resumed reading a slim European novel that had been both well- and ill-suited for the plane: impressive looking and easy to slip into her purse, but too slow and challenging for distractive settings. As usual—even in hotel beds—she wrote down unfamiliar words on an index card that doubled as a bookmark. Later she would type the words and their definitions into a document that she called a commonplace book, though it was mainly a word list. She'd been doing this for years and liked seeing the words get more recondite as the document enlarged; many of the recent entries ("siffleur, an animal that makes a whistling noise, or a person who entertains professionally by whistling") could be used only on rare occasions and at risk to one's popularity. Writing and typing the words and definitions was supposed to aid retention, but that wasn't always true; she often encountered a word that was no clearer to her than it had been before she had typed its definition a year earlier, or vocabulary that made repeated trips to her index cards but always seemed too common for her commonplace book. In those latter cases, before scribbling on the card, she would include a qualifier: "again," "clarify," "whet understanding of," "check etymology," or some other frequently dishonest indication that she possessed at least a weak grip on the entry and was only seeking a refresher or mastery. As if she needed to persuade readers of her private index cards to judge her linguistic gaps more compassionately. This finical self-absorption, this timorous, circular miniaturism, often seemed emblematic of her shortcomings as a writer, even as a person. The consensus in grad school had been that nothing was at stake in her well-written but amorphous stories of longing, bewilderment, and acedia. Of course, she thought *everything* was at stake in her stories, though she also worried that her everything was nothing, that her passions were misplaced. Given the opportunity, she could talk for hours about when a comma might justifiably be placed between parts of a compound predicate—and when its placement there was purposeless and arrhythmic!—but she was laryngitically silent, because short of deep conviction, about Israeli settlement of the West Bank.

Tonight, though, her index cards didn't seem pathetic; they revealed one aspect of her character, her pettiness perhaps, but also her devotion, her devotion to something—she couldn't always say what—maybe to the English language. And it hadn't been wasted effort! For a long time she had thought that if she could follow her passions, such as they were, do her thing, as Aunt Marion might have put it, someone would take notice, single her out, pluck her from the throng. More recently she had thought that no, she was a fool, it didn't work that way at all. But it did! It really did!

June 2011

"I thought maybe I could swing by with my suitcase," Lucas said over the phone, "then just bike over on the morning we leave."

"I'm not following."

"My friend has a car," he said, and explained his plan again, how it would save Karyn from having to pick him up, though it seemed obvious to her that his plan would only make things more cumbersome when they were returning exhaustedly home.

"I don't mind picking you up," she said.

"Yeah, but I'm in the opposite direction."

"The opposite direction from Winnipeg? I thought you said you lived in Stevens Square."

"Well, yeah. I wasn't thinking of, like, literal compass points."

After she got off the phone, she put her dinner plate in the dishwasher, cored an apple, and carried the *New York Review of Books* into the living room. Lucas must have been calling from the road, because a car door slammed in front of her house fewer than ten minutes later. She turned around and kneeled on the sofa, watched through the window as he unstrapped his bike from the rack. A swatch of wokbelly was exposed when he carried the bike to a boulevard ash recently ringed with terminal green paint. He fetched his suitcase—some would have called it a hockey bag—from the backseat. For a moment he talked to his friend through the passenger-side window, leaning like a streetwalker, the sun shining in retiring amber through the leaves. It was the sort of light by which people stand in long lines at Dairy Queen.

"Snazzy bike seat," she said a moment later.

"Yeah, classic," he said, caressing and slapping the leather seat. It was long-nosed and honey brown. He leaned the bike against a recliner she had inherited and ostracized to the porch with other renegade objects: unread community newspapers, a cracked plastic sled, a tote bag filled with tote bags. "You pay a weight price with this model," Lucas said about the seat, "but there's a payoff in beauty and comfort."

"In comfort?" she said, bending down a few inches to touch it. "It seems *un*comfortable, seductive and uncomfortable, like five-inch stilettos. Not that I have experience with heels that high."

"No."

"What do you mean, 'no'?"

"Just that they come with . . . podiatric perils." He seemed pleased with the alliteration.

She returned his smile. "I was at this posh hotel in LA where the women were wearing heels for everything," she said. "At the pool they were wearing heels."

"Oh God, I love that."

"Mm-hm. One night we went out to see this band my ex-husband used to be in, and we were waiting for our rental car at the hotel's turnaround. Which was cobblestone, so the women could barely walk in their stilettos. They were like sex foals—sex toddlers—boyfriends and bellhops rushing to their sides. Of course that's part of the appeal, right, that the woman is fettered?"

"Um."

"But I like wearing heels. Sometimes. It takes me a while to reacclimate in the spring."

"These saddles, though, they're actually pretty comfortable," he said. "Stiff at first, but eventually they conform to the rider's sit bones." He pointed out the saddle's indentations.

"It's like an intaglio of your . . . sit bones," she said.

"I left my bag on the sidewalk."

After he'd stored his things in the coat closet, he stood expectantly by the front door. There were sumo wrestlers printed on his sweat-spotted shirt.

"You want an iced tea or something?" she said.

"Ice tea, wow." He seemed unreasonably impressed. "Is it in one of those glass pitchers with lemons on it?"

"Uh, no, it's in one of those pastel Rubbermaid pitchers with the white top that either strains or pours freely." They made their way to the kitchen, his bike shoes clicking the Pergo.

"Maybe just water," he said.

"My pitcher's not good enough for you?"

"I actually think ice tea's kind of yucky. Where's Maxwell?"

"With his dad."

They sat on stools on the same side of the kitchen island, not quite facing each other. He pushed up his huge black glasses. She could make out a thumbprint on one of the lenses.

"The truth is," she said, "I've had some previous run-ins with those bike seats, or saddles—is that the preferred terminology? I made it seem like it was all new to me, but that's not quite true."

He tipped his head rightward. "Weird thing to lie about."

"I didn't *lie.* I'm not sure I've ever touched one before. My ex had one, but I get tired of referring to him."

"Although you just did—the band he used to be in and all."

"But that seems less about him than the bike seat," she said. "I never saw him as a legit musician; it never seemed to *come out* of him, you know, or maybe I just can't remember when it seemed that way. But he was, I don't know, into *things.*"

"A materialist."

"In limited areas. He was—well, the line between connoisseurship and consumerism gets blurry for most of us, right? With him the distinction seemed nonexistent. He was always digging up arcane objects of desire, making them seem hidden and cultish and timeless, and then I'd come to see that he just had a good spot in line for some broadening niche market." She worried for a moment that, while critiquing Jason, she was unwittingly critiquing Lucas. "Not to knock your bike saddle," she said. "It really is pretty."

"A friend of mine has a Tumblr devoted to pictures of them."

"You're joking."

"Not really, no. He's the guy who built my bike"—he gestured toward the porch—"Archer's old roommate. He'll be at the wedding."

"I'll get the Tumblr URL straight from the source, then," she said. "Anyway, I'm trying not to talk about him, my ex, trying not to define myself against what I used to be." She rubbed her jaw. "For a few years in my twenties I was an actor. Years after I stopped doing it, I'd still find myself at parties saying, 'I used to act,' 'I used to be involved in theater.' It had only been seven, eight shows."

Lucas held a blink as he nodded. "You miss it?"

"I don't, which is funny because for a while it seemed so all-consuming."

After a short lull, he said, "I'm in sort of a funny mood." He seemed content, at first, to leave it at that, then confided that his mother was asking him for money.

"She's having financial problems?"

"In a way, yeah. Although the money she's asking for is money I borrowed." He rubbed his right forearm. Karyn wondered if there was a connection between his apparent carpal tunnel and that Jessica Rabbit site. "I had this idea," he said, "forever I had this dream of making reusable grocery bags."

"All right." She hoped she wasn't registering foreknowledge. Then again, her ignorance might imply apathy. She thought about her life's ungoogled names; these were people about whom she truly gave not one fuck.

"Yeah, I even tried to get Archer to invest."

"Really?"

"Not interested. Things kind of languished," he said, "but when I lost my job, I went for it." Karyn overrode a smile when Lucas revealed the name, but the venture became less of a joke as she took in his enthusiasm, his pride in the bags' construction ("incredibly sturdy") and design ("there's one with tigers"). There was a shakiness to his voice that seemed to admit failure but not defeat. He had turned his chair to face her, and she noticed again how the corner of his lip sometimes curled upward when he talked, a gentle tic more than an Elvis-like sneer, as endearing as a missed belt loop. "So I borrowed ten grand from my mom," he said, "who doesn't have much money, almost none. I should never have asked her, but I was so confident I'd make it back."

"Sure."

"Yeah, so: had the bags manufactured, hired a friend to build a website, did some SEO. Only, by the time we were ready to roll, reusable grocery bags were the new T-shirt, like people were constantly getting them for free."

"Right, right."

He took a deep breath through his nose.

"I'll buy some of your bags," she said. "If you still have any."

"I do. I made five thousand of them, so I should have, let's see, just under five thousand of 'em in the basement. My mom's basement."

"I'd probably want a marginally smaller quantity."

"Up to you." He changed the subject: "Have you been gardening a lot?"

"Garnering a lot of what?"

"No, gardening. I like your profile photo, with the gloves and all."

"Oh, right," she said. That photo was now sullied by its association with the systems consultant, but she thought that changing one's profile photo too often looked self-absorbed. "No, not much, not this week."

"I was thinking that, if you want, I could make some mixes for the trip."

"Yeah, sure."

"What kind of music do you like?"

"Oh, different kinds." She felt like a kid, answering a question like that. "I feel like a kid," she blurted.

"What?"

"I like a little of everything, or everything from A to, I don't know, L. Lately I've been listening to British folkie stuff: Incredible String Band, Sandy Denny, Pentangle."

He waved a hand over his head. "I guess I don't mean 'over my head,' just that I haven't heard of those people."

"I know them mainly through—" She stopped herself from mentioning her ex yet again. The String Band project grew naturally out of her divorce because it was Jason who had exposed her to the group. It was the sort of music he listened to in college with his set of fellow geology majors, high-testing, tentative neo-pagans or, in campus parlance, "cloak people," though maybe that designation was for less tentative types. Some of the soundtrack from her marriage was too painful to return to, but Jason's British hippie folk had taken the opposite course; she embraced it only after he and roughly half of his records were gone. The String Band's music was full of the dichotomies she loved—earthy/ethereal, local/ecumenical, plus the usual sublime/ridiculous—and their songs affected her more than any had since she was a teenager. They were "songs as empathy evacuation engines," as Rae Armantrout put it. Karyn looked at Lucas and restarted: "It's been an obsession because, well"—so far she'd told only Maxwell about her project—"I've been writing a play about a woman who's part of a group a lot like the Incredible String Band."

"A playwright! Like Yeats."

"Yes, I recall our common expertise in Yeatsian dramaturgy. I guess it's a play—it is, but it started with me just acting, escaping into this, I don't know, this kind of dreamy, forestlike world."

"Forestlike?"

"Nothing takes place in a forest, but it *feels* like a forest."

"Like *Midsummer Night's Dream*?"

"Well, I might prefer to lower the bar of comparison. But I loved it, loved acting the stuff out. When I said I didn't miss acting, I really meant that I don't miss it now, 'cause I've been doing it, but for myself."

He was listening with a hard-to-come-by attentiveness.

"And the world of the play had all this mystery and melancholy and romance that I could disappear into; it would sort of overcome me, so that even though I knew I was making everything up—I'm not crazy—it felt like there were outside agencies at work."

"Like in a holodeck?"

She didn't know what that meant. "Maybe," she said.

"It sounds great—seriously," he said. "I've been—this isn't at all the same as what you're talking about, but I've been imagining this—let me backspin: I've been having trouble reading lately, okay, like the only thing I can concentrate on are these obsolete travel guides the previous tenant left in my closet."

"I can see those being addictive, though. A friend of mine has an amazing collection of nineteenth-century Baedekers." Why had she said that? It wasn't true, though she'd once read an essay by a man who collected old Baedekers.

"These are from, like, ten, fifteen years ago," he said. "A whole box of them, which is strange 'cause I don't see how anyone living in my shitty apartment could have such extensive travel plans. I've been picturing this wanderluster—is that a word?"

"I think."

"Yeah, who's so ashamed of how badly he wants to travel and how little he can afford to that he hides *Exploring Rome '95* like it's *Barely Legal.*"

"What's *Barely Legal*?"

"Oh, well, it's a pornographic magazine with an emphasis on—"

"Little joke; I figured it out."

"Oh. Yeah, so for me it's less a box of old travel guides than it is an epic quest novel or something, with this pathetic, thwarted hero."

"Schmodysseus. Sorry, that was awful."

"No, I'm laughing on the inside," he said. "I guess I didn't tell you, but I was once in an MFA program for fiction."

"Oh," she said, surprised.

He named the school; she hadn't heard of it. "It wasn't quite the right—I didn't graduate. Back when I was in Philly I wrote a story, really a pretty good one, about a prison guard. It came in a rush, you know, four days in the 'zone' or whatever. So kind of as a lark I sent it off to a couple programs. Well, six. One took me. I wasn't all that literary, to be straight with you; I mean, I read books."

"Travel guides."

"Yeah, and the investigative pieces in *Barely Legal.* But I wasn't a—what do they always say readers are? Copious? A copious reader?"

"That's for *notes,*" she said. "Copious notes."

"Right."

She suggested *avid.*

"Yeah, an avid reader."

"Or voracious."

"I wasn't that either. Kind of stupidly, I thought that gave me an edge, like when Tea Party candidates get all, *Vote for me 'cause I have no political experience and what's more I despise the very idea of political experience.*"

"Right."

"But I hated everyone in the program. Not *hated,* not everyone. Sara—the one who worked for Archer?—I came to like her. She was in some ways the biggest pill in my class, but also the best, the best person. We lived together awhile."

"You hadn't mentioned that."

"Not boyfriend-girlfriend," he said. "I'd love to read your play, though. I don't have much background reading plays, but I'm good at giving notes."

"I'm sure you are, but I'm not really looking for that. I don't have ambitions to see the play produced or anything."

"Hey, that's cool."

She swallowed audibly.

"So maybe," he said, "you can bring some of your Ultimate String Band on the trip, and I'll make my mixtapes."

"I don't have a tape deck in my car."

"I mean 'tape' like how we 'dial' and 'hang up' cell phones. I'll keep 'em clean on account of Maxwell."

"It doesn't matter; he's heard it all—most of it."

"I'm mainly into hip-hop, if that's cool. Some R & B and EDM, a bit of jazz."

"He'll love that. He's gotten into"—she thought for a moment—"sorry, who's the fat rapper who died?"

"Big Pun?"

"More famous than that."

"Notorious B.I.G.?" He seemed horrified that she hadn't summoned the name. She was glad she hadn't asked him to explain what EDM stood for.

"Yes, of course," she said. "He came around a few years after I stopped paying attention."

When he reached an index finger under his glasses to pull an eyelash, his eyelid made a little kissing sound. "Gemma wanted me to

DJ the wedding party," he said. "But I sold all my equipment a few months ago."

"You had turntables and all that."

"Yeah, two 1200s. It was almost my job back in the day. I was never a technical wizard, but I was good at moving the crowd, you know, giving them what they wanted without necessarily giving them what they thought they wanted, 'cause maybe the song they want most is one they've never heard before." A presumably nostalgic smile passed over him. "It's an amazing feeling, getting people to dance, watching them adjust to the next record, like if I'd done my beat-matching properly so the kicks and snares were locked, but maybe there's some dissonance in the rest of the music, some tension that hypes people up for a few measures. Which is kind of what grabbed me when I was writing that first story, about the guard. It wasn't totally autobiographical, but still the narrator and I blurred and overlapped in a way that was, like, seamless but uncomfortable, so it was like a good cross-fade."

"I've felt that onstage," she said. "I've felt it working on this play."

His eyebrows were black and peaked like the adhesive corners used by scrapbookers. He raised them. "Will you send it to me?"

"Okay."

"Though, actually, could you print it out? I don't have any paper at home, and I hate reading on a computer."

"Paper can have a nice decelerating effect," she said.

"Is this just regular water? It's good."

"Yeah, just tap."

"I knew a girl who—you could pour three different kinds of water, like tap and different kinds of bottled, and she'd be able to identify which was which every time."

"Maybe I'll print that play."

"Perfect."

May 2006

Despite having come within fourteen months of earning an MFA in creative writing, Lucas's policy vis-à-vis literary journals, with three remembered exceptions, was the standard one: he didn't read them. He wasn't among those writers, often alluded to with bridled pique in editorial guidelines, who submit to journals they haven't bothered to so much as skim, because he had never submitted his stories for publication. He hadn't even saved them, a notable renunciation in that he saved lots of nonessential things—old issues of the *Source,* broken handheld video games, two deutschmarks, punch cards for sandwich shops in cities he probably wouldn't return to—and for that matter he had made and kept PDF files of his fellow MFA candidates' manuscripts, not for their Fisher-Price stories and novel excerpts but for his own discursive annotations. He put in more effort on those annotations than he did on his fiction. For a time he even thought they could be mined for a book, something like *Pale Fire* meets *Friends,* in which the story of a romantically entangled, endlessly treacherous writing workshop is told through the annotations of its most discerning participant. The project never advanced past this germinal stage.

It was during his aborted graduate studies that he found two back issues of *Granta* in a professor's please-take box, setting up the sequential second of the three above-mentioned exceptions regarding literary journals. About eight years earlier he had read the *Paris Review* interview with William Faulkner and had wedged one of its cussed and oracular quotes into a high school term paper ("above and beyond," commended the teacher, who ostensibly didn't detect that Lucas's knowledge of *The Sound and the Fury*'s late and late-middle pages stemmed from a yellow-jacketed secondary source).

So, in the spring of '06, when he started to read an essay in the fourth issue of an instantly influential journal out of New York, his immersion was a breakthrough of sorts. He and Gemma had been browsing the stacks at McNally Jackson after dinner. He'd gotten signals that they might sleep together that night for old times' sake, as he thought of it, though only a few months had passed since the start of their friendship era. He had picked up the journal at random. Its table of contents was austere save for a tiny, unaccountable drawing of a porcupine. It took him a moment to place Archer's name. Lucas's old MFA peers stayed safely under the radar, so it was unprecedented for him to run across a piece in print whose seed, as it were, he had witnessed; it was additionally coincidental that earlier that day he had been allowed to work from home, which mostly entailed watching pornography while avoiding work, or daydreaming about Gemma while avoiding pornography. When away from the computer, he had assumed positions he hoped to be in later that night, murmuring sweet and dirty things, then with tentative transsexualism he had assumed positions he hoped Gemma would be in, at one point inserting an extraordinarily lifelike Dr. Knox dildo, complete with testicles, into his mouth. He had two tangerines with lunch, and his spine tingled when he freed them from their red net, remembering the time that Gemma, on all fours, had let him tear her old fishnets . . . then kissing her thighs, nibbling her pelvis, the first fingertip of wetness. He couldn't imagine meeting another woman with whom he was so sexually compatible and to whom he was so attracted. It wasn't reasonable, he knew, to think he was permanently spoiled for all others, but all the same that's what he thought.

He had been able to sustain such a consuming state of lust, compulsion, pleasure, and anxiety throughout the day in part because, though he had masturbated liberally, he hadn't done so to orgasm. He would get himself as hard as he could, sometimes sucking in his stomach to check his profile in the mirror, then, on the edge of coming, he'd zip himself back into his jeans, wait until he shrank to a nub, and repeat. The idea was to arrive at Gemma's apartment with as large a store of pent-up arousal as possible. The hazard in this, he conceded, was that he might arrive overeager and selfish, with a stockpile of porny demands or unarticulated porny fantasies or various signs of pornographic derangement. A gamble.

Still, with the benefit of hindsight, he wished that he had elected to masturbate to orgasm three hours before the date, so that he might stand here now with his libido relaxed but rejuvenating. Instead, when he made it to the bookstore's magazine racks, he was nervous, suffering from some bladder discomfort, and determined to give up porn again for good. At least during work hours. It seemed that Archer, besides sharing interests and concerns in this arena, had experience, too, with creative-writing pedagogy, or had at least taken one workshop at his "elite university," probably unnamed to shroud the identities of his peers and professor, though it was just the species of falsely modest, feebly tantalizing discretion that would come automatically to Archer. Of course, Lucas was looking for bones to pick; from his perspective, the essay's paramount defect was its failure to be completely hateful. The story about the aunt's panties? Fucking hilarious!

He was about five pages in when he felt Gemma's hand on his arm. He turned to look at her. Exciting to have her face so close to his again. He remembered the third or fourth time they met, by chance at a festival in Fort Greene Park, how on seeing each other they couldn't decide whether to shake hands or risk a hug (they were both seeing other people at the time), how there was this drawn-out moment when he was staring down at their waffling hands, at her hips in her turquoise shirtdress, how erotic their closeness seemed.

After checking the contributors' notes—the relevant bio was pretentiously spare: "Archer Bondarenko lives in New York City"—he put the magazine back on the rack. He vowed not to mention the essay to Gemma.

As they were leaving the store, he said, "Remember that blowhard Canadian we met with Sara and John last year? Super rich."

"Sure. Hunter, is it?"

"Archer."

"The vanguardist of wanker studies."

"Yeah, yeah."

"I didn't think he was a blowhard."

"Either way, he did write that essay."

"Did he?" She stopped on the sidewalk. "Is that what you were reading?"

"Skimming."

"Well, you have to buy it."

"It was like fourteen bucks."

"Oh you horrid skinflint."

She turned back toward the store, made the purchase, and they set off again for her apartment, his fingers spidering her thigh on the subway, their hands slowly coming together, though one of hers held the journal, over which she sometimes piercingly chuckled. The sex was by no means bad and was sometimes, despite Lucas's over-plotting, inventive and surprising (he was forced to consider that Gemma had already learned new tricks since their breakup). But it was bound to disappoint; he'd built it up too much, imagining a fizzy endnote rather than a moody epilogue. It didn't help that during the day he had literally rubbed himself raw. His postcoital sadness was pronounced—he more or less mewled into Gemma's neck as he lay on top of her, stroking her hair—and he grew sadder when he thought of how uncommon that had been when they were together, his postcoital norm having been starry happiness, gratitude, and take-out burritos.

He thought that would be the end of them altogether, but within a week they were able to talk again in an easy, friendly way, not untouched on his side by longing but not fraught with it. In the past he'd been partial to clean breaks, but this time that prospect seemed depressing and proved unnecessary. As the months progressed, Gemma considerately didn't fill him in on her love life, but he knew things were happening, and somewhere around that time, he later learned, she sent Archer what must have been an entertaining and enticing fan letter.

June 2011

Without taking off his bag, John reached into the unzipped pocket that held his scavenged balls, pulled out a dirty pink one, and underhanded it onto the fourth hole's fairway, where it fell with a tap. Often after he'd served George his Heath bar, cleared the table, and filled the dishwasher, he would sneak on the course for three or four twilit holes. He was always alone, though every so often he would see groups finishing the front nine in the distance, and frequently there'd be activity in one of the yards that bled into the course: someone covering a pool or setting up a sprinkler, teenagers laughing around a patio table. Once in a while he'd chat with the bald greenskeeper, who always asked after Mr. Crennel and never reported John to the country club's high officials.

He took the tasseled knit cover off the three-wood and dropped it on the grass. The clubs were high-end Pings from the mideighties, George's last set, finally regripped this spring for John's nonarthritic hands. He raised his arm and let a few blades of grass slip from his fingers to gauge the lilac breeze (Beaufort scale three), then lined up, rocking in place, narrowly pendulating the club before taking his shot. After practicing a sloping putt on the seventh green, he walked back to the pond that took in wayward shots from the fifth and sixth holes. Scanning the shore, he spotted a ball whose retrieval called for little wading. He sat down, took off his spiked spectators, the kind with the fringed leather flap over the laces, then his over-the-calf argyle socks, and rolled up his khakis, strict reproductions of those issued to American servicemen during World War II. With each roll he pulled the cloth taut against his leg and smoothed out the new cuff. A minute later he was back in the same spot by the pond, picking grass from his wet skin, studying a wart that looked like the nub of glue that blocks an Elmer's cap. He reached for the towel he kept clipped to his bag and carefully dried the ball and his feet. The grass felt cool on his palms when he leaned back to take in the scene, the willows swaying like those *Fantasia* mops (or maybe it was brooms), the clouds showing a touch of medium-rare pink.

He liked it here, liked Lammermuir's rolling lawns and blacktopped esses, the sound of tired acorns when he drove his Oldsmobile (formerly George's) up the driveway in fall. True, he wasn't where he had once hoped to be, but he didn't feel chagrined by his station, or he felt that way only sometimes, every so often when he was kneeling to mark a customer's cuff, when George called him Beau Brummell or Fancy Dan, when Archer posted photos online, taken at some chic gala for poor people or bees, or snapped on a lido's sun-dappled deck, reconstructed Neolithic pile dwellings and rows of pear trees flowering like steam clouds in the background. John sometimes wished the peak times from what remained his deepest friendship had been documented and made public: the time the black bear visited John and Archer's campsite, the time Archer introduced John as "the only man I know who can speak with equal authority on vests and vector fields," the party where they almost met the guy from LCD Soundsystem. Mostly, though, John had learned not to dwell on the past, not to let those best times circle in his brain like the Empire Today jingle. He saw his period of world-beating ambition as anomalous rather than unfulfilled, beyond the range of his ability, out of true with his inborn indifference to money and status. His high school dreams of becoming a serious mathematician now seemed as irrational as the square root of two, but when he thought of them, he was amused more than ashamed.

He stood up, brushed off the seat of his khakis, and turned toward home. A wide lane led from the fourth hole to a field split between country-club property and the Hansons' lawn, which George still called the Wrightsons' lawn. John crossed the field, then crossed a narrow, unlined road to the rotting wooden bridge at the foot of George's driveway. The creek under the bridge: trickling; the driveway: steep, winding. The door to the right of the two-car garage entered into a long mudroom paved with smooth maroon bricks, where John took off his shoes and leaned his bag in an alcove tidily crowded with work boots, sweat-browned tennis visors, grass-stained golf tees, giant umbrellas. The mudroom also held a washer and dryer (laundry was another of the duties for which John received room and board and a small salary), a folding table, a freezer, and, on the opposite wall, a long shelf, above which was a squishy red vinyl frame that held a half-dozen snapshots, including one of Sara as a beginning skier, her fringed yellow scarf hanging below her puffy jacket.

He passed through the kitchen and the dining room, little more than a wide hallway since the late-fifties addition of the now nostalgically named family room, in which George was dozing through a documentary about Nostradamus. There was a fat-legged dining table in the center of the busy room, and a set of bamboo furniture spread out along the room's edges. Although for years a pall had hung over parts of the house, over the unused living room, the underlit study with its obsolete exercise bike and taxidermal big game, over the shelves of forgotten bestsellers and the pink-tiled shower that still held one of Mrs. Crennel's hairnets—although the pall was obvious to the point of staginess, there were other parts of the house, such as John's little bedroom ("el cuartito," in George's coinage) and the big family room, now filled with a portentous chord, that retained a kind of pastel contentment, all chirping sparrows and distant diving boards, snow-drooped branches and wafts of fresh-cut grass. Of course, those are all things you hear, see, or smell through windows, but in a way a room directs its windows.

George was sitting on one end of the sofa, in line with the television but fourteen feet away from it. It was dark enough now that John could see the screen reflected in the sliding glass door above George's slumped head. George stirred at a swooping theremin. "Oh," he said, "what do you know?"

"Nice night," John said.

"How was work?" John put in two weekly shifts, Tuesdays and Thursdays, at Mitchell's in Northbrook Court, but George hadn't bothered to master the schedule.

"I was off today. I just knocked around a few Titleists."

"Did you play eighteen?" George's voice was warm and gravelly tonight, like it used to be. He had become increasingly ornery over the past few years, so when the warmth of his voice resurfaced, it could seem held over for show, like ticket pockets or lapel buttonholes.

"Nope, I just snuck on the course after we ate."

George motioned to the TV. "The French seer."

John nodded.

"They say he knew about the French Revolution and Hitler."

John stood watching for a while. If you foretold a revolution back then, he figured, you'd be right eventually. "He would've made a helluva stockbroker," he said, trying to play to George's interests.

"I don't believe they had stockbrokers in those days."

John still liked George, but not as much as before, and he was getting tired of these out-of-sync exchanges. He considered his own loneliness to be a product not of inadequate company but of incomplete solitude.

"Did you get in eighteen?" George asked.

"I just played a few."

George returned his attention to the TV.

John let him watch for a minute, then said, "So I reminded Kristen Hanson today about looking after things while I'm away at the wedding."

"That Greek's wedding?"

"'Member how we went over that? He's Ukrainian. Half. So she's all set to fix your meals and keep things shipshape."

Austerely: "It won't be necessary."

"Sure it will. It's—"

George, wanting to hear the show's conclusion, held out a hand like the Heisman Trophy. A plane flew overhead, and John bent down to see the wing lights through the window. "Osama bin Laden," George said.

They could pick up this discussion tomorrow. "I reckon I'll hit it," John said. "You have clean pajamas on your pillow."

"Would you put them in the dryer for me?"

"Your pajamas were just washed and dried this afternoon."

"I like how they feel fresh out the dryer."

"I understand, but isn't that a winter thing?"

"Thank you, John," George said, and closed his eyes again.

After warming the pajamas, John closed himself in his room. He had a sewing table tucked in by the window, and, since he wasn't really tired, he shortened a pair of canvas trousers by a quarter inch and moved a sport coat's sleeve buttons so they would properly kiss. He used to lean toward jacket sleeves with functioning buttonholes, but now he thought that was pretentious. Next he took inventory of his closet. Though he was sentimental about the shepherd's-check jacket he had worn on his first date with Sara, it was overpadded in the shoulder, and he decided to relegate it to storage. A dog-legged staircase led from his room to the attic. John pulled on the light and found his way to the garment rack containing some of Mrs. Crennel's old coats and dresses, now scrunched by John's second string. Still not sleepy, he found himself inspecting a stack of three boxes he'd never bothered with before, one filled with aluminum containers, another with extra bathroom tiles and what was either a candlesnuffer or something religious, though the Crennels weren't.

The bottom box held a pair of bell-bottom cords, a deteriorating newspaper—B-52S BOMB HAIPHONG—three paperbacks, and, most interestingly, a typewritten manuscript. He leafed through it for a half minute. There were 278 pages, but the last sentence didn't seem like an ending. He returned to the title page—*God's Good Side* by Marion Crennel—then to page one:

> The house was a white one-story with a gray, barky roof. Its trim had been painted the purplish green of the claws that climb toward and cover asparagus tips.

He read on for a few pages. A novel, it seemed. Sara had told him that her aunt Marion had been inspirational to her, but she hadn't explained why, really, or mentioned any abandoned novels. He figured he should ask George about the manuscript, or find out how to get it to Marion's surviving partner. More than that, though, he wanted Sara to have it. He could mail it to her Buffalo address with a concise note—"Something you should have—John"—but it would be better, he realized, for Sara to find it herself. The thrill of discovery. She could happen across it at the Thanksgiving reunion, or think she had.

January 2007

There was only one shade tree on the beach, a beefwood tree with foliage like puppet hair and woody fruit like miniature grenades. Sara sat under the tree in a padded, straight-backed chair, eating peanuts, reading a book, sometimes looking up at the water. Ugly brown pelicans dived precipitously when they weren't soiling the docks, boobies hunted farther off and from higher up, and tiny silverfish, now only faintly seen but remembered from Sara's last swim, jumped in schools like protractors of Seven-Up mist. The Caribbean was a shade lighter than travel-brochure aquamarine, the view compromised or completed by two yachts, the larger one owned by a German hardware tycoon—the Screw König, in Sara's christening—who, to judge from a chronology pieced together on the internet, had purchased the boat as a reward for overseeing a mass layoff.

It was late afternoon and only two other guests were left on the beach: the fifty-something producer of a TV show Sara hadn't heard of and the producer's elderly husband, a renowned painter. Making his way from the bathhouse to the water, the painter stopped to ask Sara one of the few questions she consistently welcomed. "I'm reading Jane Austen's *Persuasion* for the first time," she answered. Well read and still two years shy of thirty, Sara was seldom vulnerable to criticism over having inordinately put off a book, but all the same she would sooner be caught *re*reading a classic and was proud of herself for telling the truth this time, explicitly and without a suave mea culpa. Ever since overlooking that moronic misspelling of Austen's name (the publisher never rehired her, but big whoop), she had become a penitent and more dedicated fan, though not yet dedicated enough to reread *Emma* or *Pride and Prejudice.* She rarely reread books, possibly owing to the same dispositional defect that kept her from eating leftovers, though she went on refrigerating them and apparently considered it more economizing to discard a forgotten, half-eaten slice of meatloaf and its mold-dotted Tupperware than to dispense with all food scraps straightaway. It was another thing—reading a book just once, forgetting almost everything therein—that made her feel like a fraud. The writers she looked up to seemed to view the first pass through a worthy book as merely the ruminal stage toward an absorptive understanding born of multiple readings. Probably they were right, but she found the unknown more seductive than the forgotten. She would embrace the pleasures of rereading in her miraculously prosperous senescence.

"Wonderful book," the painter purred, "wonderful book." His accent was as worldly, as borderless as air. He was an American but didn't seem like one, though he didn't seem like anything else. He had been one of the thirty-two artists in Clement Greenberg's epochal *Post-Painterly Abstraction* exhibition, and while he hadn't reached the fame of Frank Stella or Ellsworth Kelly, he was famous enough for Sara to know his name. She'd seen a few of his giant rainbow canvases in museums, had seen another reproduced on the cover of an early seventies poetry anthology called *The Sound Inside.* An honor to have him sanction her reading material, a relief that he hadn't been too bored to remark on a fairly ordinary, if unimpeachable, choice. The other books she'd brought to the island were more esoteric, though not what you'd call difficult (she didn't want her beach reads to seem self-satisfied or anhedonic), and she hoped that someone closely observing her would surmise a reader neither endlessly returning, like some cardiganed spinster, to canonical crowd-pleasers, nor unmixedly devoted, like some wallflower rebel, to outré small-press paperbacks, but instead someone at home in many worlds and genres, someone who simply swept up the far-flung books stacked on her nightstand and tossed them into her rollerbag.

After a while the no-see-ums descended, and the painter was driven up to the resort in a golf cart while Sara and the TV producer, Linda, walked together to the foot of the steep hill, past the cracked tennis court, the flamingo pond, the grove of palm trees. Some of the palm trunks leaned drunkenly while others were as straight and gray as concrete lampposts. For part of the way up the hill, Sara and Linda took a coiled dirt path, their voices and footfalls sending rock iguanas rustling out of view. Linda gossiped about the island's owner, a Swiss-born investor, entrepreneur, philanthropist, and chess grandmaster ("though they give out those titles more liberally than they once did") who might arrive any day by helicopter with a retinue of lawyers and sex workers. "One of the guys from our group plays chess," Sara said, adding that she didn't think he (Lucas) could provide much competition to a grandmaster even of the new, debased standard. Gemma had beseeched Archer to invite Lucas, who was trying to be gallantly courteous when he wasn't openly salivating over Gemma and her collection of brightly colored rompers.

Originally, Archer's thirtieth birthday party was supposed to happen at his parents' place on Dominica, but it came about that his stepfather needed the house that week for a friend, or rather for a venture capitalist he was partnering with in a scheme to convert long-haul diesels to run on liquefied natural gas. So the party was moved to the small resort on this thousand-acre island, whose most deluxe and secluded cabin sometimes attracted movie stars; a chiseled, inexpressive British actor and his presumably gorgeous girlfriend had checked out of that cabin only days before Archer and Gemma checked in. At other times of year the island was the site of ongoing botanical and entomological studies, which must have provided tax advantages for the owner. The meals at the resort were sophisticated if rarely adventurous, the facilities elegant if usually rustic, the beaches pristine, the grounds beautifully landscaped. But mostly you paid for what you didn't get: crowds, noise, television, music, children, Jimmy Buffett fans, and middle-class tourists, aside from occasional tagalongs such as Sara and maybe half of Archer's other guests. "An interesting thing about rich people," Archer had once said, "is that most of them aren't interesting." On the party's first night—many of the guests still woozy from puddle jumpers, boat exhaust, and the inefficiencies of Caribbean airports—it was announced over a late dinner that Viking had acquired Archer's debut novel, making the week doubly celebratory. Lucas, pushing the gratitude act too far, initiated a chorus of "For He's a Jolly Good Fellow" and was taken aback when people actually joined in. Gemma sang the "and so say all of us" version and was flirtatiously teased.

"Now, I'm sorry," Linda said, "are you and Archer together"—Sara felt a simultaneous sting and flutter at the question—"or is he with . . . what's the Brit's name?"

"Gemma. She's been in the States since she was twelve. But yes, they're together. Archer and I are just friends. And I do some work for him—little things, proofreading and occasional research. When you saw us the other night we were just looking over something he's writing for the *Believer.*" Sara had to take care to make her work for Archer seem inconsequential, lest anyone question the totality of his artistic commitment or the individuality of its yield. In fact her work for him was full-time, though by contemporary standards the hours were undemanding. Of course, it was hard to say where a writer's work ended and where her leisure and procrastination began. Reading was part of the work, after all, as was pausing from one's reading to think; and walking pensively through Delaware Park; riding the bus with a notebook in perpetual readiness; using television to monitor the demotic zeitgeist; being a person on whom the posturings, contretemps, and misadvised sandals of Fourth of July barbecues were never lost. Really, Archer was buying all that, though more practically and currently he was asking her to write book reviews, "think pieces," light essays on the writing life or medium-light essays on other lives—anything that might raise his "platform." He paid her an annual salary of $170,000, a figure well in excess of the advance that came with his book contract. Nice work if you can get it: all the remuneration of a tenured upper-tier literary novelist without the horrors of teaching, self-exposure, public speaking, and insincere blurbing. Archer also sent her thoughtful, often expensive premiums and perquisites: a first edition of Barbara Pym's *A Glass of Blessings;* a print from Tom Phillips's *A Humument;* a signed Bobby Hull photo for her dad; a surprisingly uncomfortable Aeron chair with a slight yet vertiginous wobble.

"And are you a writer as well?" Linda asked.

"I'm gathering material." This was another thorn of her situation, knowing that people took her to be an odd-jobbing literary washout or rudderless trust-funder when in truth she was a self-made, improbably deep-pocketed Geppetto. "I haven't had much time for my own stuff lately," she told Linda, "but I hope to get back to that soon." She hoped to get back to that on this trip, in fact, but so far she'd added only nine words to her notebook ("birds roosting on airport beams, dust falling like molt"), and this afternoon's writing session had morphed quickly into a nap, her body logy from the sun, her adobelike cabin cool with the punningly green jalousie blinds shut, her pen slipping from her fingers as she reminded herself that two rested hours were often more productive than four tired ones.

Now they were on the paved road, grooved in the interest of traction like a freshly raked sand trap. The hill was at its steepest grade, and Sara was breathing heavily, feeling each step in her thighs. A light-footed gardener weeded on the side of the road in a conical straw hat. Sara and Linda didn't talk again until they reached the ridge, where the resort had its main building and its original whitewashed cabins, built in the thirties by Newport merchants with distant family ties to Benjamin Franklin. "Will I see you at cocktail hour?" Linda said.

"Unless the cocktails impair your vision," Sara answered.

Cocktail hour was a simple operation held in the lounge of the main building, which guests were encouraged to call the Great House. Two trays of hors d'oeuvres—including, to widespread puzzlement, deep-fried grapes—and a few dishes of hot nuts were brought out and placed on a teak buffet. Guests mixed drinks or grabbed beers and sodas for themselves at the honor bar a few steps down from the lounge. At present there were only sixteen guests at the resort: the Bondarenko party; Linda and the painter; a DC lawyer and her Defense Department husband; and an aged English couple, he a former Labour MP, she a versatile hobbyist with the look of someone constantly processing lorry exhaust. Sara found the swirl of wealth, power, and status intoxicating, arousing, tiring, and sometimes nauseating, as though she were experiencing all the effects of alcohol at once, or all the effects except relaxation; for that, she was turning to alcohol. Her piña colada rested on a table whose glass top displayed seashells identified by sallow, typewritten labels the size of cookie fortunes. The lounge had a high ceiling with exposed wood beams, bamboo and rattan furniture with muted floral cushions, moldy guest books, watercolors of local scenes painted by a daughter of the founding family, and a framed coral leaf of a purplish brown much like the Plymouth Reliant Sara's parents owned when they were still married.

She sat at the end of a sofa next to John Anderson. He wore a seersucker jacket, salmon shorts, camp moccasins, and his leonine beard. She hadn't seen him in two years, and his presence stirred up suppressed guilt over how passively she'd dumped him. The guilt might have engendered a cautious, expiatory tenderness toward him. It didn't. It made him twice irritating: first, for being himself; second, for stirring up her suppressed guilt. Another of Archer's college friends, a photographer of rising reputation, was now describing her latest series, for which she traveled the country photographing local semicelebrities, basically nonhomeless eccentrics known for spending a lot of time out of the house in odd clothes. "I know I keep coming back to this," Archer said to Jessica, the photographer, "but we really need to work on something together; my text in response to your photos, or vice versa, anything."

"Yes, we have to," Jessica said with what sounded like legitimate enthusiasm, though her choice of words was telling; Archer must have been her top patron; an attempted collaboration of some sort was probably as voluntary for Jessica as a sneeze. Sara liked books in which prose was augmented by photos—Breton, Woolf, Berger, Gass, Ondaatje, Marías, Sebald—though the practice seemed dissuasively faddish of late, and perhaps she didn't like all those books as much as she had once professed. "The only thing," she ventured, looking at Archer, "is that so many writers are using photos right now. There's a risk."

"A risk of what?" Archer said.

"Don't get me wrong," she said, "Jessica's photos are incredible." The compliment was unpretending—well, "incredible" overstated the case—but unnecessary, since Jessica's attention had been pulled elsewhere. "But a risk of seeming late to the party, you know? Like a rock band adding sitar to its sound in 1971."

"The ISB made brilliant use of sitars," Archer said reverently.

"But earlier than '71, right?" Sara said, trying to salvage her illustration, not as artfully pandering as she had hoped.

"There's no expiration date on sitars," he said.

"So, Archer, tell me," said the lawyer, who'd been listening in, "are you already into your next novel, or is it too soon for that? A friend of ours is a novelist—political thrillers, mainly, quite polished—and he literally starts the new one the morning after finishing the last."

"I wish I could do that," Archer said. "I . . . I have a few things brewing," he added, waving his fingers around his head. "Nothing solid yet."

"Are you an outliner?"

"Well, I make them, yes, but I grow quickly heedless of their directives."

"Men and maps, eh?"

"I suppose," Archer said. "This last book—how to put it?—it's fastidiously plotted, but the plotting came about gradually and organically." Sara tried not to roll her eyes while Archer swept a hand through his wispy hair. "It's a matter," he said, "of listening, very attentively, to what your characters want."

"What they really, really want," Sara said, referencing the Spice Girls.

The lawyer shook her head approvingly at Archer. "I so admire that kind of creativity."

"Oh, I don't know," he said, smiling shyly as he got up to revisit the bar.

Sara held up her glass. "Another?"

Several conversations flitted around her along with a moth the size of a young bat. She watched the moth and listened to Archer run the blender. Soon he returned, deftly carrying three glasses and a can of club soda as if he were an experienced waiter, though in fact he had no traditional work experience of any kind. Most of the guests had dressed up somewhat for dinner, but Archer was still wearing rolled-up Levi's, his dirty Jack Purcells, and a one-pocket T-shirt with broad horizontal stripes. He looked like he was trying out for Yo La Tengo or delivering the *Sacramento Bee* in 1966. She noticed now that his tongue was poking out irresistibly from the effort of balancing the glasses, which to Sara made up for his puffed-up replies to the lawyer's questions.

He was such an attractive mesh of arrogance and awkwardness. It was hard for her to remember how she'd once found him ugly. As a kid she'd always hated the Buffalo City Court Building, a symphonically dystopic concrete tower, not windowless but with vast windowless expanses and, around its edges, wedge-topped slits that brought guillotines to one's mind, or to one's head. Then in college a friend told her the building was a distinguished example of brutalism, and instantly she recognized its overcast beauty, became one of its staunch defenders. Her view of Archer had changed gradually, but the reversal was comparably stark. As far as looks went, Archer and she were suited to each other, she thought, both somewhat off, even homely at times, but with reserves of acquired-taste beauty. (The *Stickler* had called him "publishing hot," which Sara guessed was roughly analogous to "hockey smart.") Money was part of his allure, of course, and she wondered about the purity of Gemma's motives, and of her own, though she didn't precisely have motives. If she did, she didn't pretend they were pure. Besides, one could enter a situation with dicey motives and find purity along the way. She remembered something Mary Anne Disraeli had said: "Dizzy married me for my money, but if he had the chance again he would marry me for love."

"The thing is," Archer's friend Seth was contending, "the most interesting long-form fiction happening today is happening on television."

"I'm just reminding you that Plame's covert status at the time of the Novak column isn't indisputable," someone held in a different conversation.

"My God, look at that enormous moth!"

"Well, there *will* be climate-change winners. Mushy to deny that obvious fact."

Sara pivoted to still another group: "They're definitely related," Linda said. "Ira is Philip's nephew or something."

"Water rights is one area, sure. Mitigation and adaptation products and services is another."

"Is it indeed a moth?"

"It's not that close," Archer said, turning with an apologetically raised finger from his finance-industry friend. "It's, like, second cousin, or first cousin once removed."

"I've never bothered to learn the finer points of cousinage," Gemma said.

"We don't need to learn that kind of stuff anymore," Lucas said. "We can just look it up."

"We couldn't look it up before?" Sara said.

"At any rate, a talented family," Gemma said.

"But didn't you say you hated *Nixon in China*?" Archer said, smiling at Gemma.

Sara didn't like to think of Archer and Gemma having private conversations about art. She could only tolerate their relationship if she imagined it to be unvaryingly shallow and dull: restaurant deliberations and unfulfilling sex and voiceless games of draughts.

"I may have done," Gemma said. "I don't really care for that lot; I prefer maximalists."

"It's not quite to the point, though," Sara said, "since *Nixon in China* is by John Adams."

"No, it's by Philip Glass," Archer said.

Sara's shoulders clenched as she looked at him. He was so sure of himself that for a moment she thought *she* was wrong.

"Yes, that's Glass," said the painter evenly, permitting Archer to gloat silently in his misattribution. Of course it would seem small of Sara to drag Archer into the internet closet to resolve the dispute. She was still seething when a member of the uniformed kitchen staff entered the lounge, waiting for talk to fizzle so she could announce to the ladies and gentlemen that dinner was served.

A steep, rain-slick staircase led from John's cabin to a private deck on which there were two lounge chairs, a straw bench, and a wooden kiosk for shade. John had so far spent much of his vacation on the deck, reclining for hours at night, finding constellations and listening to the rhythmic chirps of tree frogs, reminiscent in a backwards way of industrial sprinklers. This morning he was up in time for sunrise, before most of the workers arrived from the nearby populated island, whose tree-covered northeast coast was visible from John's deck. Also in view were palm shrubs and organ-pipe cacti, the sickly green salt pond at the bottom of the hill, and the ruins of a Quaker-owned sugar mill once worked by African slaves. When John said yesterday to Sara that it didn't seem very Quakerish to own slaves, she reminded him that Richard Nixon had been a Quaker. He didn't think that answered, since Richard Nixon hadn't, after all, owned slaves. "But he would have," she had said.

He swept last night's rain off one of the lounge chairs, dried his hand on the resort's terry-cloth bathrobe, and sat down. It was strange to be here. A few years ago he had felt slighted by Archer's efficient upkeep of their friendship; now he missed that efficiency. They saw each other rarely, and when they did, there was an echoey sadness about their interactions. John understood now that, from the beginning, he had wanted the friendship more than Archer had, though dorm life, demanding little in the way of plans and overtures, covered that up; you sort of fell into talking, drifted toward the same party, tagged along to the boring Fassbinder movie. Still, there was an imbalance of need and affection and, naturally, an attendant imbalance of power. That's what kept John from doing anything that might jeopardize the friendship. He never argued with Archer, not about anything serious, because he knew Archer would win, would juke him toward some illogical generalization. For some reason John was drawn to people who wanted to make seemingly simple things complicated, when all he wanted to do was make complicated things simple. Complexity could be fascinating, sure, but John more or less believed what he'd been taught in church, not the literal truth of the resurrection or whatever, but in the universals: be honest, be humble, be nice to people, really mean it when you say "peace be with you." He wasn't saintly at enacting those beliefs, but he was trying. Hard to know what Archer believed in, except maybe that you should do the wrong thing prudently. Like: every semester back in college, he would hire out most of the work for one of his humanities courses, employing a wheezy comp-lit concentrator to write the papers, which Archer would subject to shrewdly dilapidating revision. He was proud of his small, probably unneeded precautions, how for instance he would misuse a word in class, then insert the same mistake into his next paper. (Maybe he'd meant to mix up Philip Glass and John Adams—

John had done some fact-checking last night—but to what end?) John never expressed his disapproval of the inexplicable cheating, inexplicable in that Archer wasn't pressed for time and was so smart, so quick to absorb the ideas John often couldn't wrap his head around, even quicker to adopt the jargon John couldn't tolerate.

Archer hadn't abused his power, though, or at least he hadn't made John feel unappreciated, and it was a touching sign of his loyalty that John had been invited at all to this small but lavish birthday party. He had even been given a favored friend's cabin, spacious and within spitting distance of the Great House. And maybe Archer was looking out for John when he booked newly single Jessica Kim into the room next door. It was true that when John heard her shower running one morning—it sputtered intermittently like a machine gun—he imagined her lathering herself in a more seductive style than cleanliness and sand removal would require. But he only thought of Jess that way in flashes. Sometimes—it probably wasn't cool—but sometimes he still thought of Sara in that way. It was awesome to see her. He'd told her so when they hugged on the dock the first night, he having walked down the hill with a borrowed flashlight—or "torch," as Gemma called it, maybe fittingly—to greet the last incoming boat; only later, when he was trying to read a book about shipbuilding while a bug ricocheted inside his bedside lampshade, did he remember that *awesome* was one of the words Sara looked down on and tried to discourage. It had just slipped out, and he'd meant it in the old-fashioned, not strictly positive sense, since it was also painful to see her, hard not to stare or seem like he was making a big point of not staring. On this trip he had learned to position himself in spots where he couldn't get a direct view of her, as if she were the sun, or the fire and brimstone Lot's wife wasn't supposed to look back at.

The first clanks and voices sounded from the kitchen. He sipped his herbal tea and stared at a tiny lizard that had emerged from the deck's cracked stone parapet. Of course the lizard knew that another creature, a large one, was nearby, but did it sense itself being watched? He started to feel a paternal tenderness toward the lizard, a warmth he suspected would prompt ridicule if articulated. From Sara, probably. Her cynicism was only superficial, but it was a thick surface.

Birds chirped, tea dribbled down his beard. So peaceful here. He whispered it, "So peaceful," and his voice sounded strange, like balled-up paper blowing across a concrete floor. He decided to let the tea dry on its own. He thought maybe he could feel it drying. He was all the time talking about leaving New York, but now, as the lizard darted away, he knew he had to make good on those threats, find a quiet place, a place where he could start building bikes again, or start building something else. "So peaceful," he said again, "so peaceful."

Sara woke up early with a hangover and settled in on one of the patios before most of the others. She hoped to check her e-mail over coffee, but Robert, the Defense Department guy, was similarly engaged at the next table, and by now she'd deduced that his laptop was fortified against inclusive use of the resort's wireless. He didn't seem to notice her exasperated sighs. She thumbed through the printer-hot *TimesDigest* and watched an army of creamy yellow butterflies—perhaps the species that gave rise to the name—float around a shrub that one of the gardeners identified as a Jamaica caper tree. After Robert powered down, she took the opportunity to visit an online retailer and arranged for a CD of John Adams's *Nixon in China* to be sent to Archer's condominium. She was still grinning over this when the painter strolled up to her table. "What are you on to now?" he asked, nodding at the paperback to the right of her plate. The cashmere sweater tied loosely around his neck was the color of underripe watermelon.

"Michel Leiris," she said, slurring the surname to hide her uncertain pronunciation. She turned the book over to reveal its cover.

"A kind of anthropological autobiography. Arrestingly undissembling." The phrase didn't excite him. "I loved *Persuasion,* by the way," she added, hoping to keep him by her table a little longer. "Overnight it's my favorite of her novels. I love how Anne is older than the typical Austen heroine and for once not only as clever but as wise as her creator."

"God, do you mean, or Jane Austen?"

She smiled. "Austen."

"Good. I don't rate the wisdom of our creator very highly. But I haven't read that one, *Persuasion,*" he said, erasing the endorsement he'd given with apparent emotion on the beach. "I don't think I've read any Jane Austen."

"Oh."

He excused himself as John and Lucas arrived.

"Did you guys sleep together?" Sara said.

"No," John said.

"Yes," Lucas said.

"We arrived at the same time from opposite directions." John exhibited no feel for the homoerotic or homophobic joking so common with straight men of his age and type, she thought, forgetting for a moment that she had started it this time.

"There's mad caterpillars on that tree over there," Lucas said, pointing. He strapped his backpack around the chair next to Sara's.

"Fat black-and-orange ones," John said, brushing dandruff off his navy linen jacket.

"Princeton caterpillars," Robert broke in. "It's a good year for them."

"Is it?" Lucas said in a tone that didn't invite embellishment. After returning from the buffet with a quantity of pastries, fruit, and yogurt that might have been called gluttonous in itself, Lucas ordered an omelet and sausage. "I'm trying to cram in my month's eating down here where the food's free."

"I don't reckon that's healthy," John said, meaning *healthful.*

Sara closed her eyes to better concentrate on the just-right temperature: breezy and, she guessed, seventy-eight. John and Lucas were caught up now in a friendly debate about whether bears truly hibernate. Her hangover was gone, and she was feeling the optimum effects of her morning coffee, high but not jittery. She wondered how many more sips she could afford.

"Oh, did you start without me?" Gemma mock-pouted, sneaking up on them. Today's romper was marigold orange. Lucas seemed to truffle in vain for an adroit response. Sara watched a hummingbird hover over a dish of mango.

"What?" Lucas said, looking at Sara.

She was smiling broadly. "Nothing," she said as Archer came into view.

When Gemma showed up for breakfast in another of her amazing baby-style outfits with the high-waisted short shorts, Lucas wanted badly to touch her, not just to touch her sleeve or hug her goodbye three days from now, but to put his hands all over her and guide her into new positions so he could put his hands in different spots. "You didn't start without me, did you?" she said. "Not in our hearts," Lucas answered. Archer followed a minute behind her, looking bleary. He greeted Lucas: "Your holiness."

"I'm not really into these papal puns, man." They didn't bother him out of other mouths, actually, and it was Lucas himself who'd dubbed his first (and last) car the Popemobile.

"All right, noted."

"It's been a lifetime of 'em, you know."

Archer repeated that he understood and was soon recruiting people for a morning hike to Franklin Beach, where there was said to be excellent "schnorkeling" (for some "quirky" reason he pronounced the word in what must have been the German way) and opportunities to "commune with nature."

"If we go as a big group, wouldn't we be more likely to commune with each other?" Lucas said.

"We could multitask," Archer said lamely but with a bonhomie that seemed genuinely interested in everyone's fun. Lucas's thought experiment for this trip was to imagine that Archer was annoying and full of himself but not a scoundrel. Really there was no reason, other than class resentment and sexual jealousy, for Lucas to be against Archer, and the sexual jealousy wasn't so gnawing anymore. He admitted that Archer seemed to be good for Gemma, good *to* her as well, Lucas's invitation to this island being a sign that he was good to her, willing to make sacrifices. Lucas tried to admire Archer for bestowing such largesse on someone he presumably disliked—and maybe Archer only disliked Lucas because Lucas had disliked him first. Which would make him all the more generous. The resort's prices were unpublicized on if-you-have-to-ask grounds, but Lucas guessed that, for the cost of a week's stay, a person could live frugally but not hungrily for the better part of a year. Lucas himself could pull off such austerity if he finally left New York, moved back home to help with his ailing father, returned to DJing in a less competitive market.

Gemma studied the water. "Too windy today for snorkeling, I fear," she said. They were on one of the patios overlooking the choppier Atlantic side.

"For schnorkeling, yes," Archer said.

"Archer tells me it was very windy in Cape Town," Sara said to Gemma.

"Horrifically," Gemma said.

"See any elephants?" John said.

"I suspect that elephant sightings are unusual in Cape Town," Sara said.

"I thought maybe they'd safari too when they were over there," John said quietly.

"No, their dry season is better for that," Archer said, but coughed up a few anecdotes from an earlier safari. He pronounced *zebra* to rhyme with *Debra*.

"You traveled over the holidays as well, didn't you?" Gemma asked Sara.

"Not really. I spent a few days with my grandfather in Chicago."

"Surely you had to travel to get there."

"Well, yes, but it was more of an errand—not that I don't love my grandfather," Sara threw in. "He's 'slowing down,' as they say, but resolved not to leave his house, so my dad asked me to check on things. Now we're trying to find someone to look after him."

"A medical professional, you mean?" John said.

"No, he needs a factotum more than a nurse," Sara said. "According to my lay evaluation, at least. And my dad doesn't want to spend much money, or, you know, doesn't want my grandfather to spend much—no doubt thinking of his inheritance."

"Is your father a greedy man?" Gemma asked.

"No," Sara said. "I shouldn't have put it that way. Anyway, best would be someone who's not a professional in any line."

"Like a bum?" Archer said.

"Just someone whose life decisions have opened the door to flexibility."

"Okay," John said, nodding like a bobblehead doll. "I know a guy in Chicago. He's in improv comedy, but, as to the professional thing, I guess I'd call him semipro."

The sun was shifting. Lucas put on a pair of pink drugstore sunglasses over his regular glasses. He was taking style cues lately from the insane.

"It'd be a live-in position," Sara said, "and quite a ways from Chicago itself."

"Maybe give me the contact info just in case," John said. "How old's your grandpa?"

"Ninety? Ninety-one? My dad wants to take his license away."

"I do think we should be more vigilantly testing the driving competence of our aged," Gemma said. "Last year I was very painfully doored by a woman of your grandfather's vintage."

"What's 'doored' again?" Sara said.

"I was cycling, observantly, when an extremely elderly woman opened the rather ponderous door of her Buick—"

"Mercury."

"—right in front of me."

"There was a hole the size of a tennis ball in her shoulder," Lucas said. He had been talked out of waiting in the lobby during Gemma's short hospitalization.

"Not a tennis ball, Lucas, a golf ball," Gemma said, showing the scar on her creamily rounded shoulder.

"Still, it must've hurt like hell."

"It was not quite hell. Perhaps closer to the duty-free shop in the Cancun airport."

"In my grandfather's defense," Sara said, "he hasn't been in any accidents. He backed into the garage door, but no one was harmed."

"Hard stuff," Lucas said, "getting old." He felt least original when aiming for sympathy.

"At ninety-one I daresay he isn't *getting* old," Gemma said.

"It is what it is," John said, working in the same mode as Lucas.

"What explains the rise of that expression?" Sara said. "*It is what it is.*"

"People have always said that," John said.

"But they're saying it *more,*" Sara said.

"I think that's true," Archer said.

Sara nodded gratefully at Archer. "There's the Naipaul book that starts, 'The world is what it is,'" she said. "And that *La Cage aux Folles* song, and even Wittgenstein: 'The world is all that is the case.'"

“I’m sure that accounts for it,” Gemma said. “Lucas, you have what appears to be yogurt on your face.”

“I’m saving it for later.”

“And God in Exodus,” John said with a slight edge, “‘I AM THAT I AM.’”

“I thought that was Popeye,” Lucas said.

“But there must be something else,” Sara said, “like from TV.”

“Popeye’s on TV sometimes,” Lucas said.

“Popeye doesn’t say, ‘It is what it is.’”

“Is that all you have to talk about?” the Defense Department guy barked from the next table.

“What’re you gonna do, waterboard us?” Lucas said.

It was hard to make out his muttered response.

“How long do you ’spect this hike to take?” John said.

The exchange with the Defense Department guy had flustered Archer. “I need a moment to gather my, uh, thought,” he said.

“Think it’ll take all morning?”

“We’ll be back by two, I guess.”

“I definitely fear it’s too windy for snorkeling,” Gemma said.

“It is what it is,” Lucas said.

Archer had originally led the way along the narrow trail, but he’d been so chary around the spiderwebs, especially those with tropically proportioned spiders in them, that Sara and he had to trade places. She now carried a long stick in front of her, using it to delicately adjust the operational webs, if there was no easy way around them, and to clear away single threads that crossed the path and sometimes glistened through the trees. “You sure you don’t want me to hold the spider stick?” he asked, in the way that Thanksgiving uncles offer to help with the dishes after most have been dried and put away.

She couldn't identify much of the flora but liked being surrounded by it, liked the whiff of fairy-tale danger. Truthfully there wasn't much to be afraid of; they had a phone and coverage, the trail was well marked, and the island offered no poisonous insects, no animals fiercer than its small population of feral goats. It was unmistakably a forest, not a jungle, but some of the trees had Tarzan-ready vines, useful for navigating slithery spots along the trail; others, maybe in the plane-tree family, had scaling red-and-white bark like muscle and bone in an anatomical drawing. It was cool in the forest, but Sara was sweating underneath her backpack. Only she and Archer had come on the hike.

"It feels good to be down here knowing the book's coming out," he said. "My parents are stoked."

"You think they'll start to worry about their wall art?" she said. *Eminent Canadians* was about a rich young Winnipegger who, for adventure more than profit, hires a Chinese forger to reproduce his parents' most valuable paintings, then attempts to privately sell the originals. Archer wanted it revealed at the end that the stolen paintings were fakes from the get-go (!), but Sara twice succeeded in leaving that part out. Despite appearances, the book wasn't substantially autobiographical, though a few passages were substantially, if undetectably, autobiographical for Sara. Archer, however, wanted it to seem lazily drawn from life. "I'd love it if everything was invented," he had said at the start, "but in such a way that people would insist on reading it as if it were an only nominally fictionalized memoir." He was unresponsive when she answered that they might insist on reading it like that anyway.

"Ha, it's possible," he said now about his parents. "But they're stoked, really stoked. I hadn't even told them I was working on a book."

"You kind of weren't," she said, waving her stick from side to side.

"Come on, I did a lot of the work."

She apologized but stopped short of corroboration.

"To me it's like I'm the director," he said, "the director and the author of the source material, and you're the irreverent screen adapter, the cinematographer, the editor—obviously—maybe the key grip."

"The *key* grip, no less," she said. "I was worried I'd wind up as one of the flunky grips."

He laughed.

"Well, that's one way to look at it," she said. One wrong way. Really he was the star and producer, she the director, screenwriter, and everything else. But he was an essential star, an atypically inspiring producer. Concretely, he had given her a burlap-rough outline that she only partially observed, a few dozen suggestions of wide-ranging quality, and many authenticating details, most of them extracted from interviews she conducted with him over a long weekend in New York. He had put her up again in the tackily stylish hotel, and for three consecutive nights she came over to his apartment around dusk. They would sit on his sofa in the dark, the light of the digital recorder sometimes rouging their hands. He faced her but kept his eyes closed and seemed very relaxed, his normal casual dress having descended into out-and-out dishabille: bathrobes, flip-flops, oxford shirts unbuttoned with gigolo abandon. After a while his answers began to take on a flavor of hypnosis or somniloquism, and she would press him, often leadingly, for detail and precision: How long was the ride to school? What sights did you pass on the way? Was the gear lever unadorned? Well, was it just a stick, or was it surrounded by that baggy, kind of testicular leather? Or did it come out of the steering wheel? Was the back door's interior nubby and pale or was it blue and felty like a Yahtzee board? Did the door have a little silver coin-purse ashtray? Was there ever anything inside it? Regular or bubble? Pink?

It was a kind of phenomenological therapy with no therapeutic aim. She never asked Archer how he had felt about something, never asked for or advanced an interpretation; she only asked about objects, surfaces, colors, textures, trivia, some of which she could have researched on the internet. It was the resulting mass of mostly useless information, somewhere between dream fragments and the directions on a bottle of shampoo, that gave her the confidence to start writing. She wrote the first, faltering chapters during a September in Winnipeg, briefly accompanied by Archer, who introduced her to his parents and to five-pin bowling (a more enjoyable game than standard tenpins, she thought, the light, holeless ball gentler on her arms). After three days he flew back to New York, and she carried on alone, working during the day in a sublet apartment in Osborne Village, eating too many midafternoon crepes, sometimes making dubiously research-driven excursions to Aqua Books or Assiniboine Park, where she would write in longhand on a bench not far from the East Indian cricketers. She returned to Buffalo with about 150 pages, pages too scattered and remote, it seemed, to make much of, but within three or four months she started to understand the book—the voice, the characters, the (drapey) form. After that it was mostly play, not easy but devoid of the drudgery, self-doubt, and inertia that had defined most of her writing life up till then. It had taken a while for the situation's creative benefits to sink in, but when they did, they almost equaled the financial benefits, and not only because it was difficult to take immediate advantage of those financial benefits without raising suspicion. It was freeing to know she wouldn't be judged directly by the book, except by Archer, and she found herself taking more risks, leaving stuff in that her overcautious inner critic would have excised from her own work. Energizing, too, to guiltlessly make use of someone's life, to have carte blanche to steal traits and reform memories. Leading up to when she started working for Archer, especially during the gray months following her sojourn in New York, she had come to think that her tragic limitation as a writer of imaginative prose was her dearth of imagination. Basically, she loved to write sentences, carefully, but she wasn't brimming with ideas as to what they should conspire to be about. Archer was the corrective. He fed her material and let himself be the material, resulting, pace his analogy, in auspiciously mixed paints more than a piece for adaptation. He pushed her, somehow, to be better. Strangely, a full year went by before she saw that he was her muse.

She stepped over a family of crabs. "I'm wondering about interviews," she said, knowing she would have to get more specific but not knowing how to proceed. She never wanted him to think she was giving much thought to his career or her place in it, even though that was part of her job. "Obviously you'll need to do phoners and in-person interviews yourself," she said, "but d'you think you'll want me to handle the written ones?"

"I think, hmm, I think I'll want to do all the interviews," he said, apparently considering this for the first time. Sara, in contrast, had spent much of her life conducting interviews with herself: in the shower, on walks, as she drifted off to sleep, imagining her dazzling repartee with Michael Silverblatt, her winning humility with Terry Gross, her feet-up elegance with Joshua Kehr. "I'll want you to tidy up the written ones," Archer went on. "We should aim for consistency of voice, so maybe you could interpolate some of your pet words into my answers."

"I don't have pet words," she said.

"Yeah," he said. "Except you do."

"Like what?"

"*Conspicuously* is one."

"Oh. Maybe you're right. God. I'll do some finding and replacing."

"No, no, I *like* it. It reminds me of Gemma. I like *all* your pet words."

"All of them!" She took a moment to calm down. A bird or rodent made a coffee-slurping noise. "As long as we're offering notes," Sara said, "I'll just mention that in interviews you might want to avoid saying things like 'This book is meticulously plotted.'"

A measure or two of quiet. "Of course that was just a conversation," he said, "not an interview."

"But those conversations are preparation."

"And I didn't say it was *meticulously* plotted; I said it was *fastidiously* plotted. Plus, it's good, what I said. It makes people want to read the book. No one wants to read a slovenly plotted book."

"Some of us do, actually. Some of us want precisely that."

"Most of you are pretending. Besides, *fastidious* isn't laudatory. It implies excess."

"Well, yes, often it does," she said. She loved this part, really: squaring off with the louche debate captain. "But isn't that sense reduced if you're using the word to describe your own work?"

"False modesty is tiresome."

"The other reason not to say it is that the book *isn't* fastidiously plotted."

"Sure it is."

"Are you kidding? I don't know anything about plotting—I mean, I do, I do." She worried that she'd confessed too much. Archer didn't have an immense knowledge of narrative theory, nor did he read much fiction; it was possible that he really did think the book was fastidiously plotted. "But this book's more in the episodic tradition, no? More of a yarn."

They listened awhile to their steps.

"You think it'll be a hit?" he asked. Though she had come to see that he wasn't a terribly glib or ironic man, his earnestness always seemed like an achievement—her achievement, another winning of his confidence. It was attractive because it always seemed rare, whereas John's earnestness—as this vacation reminded her—was off-putting in its constancy.

"Probably not," she said. She had written the book to please, but she doubted her genius in that line.

"Wow." He tripped on a vine but quickly recovered. "Ye of little faith."

"Don't get biblical on me again. Most books aren't hits, is all."

"But you'll jinx it."

"I always strive to blur the edge between realism and defeatism. Anyway, does it matter?"

"Does what matter?"

"The book's success." It was as close as she'd come to probing his motivations. She doubted he was spending so much money in hopes of experiencing the occasional air-kisses of public indifference. On the other hand, he had put few commercial pressures on Sara, had taken a smaller advance to work with a more literary editor, and seemed to get most excited when talking about the book as an experiment, a game, rather than the start of a writing career. Also, it wasn't a lot of money for him. She'd heard two rumors regarding his net worth; the less exclamatory figure was seventy-two million.

"No, it doesn't really matter," he said merrily, as if he'd only now grasped how unimportant it was.

They were getting closer to their destination. The first ocean sounds made Sara think of the surf scene in *From Here to Eternity.* She was about to ask if Archer had seen the movie—she hadn't, only that clip—but stopped herself. She let out a light laugh at the thought.

"What?" he said.

"Nothing."

Grumblingly: "I hate that."

"I know, I know. Isn't there an old Ukrainian proverb: 'She who leaves her chuckles unexplained finds her tears unconsoled'?" They walked on in happy silence. Her arrangement with Archer had its drawbacks—the anonymity, the secrecy, the jealousy—but for now it suited her, and in certain frames of mind, such as the one she was in on this walk, the advantages overwhelmed the drawbacks. She was doing the best work of her life. The conservative mutual fund Archer had led her to would be a benison during the water wars of her senior citizenship. Having finally found the right allergy medication, she was putting her mouth-breathing days behind her. (That was only coincidental to her work with Archer, but it felt causal.) She was going out: to readings, restaurants, yoga classes, nightclubs. She was having sex, good sex, mostly with an IT guy whose lazy eye and atavistically leading-edge mustache made him look like a recently punched Orville Wright. He was boyfriend material in few respects, the sort of jagged playboy who couldn't be trusted to remember a birthday but would inevitably come through with the gift of chlamydia. His strong-and-silent posturings—an encyclopedia of nods and monosyllables—were at once seductive and risible. But mostly seductive; she let her birthday pass unannounced and hoped for the best, enjoying his skinny intensity, his eyebrow scar, his slight scent of having spent many hours untangling cables under dusty cubicles. Though she knew his desire was dispersed across several subsets of womanly Buffalo, she didn't doubt that it was strong for her, and while she hadn't in the past been a great fan of bedroom talk, she loved how he got talkier during sex, full of blandishments, compliments, and instructions. His name was TJ, which she found funny and unspeakable. She hadn't mentioned him to Archer. They didn't talk much about her personal life, but she preferred for Archer to think of her as chastely single, or patiently steadfast. Mentioning TJ to Archer would have felt like confessing to an affair.

They came out of the forest to a more exposed part of the trail not far from the shore. Now the ground was sandy, the plant life desertic. The flat red tops of the Turk's head cacti indeed looked like fezzes. Some needles from a different species penetrated the sole of Archer's running shoe, and when he decided he couldn't wait till they got to the beach to pluck them out, he sat—it was slapstick—on more cactus needles. Sara stood in the sun trying to offer moral support, the small of her back pooling with sweat. "Just leave me here for the goats," he said, but he recovered. After passing quickly through another more forested area that was in one spot slimy and putrid with pelican guano, they were on the beach.

The sun made TV static on the water. "Swim first, eat first?" she said, pantomiming a fluctuating two-pan balance. He said he was hungry. They leaned on a rock, eating their sandwiches, apples, and witch-finger carrots, sipping water and lemonade from complicatedly sealed bottles.

"Oh, did you catch my line this morning, 'gather my thought'? Singular. Self-mocking, right? Try and work that into *EC* during edits. Or you could say '*collect* my thought.'"

"Where were you thinking I'd work it in?"

"Not sure."

"I wonder if it's funny enough to insert, you know, this late in the game."

"It's definitely funny. And it's the kind of thing—people will say, 'That's *so* Archer.' Even if they don't remember me saying it, it'll trigger something." He wiped his hands on his jeans and took off his HIGHER IN CANADA T-shirt.

"Might look like a typo," she said.

"You'll know how to set it up."

"Yeah, okay."

They were both wearing their suits underneath their clothes. His patchwork-patterned trunks were short, loose, and boyish, the boyishness echoed by his inability to thoroughly apply suntan lotion. "You have blotches of lotion on your nose and cheek," she said.

He put a few more seconds into the job. "Better?"

She made a shrugging sound.

"Do you need me to get your back?" he asked, and she turned around.

Franklin Beach, she discovered, was less gradual than the resort's main beach, the water colder and rougher, which made sense since it was the Atlantic not the Caribbean. She shrieked when the first splashes reached her thighs. "Do you hate it when people say that cold water is 'nice once you get used to it'?"

"Would you like it if I shared your irrational hatred for this innocent expression?"

"Yes, it would mean a great—"

While she was talking he dived in with a yawning bellow that seemed to emanate from the Ghost of Christmas Future. She followed, and they trod water not far from each other. "It's nice once you get used to it," he said.

"It really is."

She tried to slacken her features into their most invitational positions.

The beach wasn't as remote as promised, in that once in a while boats sped or sailed by in the middle distance, and sometimes small planes flew overhead. She got out of the water first, without saying anything or looking back at Archer. He followed her. She set her sights on a spot behind a huge rock, craggy and brown. Her swimsuit rode up her ass as she walked to the rock, but she kept herself from pulling the suit down, not sure if that was the right move. TJ was forever extolling her ass, urging her to present it in specific ways ("Oh God, baby, arch your back, arch your back!"). She sat on a smaller rock in the shade of the big one. Archer was walking slowly and uneasily, his trunks failing to screen his erection. When he caught up to her, she pulled the straps of her one-piece suit off her shoulders and looked up at him.

All the guys now—TJ and one of the others, at least—seemed to want dramatically salivary blowjobs sometimes performed in odd positions, so she concentrated as best as she could under the circumstances on that, taking Archer deep in her mouth and at one point crouching in a crablike position, letting a strand of drool drip off her chin onto her breasts. His penis was somewhat hook-shaped and sprang back toward his navel whenever he pulled out of her mouth; she almost expected to hear a *boing*. For a while they were situated so that much of his weight was on his left leg, with only the ball of his right foot touching the sand, and because of that, or because of his excitement and the slight chance of exposure, or because he was cold (though that didn't seem likely), his right leg started shaking like a washing machine in its final spin. She tried to hold his tense thigh to still him, but she didn't really want it to stop, and she liked what the tenseness did to the muscle around his femur. She loosened her grip on his leg, lightly tracing the seam of his testicles with her fingernails.

"I'm shaking," he said shakily.

"Mmm."

"I wish we had a condom."

"I know," she said. As it happened, she did have a condom in her backpack. She had brought two of them on the trip, just in case, though she usually let the guy deal with that. When she learned that Archer and she would be hiking alone, she had returned to her cabin to discreetly tuck one in the pack. She hadn't really considered, though, how she would explain, even silently, the condom's presence, and she perceived now that retrieving it could be destructive.

She stood up and they kissed, at first with enough force for her to feel it in her teeth and jaw. He pushed her hair aside to kiss her neck, instinctively choosing the more sensitive side, and before long she found herself lying in the shade on the gritty sand while he licked, rubbed, and fingered her. He had a good sense for delay, knew for the most part when to concentrate directly on her clit, when to increase pressure, when to add another finger. They were very long, his fingers. She vised his head with her thighs when she came and trusted that the speedboat passing by was too far away to see them, much less to record them and post the results on the internet. It all felt more urgent than rushed, though as they sat looking out at the ocean again, close enough to touch each other but not touching, she knew that the urgency, or any other part of the experience, wouldn't be repeated, wouldn't even be spoken of, and she started to regret that their probable one time hadn't been a more extended once. A night, a weekend, a long weekend.

Real sadness and guilt might have set in over a long weekend, though, and she was visited by little of that now. A trace of melancholy, yes, but mostly pleasure and some relief. And it was perhaps better—considering Gemma, considering everything—that in the Clintonian sense they hadn't even had sex.

"I sorta don't want to go back," he said.

She was slow to respond.

"But we should," he said. Partly to wash away the evidence, they took another swim, and in the cool water she felt deliciously slippery.

June 2011

Karyn stood in the passageway between the kitchen and the dining room, holding out a four-dollar can of carbonated energy water. "Seems late for energy," Lucas said. Rejecting a coquettish response ("Is it?"), she fetched him a spotty glass of tap water. He was standing at the table behind Maxwell, who for two weeks had been designing uniforms for his alternate-universe football league. "Ooh, Barracudas," Lucas said. "That one's off the chain."

"Thanks. It's my third favorite."

Premature, surely, to suspect Lucas of launching a stepfather audition, but the thought occurred to Karyn. If so, he had a knack for it; his friendliness toward Maxwell, at least, didn't seem especially exhibitive.

"I was gonna do silver pants," Maxwell said, "but then it's biting the Lions."

"Try white with a blue stripe."

"Color it white or just paper white?"

"I'd color it."

His text had come through on her lunch break. Could they, he had wondered, get together, maybe tonight, to talk about her play? She considered responding with caveats: she wasn't interested in lengthy, in any, discussion of her essentially private play, nor was she up for cooking dinner. In the end that seemed overwrought. She wrote, "Sure, drop by at 8."

Lucas gave Maxwell one last helmet suggestion, passed through the archway to the living room, and, establishing a certain familiarity, took a seat near the center of the two-cushion sofa. Karyn joined him as he pulled out the play from one of his vinyl bags, this one decorated with zebras.

"That one's off the chain," she said.

He thanked her. For fun, she guessed, he pronounced *zebra* in the British way. He tapped the play's (un)title(d) page. "I love it," he said.

"I'm not really—"

"I know you're not looking for praise or pointers or anything. I just want to say I love it."

"Thank you."

"It's funny, I started kind of mechanically writing notes, but they were, I don't know, mostly tangential." He rested his foot on his knee. "Like the scene with Derek and the patched-up overcoat got me thinking 'bout this guy from Bright Lake, the Gum Man." Karyn had a vague sense of Bright Lake, a Twin Cities exurb that must have been more of a farm town when Lucas was a boy. "He was this hunched old man," he said, "not homeless, 'cause he had—it was a shack. Maybe not dictionary *shack,* though I think probably. He would shuffle down Main Street tossing sticks of gum at the townschildren's feet. We'd pick them up and eat them. Which seems so strange now—that the transaction wasn't hand to hand, that our parents looked on as we stooped for our gum like urchins."

"They were wrapped though, right?"

"Yeah, yeah, silver foil. Wrigley's. Stale. I guess with stick gum staleness doesn't much matter after ten seconds, but you don't want it to snap or crumble when you first put it in." He paused. "I'm still not sure if throwing the sticks on the ground was the Gum Man's way of being subservient, presenting himself as a kind of untouchable. Or if it was more the opposite, like, contemptuous."

"*Chew up, you little fucks!*"

"Or just super low pressure: *Hey, buddy, I'm gonna toss this gum here. If you want it, great; if not, that's cool too.*"

"And he wore a patched-up overcoat?"

"Well, it seems like he would have. Later, I thought the whole thing must have been a gift-economy situation, you know, where he's tossing the gum in exchange for handouts from the parents, like stealthy"—he finished the thought with his hands. "But I asked my mom about it a few years ago, and she said no, as far as she knew that wasn't it."

For friendship or otherwise, Karyn hadn't often been attracted to voluble people like this. On the contrary, she was often turned on by reserved, word-sparing men. Her only perfect one-night stand unfolded nearly in pantomime at the end of her twentieth summer, a summer spent in Germany drinking too much while learning too little of the language. Her host family had brought her along to a resort on Norderney, one of the East Frisian Islands, where she found herself watching the sunset near a man who had sidled closer to her over the preceding minutes. He seemed old at the time, though he was probably under thirty. Looking straight ahead, she said, "Der See ist sehr schön." She didn't have the linguistic resources for a more inventive opener. He agreed, said something about salmon, or laughter, and asked in English about the length of her stay. Though his English seemed flawless, they said almost nothing else. His chest was shaved.

"But there might have been some less immediate quid pro quo," Lucas said. "One time my mom and dad brought the Gum Man a turkey, which was pretty admirable since my dad was having all these musculoskeletal problems at the time, so he was still doing carpentry but not much of it. I'm pretty sure we were on assistance ourselves." He pulled his shirt away from his chest. "Sorry, this story doesn't have a point."

"They don't always have to."

"Or any real bearing on your play. That's why I stopped writing notes."

"Well, I'm glad I let you read it." Too shy to look at Lucas, she stared into the dining room. Maxwell seemed to be arranging his drawings into conferences.

"We should do a scene," Lucas said.

"How do you mean?"

"Act it out."

She hesitated. She wondered if his idea was planned or spontaneous, and if that mattered. Probably she spent too much time wondering if people were being "natural" or not.

"Like, I love the part"—he looked for the page—"where Callum wants to cut Anisette's song from the record. 'It has nothing to do with quality, it's simply a matter of conceptual cohesion.'"

She was sheepish about smiling over her own line. "I thought about having 'Kissing Bug' become a fluke hit," she said, "their signature song. But."

"No, too pat." He flipped back to the start of the scene. "You have an extra script?"

"I'm off book."

"Wow, okay. Want me to do a Scottish accent?"

"Um, sure."

He broke off in the middle of the scene's first line. "That's not quite Scottish, is it?" He resumed in his own voice, and Karyn answered in Anisette's.

"What are you guys doing?" Maxwell said from his workstation.

"Your mom and me are mummering." He turned to Karyn. "Sorry, I'm not profesh."

"You're fine," she said. "In this setting, you probably don't need to project so much."

"Ha, yeah. Sometimes, the harder I try, the worse I get."

"That's how it was with me and the violin," Maxwell said. "I was really good when I was just messing around."

That wasn't true at all.

They ran through several scenes twice, doubling up on roles where necessary. Though she had recited some parts of the play a hundred times, hearing Lucas read uncovered a few ungainly phrases, and they explored variations. They seemed to be working toward something, which was fun but worrying; the project thrived as art and therapy because it had no aspirations. It was vulnerable to even the most fleeting ideations toward production.

She had sworn to end the evening by ten, but it was Lucas who, at quarter to eleven, let out a sighing, "Well."

"Yeah," she said. "You too, Maxi Priest."

"She doesn't actually call me that," Maxwell said, getting out of his chair.

"Cool kicks," Lucas said.

Maxwell looked confused.

"Your shoes. Those new?"

"No, I just stopped wearing them for a while."

"It's a dope color," Lucas said.

"Thanks!" He trotted up the stairs.

"So, I have a job interview tomorrow morning," Lucas said to Karyn.

"Hey!"

"Yeah, I'm amped. Marketing director at this company, Aria, that makes hot-air dryers." He walked toward the door. "Lot of times I'm a wipe-my-hands-on-my-khaks guy, like I'm too busy or something, but these are the most effective"—he described the dryer's innovations. "Check it: I vividly remember the first time I used one—MSP airport men's room, probably the same one with dude and the foot tapping."

"Larry Craig."

"I figure that's a good story for the interview," he said, carrying his bike off her porch.

"Maybe not with Larry Craig, though."

"I'll leave him out of it."

She leaned down to pick up a damp newspaper from her stoop. "Thanks for coming over."

"Yeah, it was nice." He started to pedal.

Perhaps for the first time in her life, she said, "Bon chance!"

"I don't speak French," he said, looking back and smiling, "but wish me luck."

November 2009

Not only did skipping out on Thanksgiving relieve Sara from impending brushes with John Anderson and cranberry sauce, it freed her to spend the day guiltily, miserably alone. By midafternoon she at least summoned the strength to turn on internet-blocking software, for fear that she would spend the rest of the day looking at pictures of turkeys baked by peripheral friends, most tantalizingly one served less than a mile from Sara's apartment to a table of unmarried creative types not native to Buffalo. Two weeks ago, when Sara still planned to join the reunion in Lammermuir, she had turned down an invitation from her friend Emily, whose household had recently burgeoned to five. Thanksgiving there might place too much emphasis for Sara's taste on giving thanks. She was willing to take that chance but didn't want to admit to Emily that she had shirked her familial promises, nor did she want to perpetuate the lie about her pressing deadline.

"Who," asked Donna Crennel three days later, "sets a deadline for the Monday after Thanksgiving?" Or she wanted to keep the lie in the family. Her mother was standing at Sara's stove, making an exploratory incision into a Cornish hen. Sara had her own apartment now, the rented upper unit of an Elmwood Village Victorian whose first floor was a consignment shop.

"I'm sure it's not unusual," Sara said, shaking almond slivers over the green beans, "but *I* set the deadline. I needed an extension and couldn't push it more than a week."

A tsk. "I'm sure your father and grandfather were disappointed. I'm giving the hen another ninety seconds. Oh, speaking of your work, I mentioned you to Tom's kid brother—of course he's no kid." Donna had just returned from meeting her boyfriend's relatives in Little Rock. "He's getting ready to shop around a novel of some kind. About the outdoors, he says."

"The outdoors?"

"I think he means hunting. He wore a camouflage hat—not during dinner; he was very polite." She picked up two plates and a gravy boat. "I said you'd be an excellent freelance editor."

Sara followed her mother into the dining room, a small, lopped-off hexagon with white trim and robin's-egg walls. "Did he seem to have money?" she said.

"He's a male nurse."

"You don't need to clarify that he's a *male* nurse, Mom. That's like 'lady doctor.'"

Donna may have been silently counting.

"Anyway, I'd hate to take advantage."

"He's not a child, Sara."

"Most of these books don't have a prayer. Maybe tell him—"

"I gave him your e-mail, so you can patronize him yourself."

"Mom."

After a moment, Donna asked, "Is your deadline for Lord Bondarenko?"

"No, proofing an academic book, a history"—she improvised—"of railway timetables."

"I suppose I can see why you blew the deadline. I love this dining set, honey. So sleek."

It wasn't a set. "Scratch-and-dent sale," Sara said.

Donna followed Sara's finger. "You hardly notice."

Sara had gently taken a tack hammer to the table on the day it was delivered. She mainly concealed her money through the no-fun trick of not spending it, but subterfuge was sometimes necessary; she had inflicted moderate do-it-yourself damage to several pieces of exorbitantly expensive furniture, all purchased with a future, more modern residence in mind. She sometimes thought of buying a house while she could afford to, though that would entail explanations far more elaborate than scratch-and-dent sales, since everyone except Archer thought she was precariously balanced one or two rungs above plasma donors. There wasn't a strong argument, anyway, for acting quickly. Buffalo's real estate market had so far been stable—no boom before the recession, no bust during—and, despite her new weakness for high design, Sara wasn't convinced that she would take much pride in owning a home or much pleasure in maintaining one. She had always imagined buying a house with someone else, or pointedly *not* buying a house (or a home-entertainment system or a Baby Björn or a rake) with someone else. TJ had left her (and, presumably, other members of his seraglio) to get shockingly, hurriedly married, and Sara's on-the-town, wild-oats experiment had lost its sheen. She was letting herself become increasingly isolated. Before her mother arrived late this afternoon, she had passed not more than ninety minutes of the last ten days in spoken communication with the rest of the world, the majority of those minutes spent in fits-and-starts dialogue with a lethargic representative of an internet-service provider.

"But you're still doing some work for him?" Donna said.

"For Archer? Not too much at the moment; some research for his next novel. *The Second Stranger,* it's called. Pretty good title, I think."

Donna shrugged.

"It's a weird little sophomore novel; I told him it should be called *The Second*—comma—*Stranger.*"

"I don't think that would work."

"Well, no, I was joking."

"You were joking just now or to him?"

"To him," Sara said.

"I finally got around to reading the first one."

Sara waited a moment. "Oh?"

"I didn't see any mistakes." Alas, two were known to have slipped through; corrected, at least, for the paperback. "So you must have done good work, no surprise."

Here was a time to change the subject. "But..."

"I'm sure it's very clever," Donna said, "but that's all it is, you know." She wrinkled her nose. "And so *proud* of its cleverness. I want to read books with... with some soul."

"But, I think"—trying to keep a tremble out of her voice—"I think that develops toward the end, you know, as Bowman matures."

"Tacked on," Donna scoffed. "The scene by the old church, the hole where the stained glass used to be." She pressed the back of her hand to her forehead. "The void!"

"That's not what it's supposed to mean."

"I'm sorry, honey; I know he's your friend. And of course I'm glad he's giving you work. But I just don't see it."

Sara stood up, tried to relax her neck muscles. "Should I make coffee?"

"I might survive half a cup," Donna said, and excused herself to the bathroom.

Though some readers were more taken with *Eminent Canadians* than Donna Crennel was, the novel fell sacks short of earning back its advance and was remembered, in suspicious company, on only one year-in-review list. The book, as goes the old joke, made quite a ripple. About six months after its publication in early 2008, Sara had tried to work that ripple line into an interview, a protracted interview conducted over e-mail with a man whose questions were written in a slurry, free-associative prose that Sara hoped stemmed from actual drunkenness. Archer, in one of his rare executive mandates, nixed the joke. Perhaps the ultrarich have to be especially on guard not to overindulge in kvetching and self-depreciation, or perhaps he was punishing Sara for not finding a home in the novel for his gather-my-singular-thought witticism.

It was probably for the best: self-depreciation about the book's reception would be, like the bulk of Archer's money, unearned, since a chasm roughly the width of three dozen press clippings and four thousand books sold in the United States and Canada separated Archer from truly overlooked novelists. And maybe, as Archer contended, he and Sara were indeed building a strong foundation. In his mind, *EC*—his penchant for initialism drove her nuts—was the kind of book that hip collegians, MFA candidates, and freelance graphic designers would want to be seen reading on quadrangles and subways, while eating paninis in Canadian museums. An accretion of fans would follow from these tastemakers, setting up a breakout second or third novel. "Diffusion of innovations," he had proclaimed, settling the matter. Signs that this pattern was in progress, however, were more hunchy than empirical.

The good news was that Archer's contentment with the book's performance indicated contentment with hers. Probably his thinking was off on that head too. She knew there was more she could do to advance his career, more than the journalism she wrote competently but unspectacularly in his name or the Twitter and Goodreads accounts she managed for him spiritlessly and erratically. At the start, they had produced a quartet of personal essays, each infused with sociological musings and undemanding historical research, but Archer tired of that before they had enough material for a collection, and Sara never came up with ambitious essay ideas on her own—or she did, but rejected them as unoriginal, untenable, and uninteresting. Her big managerial idea—a thicket of underdeveloped ideas, really—was that Archer should be launching literary journals, micropresses, film festivals, boutique record labels, pop-up galleries, medicine shows—it didn't matter what, just that he spearhead and bankroll a few presumably money-losing ventures that might generate feature articles, "get his name out there," establish him as a Renaissance culture baron of the firing-on-all-cylinders type. She left these ideas undivulged, fearing he'd cotton to one of them and delegate all the work. He wasn't, after all, the firing-on-all-cylinders type; the metaphor would rarely fit even if one had in mind the engine on a small pressure washer.

In the dining room, Donna sipped her abstemious half cup of coffee while Sara plowed through two large mugs, explaining that she would need to stay up late to meet her deadline.

"Not an all-nighter, I hope," Donna said.

"No."

Donna stood up. By the coatrack she canted her head to the right. "I'm sorry if I offended you about your friend."

"It's fine."

"I just wonder sometimes if proofreading these wishy-washy books is the best use of your talents."

"Mom, you just offended me a second time."

Donna picked up her purse. "Well, I guess I can't win with you." She called to apologize again as Sara was checking her e-mail. Sara hoped her mouse clicks wouldn't be heard over the phone as she assured her mother that there would be no hard feelings, by which she meant (and she didn't mean it) that feelings wouldn't be harder than before. There were two new e-mails: a photo of the Crennels' reunion badly framed by John Anderson ("You were missed"), and a note from Archer:

Quick Turnaround?
FROM Archer Bondarenko
TO Sara Crennel

Hope good vacay. Hey, my friend Matt(hew) asked for an endorsation a few months ago and I totally spaced. If you could bash one out in the next coupla days that'd be fantastic. I haven't read the whole book yet but I gather it's a Long Island family drama delicately fused with tales of Hatian revolutionaries and the French aviator and inventor Louis Bleriot, all adding up to a panoptic story of hope and betrayal. (For that summary I delicately fused my own words with a few from the publicist's email—working from memory!) I know Matt wsa kind of douchey the time you met him but his mom had cancer then (now in remission). Anyway, good guy, debut novel, should be fun. I'd do it myself but we're skibobbing. PDF attached.

Thx,
AB

It was only the second blurb Archer had been asked to write, an infrequency suiting Sara's high critical standards, or parsimony of spirit, though she wished Archer were more in demand. To deter him from late notices in the future, she tried to craft a response to his e-mail that would read like an affectionately tolerant sigh, as if she were obliging an interruption. In the second graf she passingly mentioned a friend who had studied Haitian Creole; she had no such friend, but it seemed like a believable way to work in the correct spelling of *Haitian*, though Archer was apparently ineducable in that area ("i find spellcheckers fallable [sic!] & hostile to experimentation," he had explained once by text). She promised to submit the blurb for his approval by midweek.

In truth she was more than open to an intermission from tinkering with *The Second Stranger.* At this stage in her revisions, she was spending a good amount of Tuesday morning reinstating commas that had been expunged after much deliberation on Monday afternoon. Archer knew little of the new book and had contributed less to it (mostly unheeded advice and some helpful notes on bullion speculation), but a few weeks ago she had told him the manuscript was nearly ready for revelation, asked if they could schedule a time to discuss it at his apartment. His philanthropic, touristic, and venture-capital commitments, however, prevented a meeting for an undetermined while. Ever since their hookup on the beach, he had been reluctant to be alone with her. In a way she admired his restored fidelity to Gemma, and she was flattered to think she presented a temptation strong enough to demand strict distancing measures. A temptation too strong to be resisted would be better, but this was something. She thought about him all the time. It was like being in love with the pebble in your shoe.

Too activated for sleep, she decided to read the book in need of hasty blurbing, *This Overhanging Firmament,* in a single stretch, taking whatever skimming course was needed to be done by three in the morning. It turned out to be a better book than her one interaction with Matt led her to predict, notwithstanding its frequent banality, du jour time leaping, and laughless comic relief. She read until dawn, even found herself shedding tears near the end, tears that didn't just pool in her eyes but streamed down her face. It was then that she broke to draft the blurb, hinting at those tears ("deeply moving") and hazarding a cool-sounding if not strictly apposite reference to Nietzsche's eternal recurrence. As she added the manuscript's last page to the messy stack on her hard-cushioned sofa, she wondered if her own work's avoidance of unabashed heart tugging betokened timidity more than sophistication.

With that question in mind, she spent a week making more substantial changes to *The Second Stranger,* revising the plot and casting the book more bluntly as a restless hammock dream of longing and unrequited love. It was a short book, and its brevity seemed to her very refined. If it made it to print, the publisher would need to employ compact pages and various tricks of spacing, margining, and pagination to fend off accusations of novelladom. The book eschewed the first novel's tone—"so *proud* of its cleverness"—in favor of an introspection that, she hoped, dodged lugubriousness. Its narrator, a young woman, name withheld, lucks into a landscaping sinecure on a privately owned Caribbean island, then starts an affair with a corrupt official from a larger neighboring island. Though Sara didn't fully understand it at the time, she saw now that she had written the book in a state of bristly independence, trying for something as removed from Archer's sensibilities as she could get without being completely removed from her own (because really their sensibilities weren't so far afield). Stylistically, the latest draft furthered this uncoupling from Archer, but with its heightened intimacy, she felt she was reaching out to him. She wished she could watch him read it, watch him react to every sentence, at least furtively glance at his reactions from another room.

A part of her hoped he would reject the manuscript and facilitate the change she couldn't initiate on her own. His rejection, however, would in fact be an embrace; he would fall in love with her as he read the book and in doing so realize that it, the book, was unquestionably hers. His newfound duty, he would see, was to help her publish it as her own. From there they would work side by side on the next Archer Bondarenko novel (a romp, quickly written, easily adaptable for the screen).

It was the most percolating week of creation she'd had in a long time, maybe since ghosting Archer's first essay, but she finished only exhausted, not reinvigorated. She imagined spending the rest of her life in this loop: working alone at strange hours with neglected hair, drinking many-times-microwaved coffee, eating Styrofoamy stragglers from yesterday's popcorn, trying to enamor Archer by alienating him, sending off these missives with a dry-mouthed caduceus of pride and fear, convinced that she'd at last struck the thing that would either dissolve their relationship or make it infinitely richer. She couldn't go on like this forever, but that's what scared her: that she probably could.

June 2011

When George and John were called by a male bank teller, George turned to the workman behind them in line and said, "You go on ahead, I need to talk to Brianna." This wasn't true in any sense having to do with banking. George needed to flirt with Brianna, and be flirted with in a well-meaning but condescending way to which George was either oblivious or, more likely, resigned. John disliked these transactions and on previous trips had tried to wait in the corner that passed for a lobby while George got the money. George couldn't drive anymore, but he could still walk okay, slowly but without regular need of support (his walker's tennis-ball trotters were still bright and whiskered in a broom closet, and he usually rebuffed John's solicitously crooked elbow). At the bank, however, he always managed to keep John close at hand. John got his monthly salary of one thousand dollars by check, but for routine expenses—groceries, household supplies, alcohol—he was given cash (also a thousand dollars, but paid biweekly), supposedly necessitating these withdrawals every other Thursday afternoon. George could have simply written John a biweekly expense check. Or John might have been given a credit card. Most people in positions like his were given credit cards, John had argued, just guessing. The statements would go to George's financial planner; everything would be double-checked and accounted for. George objected. With a cash system you knew exactly where you stood, he said. Any system other than a cash system (he kept saying "system") would encourage overspending, lead to spotty bookkeeping. John was supposed to save every receipt, and if the two weeks outlasted the thousand dollars, he was to document and justify the shortage. If there was money left over, it was given back to George and put in a safe hidden behind an oil painting of three bloodhounds surrounding a bleeding stag. George periodically tapped this slush fund for expensive wine and steaks, over which John tried to share in some of George's pretended oenophilia and honest carnivorous ecstasies, though John preferred beer and the cheaper meats.

Brianna complimented George's red Lacoste cardigan. "He"—George indicated John with a shake of his forearm—"says it makes him hot just looking at it." She smiled, counted the hundreds, the fifties, the twenties, and gave the stack to George, who smugly handed it to John. "We'll see you," George said, winking.

After George had settled into the Olds, John said, "While we're in town, we need to stop at the dry cleaners and Jewel."

"No, I'm too tired," George said, and let out one of those loud, phlegmy coughs that provoke gerontophobia in restaurants and waiting rooms.

"It won't take but a minute," John said. "I at least need to get something for dinner."

"Planning ahead, I see."

"It won't take but a minute."

"You said that, but it's taken but a minute for us to leave this parking lot." He coughed again. "It's your job to get provisions, John, not mine." John felt he was close to ripping the steering wheel Hulk-style out of its socket. They parted without words when John dropped George off at the house.

Every visit to the dry cleaners affronted John's belief in home care, but his employer's often invisibly spilled-on woolens were smorgasbords for moths; judicious to burn off the larvae before they migrated to John's closet. Though a far cry from Jeeves on Madison, Very Best Cleaners did capable work in the strip mall it shared with a tax preparer, a jeweler, a Thai restaurant, a medical supplies shop, the obligatory nail salon, and an ice creamery that John doubted would survive the fall. After buying and not finishing a sympathetic cone, John picked up two days of groceries, then idled in Jewel's parking lot with the easy-listening station turned up, eating a cayenne-infused chocolate bar and watching a bare-chested man trim a hedge across the street. John had separated the candy bar's twenty tiles and arranged them in even rows on an *Esquire* he'd thrown in with the groceries. He sometimes forgot to reimburse George for impulse buys, which was wrong. As a wedding present, he was going to ship 100, maybe 150, chocolate bars to Archer and Gemma. It was best to buy rich people consumables, he thought, his only misgiving here being that Archer probably wouldn't know how to properly savor the chocolate, wouldn't understand that every tile, eaten mindfully, was life itself. More and more John understood that the legacy of his days as a math hopeful was an aptitude for fathoming the spiritual, for seeing that God was immanent, accessible not only through prayer, love, friendship, and math, but through the satisfying click of a smoothly hit golf ball, the slightly asymmetrical dimple in a well-knotted necktie, the feel of cool grass on your palms, the perfect coating of sea salt.

When he returned from stage two of his errands, there was a rented sedan parked under the rusty, netless basketball hoop.

August 2010

Sara ate a juicy pear over her chipped kitchen sink, trying to inhale the fruit deeply enough to veil a stench entering its fourth day, something to do, she guessed, with the inaccessible carcass of a recently deceased mouse. She wiped her hands on her jeans, did a quick standing forward bend, and tapped out Archer's number before she had time to dissuade herself.

"Crimean War," he answered.

"Hello?"

"Third novel. On the Crimean War. I'm thinking 560 pages, swinging for the fences."

"Well, we could talk about—"

"Florence Nightingale in there somewhere, but unnamed; she's just 'the Nurse.' That's all I've got so far, but, you know, mustard seeds. So what's shakin'?"

"I'm calling to demand an audience with you."

"Just a head's up, I'm about to drive into a tunnel."

"But you can hear me?"

"For now."

"I need to see you in person."

"Hey, anytime."

"Well, would—"

"Sorry, losing you."

She expected "anytime" to mean something more like, "Anytime after we're back from Bali and the kitchen remodel's done," but two mornings later she was on a flight to La Guardia. Everything had changed, a little, and she wanted everything to change a lot.

He had called early one afternoon in January, about three weeks after receiving the manuscript of *The Second Stranger*. Sara, microwaving a naanwich, had answered with a breathy, unsteady voice, as if winded from weeks of preparing her greeting's cheery nonchalance. Outside her kitchen window's linty screen and spotty glass, snow was falling in fat, wet flakes. "It's odd," Archer had said, "I like this much less than the first book, but I absolutely know it's a better piece of work." It wasn't the warmest praise he could have given her, but it was sincere, and his sincerity was, as always, validating. They talked more about the book, though not as much as she had hoped; his brevity, as far as she could tell, didn't arise from discomfort. She had expected him to allude to the novel's personal subtext, to acknowledge, if only indirectly, that the lovesick narrator was her surrogate. There was none of that. At one point it became clear that he had missed something key to the book's conclusion and interpretation, and they entered an unresolved debate as to whether the book was too subtle or Archer's reading too inattentive, both parties taking the humbler and more diplomatic side, though perhaps without full conviction. He had practically nothing of substance to say. He intended to let the editor request any changes and had already passed the manuscript on to his agent, who was reportedly approving. "I mean, I don't think anyone's eyes are turning to dollar signs with this one," Archer said, "but I think she digs it." Sara hung up feeling heartened that Archer recognized the book's quality, but the about-face she had previsioned obviously wasn't forthcoming. He wouldn't gallantly surrender credit and copyright, nor would he pursue the status quo with enthusiasm. The book would sell even more limply than the first, and soon he would lose interest in the whole undertaking. Decades in the future, when his latest social-media enterprise or seawall-manufacturing concern was about to go public, or he was one of three futuristically tuxedoed producers accepting the Academy Award for Best Documentary, his early literary career would be little more than color for the late paragraphs of a business-section profile, a badge of youthful idealism.

So she had been surprised—*shocked* might be employed without hyperbole—when Archer called a month later to tell her he'd been short-listed for inclusion in "20 Under 40," the *New Yorker*'s forthcoming honor roll of notable young and youngish fictionists. "They do it every decade," he had explained, superfluously, since Sara remembered when the first list came out in '99, "except the first list came out in '99," he added, "so it's more like a baker's decade." He was mainly calling to prepare Sara for extra work. He didn't sound excited, and she couldn't tell if his neutrality was self-protective, as it would have been for her, or if he really didn't care. It seemed more like the latter, but why would someone orchestrate a man-of-letters sham if not to reap honors, awards, and status markers? (Archer's options for such things were restricted, since as a matter of principle, or to avert bad PR, he didn't apply for grants and fellowships and had made a vow, thus far hypothetical, to refuse any award that came with a cash prize.) She knew he *did* care—she remembered him asking if she thought the first book would be a hit, his intonation related to the one children use to ask about Santa's methods and reliability—but either his interest was waning or he was getting better at hiding it. At times, she understood him well enough to write as him, through him, but she had never unraveled precisely what he was after, why he had hired her. Was he just too lazy to put in the years it takes to maybe get good at something, and was it especially embarrassing to be a rich novice, a smooth talker without the chops to silence jealous skeptics? Could he only imagine himself as a fully formed minor genius, all semi-intellectual sprezzatura and sidelong euphony? Given his means, why didn't he tap someone with stronger credentials? Because he wanted her around?

Those on the short list had been asked to submit something for consideration in the special "20 Under 40" issue, so Archer's agent and Sara qua Archer refashioned what they agreed was the strongest section from *The Second Stranger.* Sara wasn't convinced that the excerpt stood on its own, an opinion she hoped would cushion the predictable slap of rejection. Her pessimism helped her preserve some degree of sanity while waiting for the magazine's response, but only some. Normally still-bodied, metabolically conservative, she was now full of nervous energy; by summer she'd lost six pounds by twitching alone.

Archer squeaked in as a dark horse. When he called with the news, Sara said "wow" several times in a row, and he responded with contrapuntal *yeahs;* it sounded as if they were rehearsing a piece of experimental theater. She asked if she should fly to New York to celebrate. "Sure," he said discouragingly. She stayed in Buffalo, treated herself to a massage, redoubled her commitment to surfing the internet. She'd become a master of vanity searches by proxy, someone whose most humiliating insomniac hours involved spelunking to search-results pages well into the triple digits. She saw everything the internet had to offer about Archer and his, which is to say her, work. When the *New Yorker* list was announced to the public, at least seven internet commentators seemed to share her initial surprise at Archer making the cut. Most who went beyond mentioning his name were supportive or agnostic, but a few were unapologetically acrimonious. The pseudonymous wag who tweeted "Archer Bondarenko? Really? #agentblowseditor" is a fair representative of this second group. Sara spent several days trying to puzzle out Archer's position on the list. Drawing on her own perception and three or four hours killed on Google Analytics, Googlefight, Amazon, and other sites, she guessed that he was the list's eighteenth most famous honoree, his numbers trumped even by a woman with a debut novel still months away from publication. Nor was he at home with the prestigious obscurities. There were others on the list whose critical reputations were insecure, but they were among the comparatively popular writers; Archer was the only commercial laggard without a compensatory succès d'estime, reviews for *Eminent Canadians* having been divided, with praise never coming from critics of the first tier. Going over these facts, Sara started to think that Archer's inclusion was in some way capricious, that he didn't really belong on the list (which of course he didn't), and that the real, if widespread, honor would be exclusion, the premise and purpose of the list being too crass and bourgeois for the serious to take seriously.

And then, come June, there were her words in the *New Yorker,* there was the preening diaeresis over the second *o* in *coöperation* (a word she'd added to the excerpt only to see it so rendered), there, it could be imagined, was Ruth Bader Ginsburg perusing her words in the bath. It was a lonely sort of pride, pride that gave her a few days of renewed joy, then deliquesced into anger and anxiety. The magazine's imprimatur raised her regard for *The Second Stranger,* but now, maddeningly, she feared that her talents had reached their scale-model Everest while she was writing the book, that her artistic degeneration had started the moment she sent Archer the manuscript, and that if she ever got around to writing again under her own name, the results would be so inferior to her deputative work for Archer that, were the secret to get out, everyone would think she had truly been a proofreader and research assistant rather than an unusually autonomous ghostwriter.

Her flight to New York was delayed by a faulty backup transformer rectifier that concerned Sara's first-class neighbor not at all ("Let's take our chances!" he yelled). As a result, she didn't arrive at Archer's apartment till early evening. Something Indian was simmering on the stove, but Sara hadn't been invited to stay for dinner.

"What I'm leading up to," she was saying, "is that the work—really the work is mine, mainly mine." Already she was lapsing into the equivocation she had warned herself against. "And I don't think I can go on much longer not getting credit for it." Though they had always sat together on the sofa when they worked here, this time she sat across from Archer on a plywood chair swathed as a point of design in bubble wrap.

"I can appreciate that." He rubbed his patchily progressing beard. "I was planning to really highlight you this time in the acknowledgments."

"That's not what I had in mind."

"But I might say that, you know, I fed you all sorts of strong material for *TSS,* and you pretty much pissed on everything."

"I did no such thing." The words had come out too primly. "I tried to use what the book needed, and its needs evolved with its topos."

"Its topos, yes. Well," he sighed, "we're in the same boat."

"That's just it, though: we're not."

"We are in that this isn't the collaboration I had in mind either."

"Archer, it's not a collaboration."

"It is, Sara." He partially concealed his disgusted expression by leaning over to tie his bootlaces. He was dressed in his full "heritage brand" costume, ready to chop wood in a catalog. He stood up and walked to the kitchen. The domesticity of the scene made it harder to stomach, made her pine to talk instead about some happily mundane thing: whether forks should be placed prongs up or prongs down in the dishwasher, whether Tucker and Clare had been bickering or just teasing each other at dinner the other night. "You say you don't get enough credit," Archer said while stirring the curry, "and I'm sure that's true—"

"I don't get *any* credit," she said, raising her voice to reach the kitchen.

"And yet you give yourself way too much." He paused, filed the edges off his tone. "There's this team of translators, Richard Pevear and Laura Volokhovsky. They've been doing all the great Russian—"

"You don't have to fill me in, Archer. They're extremely famous."

"I wasn't condescending to you," he said, bringing the tasting spoon to his lips. "I didn't know how famous they were."

"Very famous, and it's Larissa, not Laura. Larissa Volo . . . You have the last name wrong too."

"But what is it?" He was adding a pinch of turmeric or something to the sauce.

"I can't remember. You're close, but off."

He walked back to the sofa. "If they were extremely famous, you'd know the name. When you see the vice president on TV, you don't think, Oh, yeah, what's his name again, Bolden?"

"But it's a bad—"

"Biddle?"

"I get it. But it's a bad analogy because I have trouble with Russian names. When I'm reading a Russian novel I often don't consider how the names should be pronounced. I just remember what letters they include and keep track visually."

"Your Russophobia is secondary to your skewed sense of who's famous."

"Fine, they're famous in literary circles, though their *Anna Karenina* was an Oprah pick, so it's a big circle. The point is that you don't need to explain them to me."

He leaned forward, held his mouth open, and widened his eyes to ask silently, sarcastically, if she was done. Then he said, "And the point I was about to make is that Pevear, according to an article I read, has an impressive facility for languages but doesn't have a full command of Russian. Laura—Larissa—does the initial line-by-line translation, and then he refines the English."

"Without gravely compromising its fidelity to the original," she said.

"Yes, right, good. And they consult, argue certain words, whatev."

"Again, I know this."

"I'm saying it's supposed to be like I'm Larissa and you're Richard. I give you the raw material, a kind of literal translation, and you refine my wheat into flour."

"You're mixing metaphors. And I thought you said you were the director to my screenwriter. Which is completely different."

"This is a new analogy," he said. "And it was kind of like that at first, but then with *TSS* you went rogue. And fine, great, it's starting to work out; Gemma, my parents, they're all stoked. But it's not as if you're the only one with a grievance."

Sara's chair popped when she recrossed her legs. "Haven't you had this stupid chair for, like, two years?"

"It's not stupid."

"How is it that some of the bubbles are still unpopped?"

"They just came by to rewrap it."

"They?"

"Yes. If you anticipate a lot of fidgeting, maybe choose another seat."

She took a deep breath. "Look, I think things would be better for both of us if we—what I want to propose is that we share credit for the books."

He narrowed his eyes. "In what way?"

"In the most conventional way. Gilbert and George, Lennon and McCartney, Sacco and Vanzetti."

"So . . ."

"So the new book would be released under both of our names. Your name would still come first." Her voice wasn't as unwavering as in rehearsal.

"Sara—"

"That's alphabetical anyway."

"You're serious?"

She nodded.

"An excerpt has already come out under my name in the fucking *New Yorker*!"

"I know! And that was *my* work. How do you think it feels to get that kind of recognition, the kind I've wanted since I was in high school, but not really get it?"

"You don't even respect the other writers on that list, so why should the recognition matter to you?"

"Of course I respect them!"

"No, it's all resentment and jealousy and competition with you, never respect or goodwill."

"If any of that's true, it's because I don't get the credit I deserve," she said with hard-won evenness. "Anyway, let's not get hung up on the excerpt. Maybe that section was your work, but the book as a whole was jointly composed."

He shook his head. "I don't think I should have to explain to you how impossible this is."

"It's not impossible. It's a good publicity angle."

He laughed. It was one of his gummy laughs that brought her back to when she found him unattractive.

"Just this one, Archer." She was pleading now. "Take most of the credit. Say that when you were going through the pages after a two-month break, you realized that my contributions were more than editorial, that it was only right to acknowledge that, belatedly. It'll make you look magnanimous."

"Sara." There was, at least, some tenderness in his voice. If he gave in, he would also invite her to stay for dinner, and until Gemma or whoever arrived, they could be together less combatively.

"Just for this book," she said. "I just want this one. I'm good at what I do."

"Of course you are."

"I want people to know it. Maybe that's shallow, but I want it. Just this one. The next will be all you, and I'll stick to your ideas and it'll be great, a great book."

He seemed to be studying her face. "It's like"—he delayed for a moment; that glimmer of tenderness had passed—"it's like all of a sudden you don't grasp the nature of the deal. You're basically asking for a change from employment to patronage."

"Not exactly."

"I said *basically.* You understand, right, that you're making a lot more money than you could otherwise make writing?"

"Duh."

"And frankly a lot more money than you could make at anything."

She sniffed away tears. "You don't know that."

With smiling asperity: "It's an educated guess."

She stood up.

"You're not a genius, you know. You're smart. There's millions of smart people."

"Fuck you."

"You're leaving?" When she didn't answer, he said, "Are you leaving in an 'I quit' way, or just leaving?" He hadn't even risen to his feet.

"I'm not quitting."

A minute later she palmed open the door to the sidewalk as if she were in urgent need of air. She had sneakers on and decided to walk back to the hotel. She wasn't crying, but there were tears in her throat. *There's millions of smart people.* There *are* millions.

She won no concessions, though her next check reflected a generous raise. She returned to *The Second Stranger*'s last round of revisions somewhat richer, but in a spirit of aggrieved recklessness.

June 2011

John looked back one more time at the rented sedan, walked slowly through the mudroom, and set the groceries on the kitchen counter. He stood still for a moment, listening to the sounds coming from the family room, keeping one hand poised inside a grocery bag so that if someone were to approach, he could quickly return to a reasonable action. His bowels roiled when he recognized Chick Crennel's distinctive quack. Chick lived in Redwood City, California, and hadn't been expected.

The planks of the dining room floor seemed wider and waxier than usual as John made his way to the family room. Chick stood up. He was wearing chinos and a red candy-stripe dress shirt of light broadcloth. His handshake would sooner be called abusive than firm, though John's hands were bigger. George was sitting on the sofa, crushing mint leaves into his drink and fiddling with his hearing aid. Fuzzy Zoeller was being interviewed on the muted Golf Channel while a scratchy jazz record played softly on the stereo.

Looking out on the garden, John saw that Sara was getting up from one of the Tamiami chairs. "Oh, Sara's here too," he said, which served as a greeting as she slid open the screen to the family room. "Hi, John," she said. She made his name sound like an accusation. She was holding a paperback at her side, marking her place with her pointer finger. She sat down on the long sofa, not quite within reach of her grandfather.

"One of my old records," Chick said, jutting his chin toward an LP jacket resting on the dining table. "Three eighty-nine at Hoke Brothers. They had preview booths where you could listen to anything in the store."

"Nice. Who is it?"

"Toots Thielemans," Chick said.

"The Belgian harmonicist and siffleur," Sara inserted.

"You still making ten-speeds?" Chick asked. "I keep meaning to put my order in."

"No, not hardly much," John said. "I don't have the equipment."

"I thought you were going into business with a guy from around here."

"He moved," John said, then asked about Chick's work.

"You didn't hear? I'm suddenly retired."

"Oh. Is that bad?"

"It's a year or two early. But they gave me a decent severance."

"So are you staying awhile?" John said.

Chick laughed. "I still have a place to live, if that's what you're getting at."

"No, I just—I didn't know you were coming."

Sara looked up. "You didn't?" She had been reading again, or pretending to, which either way seemed teenage.

More loudly than necessary, Chick said, "Dad, you didn't tell John we were coming?"

George shifted in his seat and looked out at the patio. "Yes, I told him."

"He didn't," John said. There was a brief nonverbal exchange between Sara and Chick.

"Maybe he should get started on din-dins," George said.

"I only have two chicken breasts," John said, "but they're good-sized."

"No need for loaves-and-fishes theatrics," Chick said. "We'll just order a pie. Does Al's still deliver?"

"Al's does *not* still deliver," George said, "and I can't for the life of me fathom why."

"They went out of business," John said.

"Christ," Chick said, as if Al's shuttering symbolized everything wrong with the world.

"There's another place," John said. "I'll call."

While John used the kitchen phone to order the pizzas, he heard George say, "I told him!" He returned to the family room with a bowl of almonds and George's celery juice. "It's supposed to help with his arthritis," he told Chick.

Chick was pouring himself a bourbon at the bar. "Have a seat, John."

George, ignoring the celery juice, shook the ice cubes in his original drink.

Chick sat down and folded his hands between his legs. "So I'm sensing my old man's left you in the dark here."

"How so?" John said.

"Maybe I should leave," Sara said.

"You can stay," Chick said.

The seating in the family room was spread out. John and Chick sat about five feet from each other, both facing the garden but angled slightly toward one another like stereo speakers.

"Well, John, I found George an assisted-living facility," Chick said.

"Oh."

"A nice place over in Barrington."

"That *is* news to me," John said.

"On the phone he told me you had a new pad lined up and everything," Chick said.

"He does," George said. "Fully furnished, he says. Nattered on and on about it over dinner. His memory's worse than mine."

"See, this is why he needs trained caretakers now," Chick said.

"The doctor says he's doing very well for his age," John said. "As for now, with all due respect, I think he's just, you know, lying. It's not a memory thing."

"John," Sara said, "you really don't know what you're talking about."

"I understand he fell not long ago when you were at work," Chick said.

"Yes," John said.

"Why you didn't call me that night, I'll never understand."

"I called Sara."

"Sara's not your contact."

"He wasn't badly hurt," John said.

"Thank God!" Chick said. "Look, it's been great, what you've done, it's been great. You reached out to us at just the right time. I know Dad's liked having you around. But it's not safe for him to live here anymore." Chick turned to George, notched up the volume: "It's not safe here, Dad."

"There's no crime," George said.

"There's crime," Chick said. "Remember when you and Mom were robbed?"

"Burgled," Sara said.

"Anyway, I wasn't talking about crime," Chick said.

George waved dismissively.

"So what's the time frame?" John said. He watched his own feet tap the edge of a black-and-white rug whose strands reminded him of sea anemone tentacles.

"I've got a Dumpster coming tomorrow," Chick said, "movers on Saturday."

"Saturday?"

"For the movers. I'd like you out by Sunday. Sara's here to help organize the small stuff. It'd be great if you were free to help too. By now you probably know better than anyone where stuff is. I thought we could start tonight, put in a long day tomorrow."

"You might've spoken directly to me 'stead of trying to send a message through Mr. Crennel."

Chick held out his hands like a bank teller in crisis. "I realize that now. But he told me you two had discussed everything. He seemed very lucid that night on the phone."

"I'm sure he was," John said.

"Okay," Chick said. "Let's not . . ."

"It's just, it's abrupt." It was all the more humiliating to be expelled like this in front of Sara.

"You know what you should do?" Chick said.

The question dangled like legs on a ski lift.

"Take a vacation," Chick resumed. "Take one on me. I've got miles coming out my rear end. Go to Jamaica, wherever—maybe not the Far East."

"No, that's not needed."

"I told you I got a nice severance from those assholes. Here's yours."

"If it's a severance package, I'd rather get money."

"I can't do cash."

John adjusted his neck. "Could you book me a hotel room in Winnipeg?"

"Winnipeg? Why not Montreal or Toronto. Whistler's gorgeous this time of year."

"I'm going to my best friend's wedding in Winnipeg. As of now I'm booked into a rattrap."

"Well, why the rattrap, John? We pay you."

"For now," George put in.

John shrugged. He had figured that cheap lodging would leave him with more to spend on the chocolate package.

"It's Archer's wedding," Sara said.

"Oh, of course," Chick said. "Well, I can check for participating hotels in Winnipeg."

John's thank-you barely sounded.

"But if I put you up at a Sheraton in Winnipeg, that's it. You can't come back to me a month later saying you want to go to Venice after all."

John stared at Chick.

"Let's assemble some boxes before the food comes," Sara said.

The next afternoon, John followed Sara up the dog-legged staircase that led from his room to the attic. Through some maneuvering on John's part, he and Sara had been assigned to work together on emptying the attic's contents. Chick's view was that everything still up there should be transferred directly to the trash—"It's a shame we can't fashion some kind of chute"—but Sara, who only a month earlier had been so uninterested in her grandmother's clothes, was now inclined to be more preservationist.

That meshed with John's aims. He pulled on the light. In some spots the dust was as thick as mouse fur. He pointed: "Maybe you could take the west side there, and I'll take the east."

"I just don't want to throw things away indiscriminately," she said.

He watched her clear cobwebs from the pie-chart top of a golf bag. He said, "So here we have a box of Christmas cards and an old kite."

"An interesting old kite?" She went on inspecting boxes, didn't turn around to look.

He held the kite. "Bent. Not sure how flyable."

"Interesting?"

"It's hard for me to judge; I'm not really interested in kites period, so I can't say. Maybe if it was—"

"All right."

"—one of those Asian kites where—"

"Toss it."

He walked downstairs and out to the trash. When he returned to the attic after two more hauls, Sara was sitting on her haunches with her back to John, reading one of the old typewritten pages of Marion's novel. Except for the long delay, it had worked out exactly as he'd planned, a silent game of hot or cold.

"Something cool?" he said.

Her shoulders jumped slightly. "What?" she said.

"What'd you find?"

In a clearer voice: "Nothing. Just some old school assignments."

Strange that she was lying. The bell-bottom corduroys that had shared box space with the pages were now resting on the attic floor next to Sara. "Your dad's?" he said.

"Here's a box of cookie tins you could take down," she said. She turned over the manuscript and pushed the box toward him as if she didn't want him to come too close. He picked up the box, lifting with his knees though it weighed hardly anything, and returned to the rented Dumpster.

He could hear kids playing at the country club's pool, the diving board's springs. He walked over to the patch of shade by the garage and leaned against the wall between the two doors, remembering how one of his Burger King duties had been to stand in the overflowing Dumpster on busy Saturdays, compacting the saucy garbage with his black, bag-covered Reeboks. It had been nice on those afternoons to be outside, away from the customers, but the task was degrading. Once, when he stepped out of the Dumpster with daubs of milkshake on his blue, elastic-backed uniform pants, he felt his chest swell up with rage and wanted to quit on the spot. Now the memory helped him see that he wasn't obligated to stay in Lammermuir, that he was only making Sara uncomfortable and irritable, that she didn't want to share important discoveries with him, didn't want anything from him. He went back to his room, quietly packed a suitcase, draped his favorite suits, coats, and odd trousers over an arm, and threw everything in the trunk of the Oldsmobile. He wasn't as tender with the clothes as he normally was, and that felt good. After releasing its front wheel, he put his bike behind the front bench. He packed a few more things, including a tennis racket that didn't officially belong to him, and called up the stairs, "Sara, I'm leaving."

"Leaving where?" she yelled.

"Just leaving."

The floor creaked. She stood now at the top of the stairs, he at the foot.

"I'm sorry," he said. "You know I'm not like this, not impulsive."

"I think you kind of are, actually."

"I don't want to be here anymore."

"I understand."

"I don't mean to be creepy, but I still love you."

"Okay."

"Maybe I'll try to teach high school math," he said.

"You'd be good at that."

"I'll see you at the wedding."

He managed to evade Chick and George on the way to his car, then started driving west, figuring he could plot a slow course to Winnipeg.

December 2010

In the unexpected letter containing Lucas's plane ticket, Gemma billed the party, to be held at Archer's condominium, as a casual and mixed celebration of their engagement and of the December holidays, "doubtless with a decorative tilt towards Christmas." The ticket seemed like the kind of gift that would end up costing Lucas a lot of cheddar, but two mornings after the invitation arrived, Gemma called to say that, for a few more months, she still had her apartment in Hell's Kitchen; Lucas could stay there with John Anderson. By this period Lucas and Gemma were still in regular but often omissive communication. "You have an apartment in Hell's Kitchen?" he said.

"For a few more months."

He had no experience with engagement parties. They seemed to be uncommon in the Midwest among his class, and he hadn't been part of a marrying crowd in New York. Not sure what he was in for, he had pictured a grander affair than the invitation spelled out, had seen himself making his way crabwise to the bar through clots of sycophants, microcelebrities, and travel-weary Canadian plutocrats. But as he stood with his back to the condo's plate-glass windows, counting heads, he wondered if he'd been wrong to think of Gemma and Archer's life together as a bustle of social amusements and obligations. He hardly credited Archer with outsize magnetism, after all, and in the past Gemma's friends made up not so much a network as a tic-tac-toe board (or noughts and crosses). Thirty-one, maybe thirty-two heads. He was surprised to have made the cut.

Despite Gemma's promised decorative tilt, the only clear signs of the season were a snow globe in which Santa and three elves were playing pond hockey, two prompt-to-arrive cards placed in a ceramic bowl by the door, and the tartan skirt worn by Gemma's approaching mother. Lucas tried to remember her first name. "Mrs. Pitchford!"

"Good to see you again, Lucas. You're looking well."

"Well *fed,* at least," he said stupidly, noting an instant later that he and Mrs. Pitchford were now comparably overweight. He asked about the Pitchfords' flight (from Seattle), how they were enjoying their weekend so far.

"We've had some excitement."

"Losing a daughter but gaining a son," Lucas said.

"That too, I'm sure. What I had in mind was that, on our morning excursion, we happened, gruesomely, upon the aftermath of Mark Madoff's suicide. Bernie's son, this is. Hanged himself. Perhaps you've heard."

Lucas hadn't. Over Susan's shoulder (the name had come to him; he hoped he could sneak it in without revealing the cover-up behind his earlier formality) he saw that Archer was passing around an exotic and, it appeared, autographed stringed instrument.

"On the second anniversary of his father's arrest," Susan said. As she fleshed out the story, Lucas started to suspect that she and Mr. Pitchford had happened upon the scene in a manner that included some rerouting. "A rueful affair all around," she finished.

"Yes."

"And did Gemma tell me you've returned to your homeland?"

"Well, to Minneapolis."

"And what keeps you busy there?"

Nothing. "I'm a shoe salesman." Of a sort. He propped up this misrepresentation with an outright lie: "And still working as a disc jockey."

"Wonderful that radio has survived all these technological shifts."

"I work more at private events and discotheques."

"Do they still call them that?"

"No. And what about you, Susan? Are you still in aviation?"

"I was never in aviation."

"Oh, I'm sorry."

"No need for apology—the field never interested me." She was a senior scientist, she reminded him, for a company that developed protein-based therapeutics.

He struggled with his fifth question—"Do you wear a lab coat?"—and she excused herself shortly after Gemma and John joined them.

"So we're roomies for the weekend?" John said.

"I already claimed the bottom bunk."

"Don't let me forget to give you boys the key," Gemma said. "John, I'll drop it in your large and responsible hands in deference to your experience in property management."

"That's not actually what I do."

"I trust you all the same." Her black ankle boots had gold floral heels and a medieval air.

John craned to check out a late arrival. "Is Sara coming?"

"She sent her regrets," Gemma said. Then to Lucas: "It was kind of you to catch up with Mum."

"My pleasure."

"I'm sure she likes you more now that your threat has long passed." Gemma's bluntness, comic but never ironic, was partly responsible for attracting Lucas in the first place, and perhaps for limiting her social sphere as well. But the charm of her whole shtick—her free-speaking, distantly monocled elegance—diminished as her circumstances enlarged. Grimier settings brought out the humor in her persona; without an incongruous backdrop, Lucas worried, she would just seem rich and affected, until she simply *was* rich and affected. "Oh, I'm glad to have you two together," she said. "Archer, taking what I trust will be a happy liberty, has reserved two seats for tonight's second set at the Village Vanguard. The Glass-Steagall Trio, I believe it is, or—it's on my phone—Robert—"

"Robert Glasper?" Lucas said.

"You have it."

"That jazz?" John asked.

"Yes, it's jazz," Lucas snapped. Brilliant pianist; what bothered Lucas most was that Archer's liberty was so well intuited. "Is he trying to get rid of us?" he said.

"Of course not," Gemma said. "You needn't search for dark designs behind every kindness."

"We came all the way out here for the party," Lucas said.

"Which will be guttering out by the time you'll need to leave." Gemma's sharpness sounded stylized but genuine. "Archer only had in mind your love of music and your straitened finances."

"I'll stand you drinks," John said to Lucas, and left for "more grub."

After a pause, Lucas touched Gemma's arm. "Sorry I was ungracious."

"You're forgiven."

"Sorry," he said again. After Gemma and Archer went public with their relationship, Lucas had worked in two, maybe three, insinuatingly critical remarks about the new boyfriend before Gemma issued a boundary-drawing rebuke. His attempts to view Archer more charitably faced a perpetual headwind, so he learned instead to avoid him as subject and person. Even before Lucas moved back to Minneapolis, he and Gemma stayed in touch mostly through the phone and occasional one-on-one drinks after work. Following Lucas's lead, Gemma talked about Archer only in passing, and as the years sped or dragged on, she talked less about her widening travels and shrinking work (she was now self-employed and highly selective), or anything else that might call attention to their diverging fortunes. Topics of conversation, accordingly, grew narrower, centering most often on Lucas and his problems. He often hung up the phone feeling like an analysand.

"Thanks," he said. "I'll make sure to thank Archer too."

"He'll want to hear all about it tomorrow at brunch."

He suspected that he wasn't, in fact, forgiven, and he found himself trying to change the mood through a show of forlornness. "I wish we still lived in the same city," he said.

"Do you have to stay there now that your father's passed?"

He chafed at mortal euphemisms. "It's a better place to be broke."

"Perhaps a change of locale would reignite the job search."

A crestfallen shrug.

"Well, I should mix with the others."

Though he had fumed about being sent away like a kid to the TV room, sticking around at Archer's till quarter to ten was a grind. He always felt on edge around money. Hard to believe he'd worked so long at banks.

Walking down Christopher Street with John, he said, "Do you miss this, man? Saturday night, a real city, petals on a wet, black bough, all that."

"No, I can be happy anywhere."

They stepped off the curb to let a foursome pass. "But *are* you?"

"I'm saying I can be."

Lucas couldn't always distinguish half-baked platitudes from hard-won wisdom, but later, in the jazz basement, while Glasper played a melody that sounded to Lucas too much like bumper music for an NPR show about personal finance, he looked over at John, who had no sense of musical history, who couldn't hear when his mandolin was miles out of tune, but whose eyes were now closed and whose head was tilted back and who was obviously hearing something beautiful and important that Lucas wished he could hear too.

July 2011

Lucas's mixtape was loud enough for Karyn to feel the bass when her left knee grazed the passenger door's armrest. "You know, I'm feeling really strong," he said. "I could easily take the last leg, push on to the Peg." Through Gemma and Archer he had secured a Winnipeg crash pad; twice already he had articulated his ostensibly budgetary interest in getting there a night early.

"It's probably too late to cancel the reservations in Grand Forks," she said again. Thinking of Lucas's poverty, she had switched from the second-cheapest place in town to the cheapest. "You should also consider my advanced age," she said. "Long sedentary stretches put me at risk of, oh, deep-vein thrombosis, pulmonary embolism."

"I'm fine with the stopover."

"Aggravated lumbago, sciatica." This breezy litany was as close as she could come to admitting how much pain she was in. It was fine to joke about being older than Lucas, but she didn't want to drive the point home too powerfully. "Temperature okay back there, honey?"

"Uh-huh."

No one spoke for a song and a half. The rows of cumulus clouds through the windshield looked like the bellies of hammerhead sharks.

"Why *is* it so flat here?" Maxwell asked.

"From science," Lucas said.

Karyn reached for her phone. "It was a seabed, right?" She shifted in her seat, tried to extend her lower back. "Spotty service. We'll research it later."

"I have a new game," Lucas said.

"Can we turn this down a hair?"

"I'll name a movie, and you have to guess, Maxwell, whether it's a real movie or one I made up."

"Why can't my mom play?"

"She'll know which movies are real."

"All right."

"*B*A*P*S.*"

"Fake."

"No, real."

"*Hey, Tony!*"

"Real."

"Fake."

"I suck at this."

"Here's our exit," Karyn said.

The down-at-heels motel was an authorized Zippo dealer and trumpeted this status in many spots around the check-in desk. The owner's T-shirt—I PUT THE "PRO" IN PROCRASTINATE—was later helpful in explaining some of the disrepairs in room 18's bathroom.

There were two tolerably comfortable beds, but the walls were thin, the lack of air-conditioning necessitated open windows, and a small but boisterous gathering of alcoholics was waxing in the parking lot. Maxwell was engrossed in his tablet, not researching the geological origins of the Great Plains. Karyn leaned against the headboard. Her pores emanated an unpleasant oniony sweetness from the soup she'd had in Hillsboro, where an old, plaid-shirted farmer, after asking about Karyn's camera, had told the group about driving from his family's nearby farm to Grand Forks—at age twelve, by combine. When Lucas asked how long that had taken, the farmer said, "Oh, most of the fall," which was now the capper to Lucas's just-published Facebook post about the droll farmer. The post perhaps condescended to agrarians, as when white people carry on too gushingly about the beauty of people of color, but Lucas's upbringing was less urban than Karyn's, so perhaps he had the right. She clicked LIKE, closed the screen, and stared at the cattle brands hanging above her room's subcompact television. She thought abstractedly about the plight of cows. By the time she was ready to go to sleep, the party outside had entered a shouting stage.

She put on a light robe and stepped outside in her espadrilles, thinking she'd make a neighborly request for quiet. Mosquitoes swarmed around bowl-like lamps mounted to the motel's yolk-yellow exterior wall. Instead of saying something to the five middle-aged men and one woman sitting in lawn chairs around a cooler, she walked over to Lucas's room and knocked twice. The television went mute. "Hello?" he said anxiously. "This party is keeping me up," she said, loudly enough for an attentive reveler to hear. One of the men got up from his lawn chair—to confront Karyn, she thought, but he only stamped a can and sat back down. Lucas came to the door, shoeless but still wearing his T-shirt and cargo shorts. He was watching one of the small talk shows that come on after the big talk shows. His borrowed review copy of *The Second*

Stranger was tented on the bed. He wasn't at all bad looking, really, with his deep-set brown eyes and long, pouty cheeks. She had no intention of sleeping with him, no firm intention, but she enjoyed the hunch that doing so would demand next to nothing of her powers of seduction. She said, "Do you think you could go out there and say something to them?"

"They're just having a good time."

"It's late on a Thursday night. Say we have to work in the morning."

"You think that's plausible? What are we, like, itinerant laborers?"

"They're not going to ask follow-up questions."

He walked to the window, pulled the curtain aside a few inches. "Yeah, I don't know. I'm getting a 'don't tread on me' type o' vibe out there."

She turned to the TV. "Is that Vic Tayback?"

"No. Some celebrity chef."

"Maybe I'll call the front desk," she said.

With a determined sigh: "Well, hang on." He stepped outside, still shoeless. The tops of his feet were hairy. Now she felt silly playing the persecuted maiden. She listened to Lucas through the open window: "Hey, uh, I don't mean to be a dick, but my sister's kid has pneumonia, and I guess he can't sleep." He was casual, diplomatic, in command of an ex-DJ's gift for reading a group's preferences and prejudices, how for instance his "I guess" hinted at reflexive skepticism of all complaints issuing from women and children. A moment later Karyn was thanking him with muffled laughter, briefly pressing his shoulder as if for support. He smelled of Pert. It embarrassed her that his show of valor—met with good-natured sympathy and cooperation—made her think that she *did* want to seduce him, which, if successful, might provide the added benefit of instigating her period, now rather late. Unpleasant to imagine, though, how the parking lot might react to incestuous noises leaking from the motel's thin walls while a boy lay pneumonic, sleepless, and alone in the room next door. "Sorry 'bout your kid," a man called to her beerily as she returned to her room, where she lay awake till half past one, feeling guilty that the party might have carried on at a livelier volume after all.

Thirteen hours later, she retrieved Lucas and Maxwell from the Winnipeg hotel's tiny, unventilated arcade. Ms. Pac-Man blipped through a maze. Concentrating, Lucas said, "Do we need to get going?"

"Yeah, I mean, I don't know."

They'd made it into town long before the rehearsal dinner was scheduled to start. Selfish of Karyn, she now saw, to let her mild social anxiety deprive Gemma of Lucas's presence at one of the weekend's more intimate events.

"I'm on the third level," he said.

She moved closer.

Maxwell looked up at her. "He has the high score, but the machine's Nerfed."

"No," Lucas protested. "Maybe set a little slow."

"It's Nerfed," Maxwell said.

After a moment, Karyn said, "On what instrument was Ms. Pac-Man's soundtrack recorded?"

"It must be—"

"A labysynth."

A run of notes descended mournfully from the game.

"Mom, you're distracting him."

She left to get supplies, promised to be back in ten. The hotel was on the four-lane road that the highway had become. She jaywalked to a discount store where she bought a box of energy bars, an early pregnancy test, and a sudoku book that Maxwell probably wouldn't find diverting. He and Lucas were waiting by the car when she returned, and the three of them started driving without specific purpose to the Forks, the park and agora where the Red and Assiniboine Rivers meet.

Lucas examined a crinkled list of local landmarks he'd printed off the internet. After a few blocks, he said, "When did you say you were last here?"

"Not since my grandma's funeral. So '75, '76. After my grandparents died there wasn't much of a lure. My dad's maybe twelve years older than my uncle Walt."

"That's Archer's biological?"

"Yeah. And they were never close, my dad and Walt." She turned up a radio documentary about a radical First Nations country singer from the seventies. A low-fidelity interview with the doc's now-dead subject segued into a Dylanesque song, unchanging and hypnotic, and Karyn raised the volume from nineteen to twenty-one, willing the song to enliven the family restaurants, auto shops, and endangered DVD-rental places to their left and right. The Canadian chains were recognizable but nominally unfamiliar, like guests at a small office party wearing inaccurate name tags. It occurred to her that, to repel posers, a bohemian Shangri-la would trouble not to look like one.

"None of the money came from your uncle, right?"

"From Walt? Ha!"

"It's all from Archer's mom and stepdad?"

"You don't know the story? It's in one of Archer's essays."

"I missed that one."

"Okay, Pamela, Archer's mom, was filthy rich from the start."

"Right, glass something," Lucas said.

"Borosilicate glass. And lumber. Her first husband was this grocer named Motrinec, Charles, I think it was. Motrinec's was the semi-upscale supermarket chain in Winnipeg and Regina, and my uncle managed the store where Pamela shopped. She came in daily rather than weekly."

"Très Old World."

"Yeah. Having adopted Continental shopping habits, it was a short step to trysts in the walk-in cooler. But that's just bag-boy gossip as reported by Archer. According to him, all these nymphomaniacal legends started years later, after Pamela married the marital-aids guy."

"What are marital aids?" Maxwell asked.

"Um, items couples use to spice up their sex lives," Karyn said.

He didn't seem to want or need elaboration.

Karyn's idea about stealth bohemias disintegrated when they entered a district of vintage-clothing stores, record shops, launderettes, and smartly designed fast-food joints for the grass-fed set. There being no solid agenda, she parked. Lucas stretched his arms on the boulevard. "Veni, vidi," he said. More to bolster the idea of independent retail than to satisfy a desire, she bought an old punk-rock CD that would have cost much less at home, and before long they found themselves sitting moddishly at a Japanesque creperie's red-and-white window booth. Karyn drank tea while Lucas and Maxwell ate Nutella- and marshmallow-filled crepes. There were big, drippy color spheres on the wall and lots of tiny food splotches on the floor. "How's *The Second Stranger* treating you so far?" she asked Lucas.

"I don't hate it," he said.

"These are awesome," Maxwell said with his mouth full, and he and Lucas gave each other a fist bump in which some Nutella changed fists.

When a group of girls took a nearby table, Maxwell jerked his head to give his hair the sweep he liked.

"Sorry, I need to text this Dave I'm s'posed to stay with," Lucas said.

"Wait, if you text him—"

"By the way, I looked up Vic Tayback. Dead."

"If you text him—"

"I just did." He made an *eek* face of cartoon concern.

"Will he be able to tell where you texted from, that we're in Winnipeg?"

He stuck out his lower lip. "No. I don't have GPS or anything on this phone. The cops could find out, but I doubt it'll come to that."

"I feel bad now about missing the dinner," she said.

"You shouldn't. If we went, I'd probably make a drunkenly profane toast, and everyone would hate you for being with me."

"You think they'd hate *me*?"

"I'm certain of it."

"That was a pivotal scene in *Three Times Caitlin,* wasn't it?"

"*Three Times Courtney,*" he corrected.

"Sorry."

"No one takes my unfinished screenplays seriously," he said, looking down at his phone.

"Do you think you guys could finish those in the car without—"

"Pow! Second interview at Aria."

"Whoa, congratulations!"

"I knew I nailed it. Not to count my chickens, but . . ."

"It must have been the Larry Craig anecdote."

"*Don't call it a comeback,*" he rapped. "Second thought, call it a comeback."

At the Forks, Lucas and Maxwell threw a baseball back and forth on a big open field. Karyn sat on an unshaded bench, enjoying the sun, following the baseball, listening to the whacks of failed skateboard stunts, trying to pinpoint the arrival of her last period. Lucas's end of the game would have been called catch only out of convention and courtesy. He claimed to be having trouble adjusting to his borrowed glove. She called up the calendar on her phone. If she was remembering correctly, she was only a week, maybe eight days, late. Not such an exercising delay, especially since her periods were already becoming irregular, though mostly in the unhappy direction of increased frequency. The course would have to change eventually, though; it could be doing so now. "Nice grab!" Lucas yelled. Weren't diaphragms supposed to be somewhat more effective than condoms? Maybe hers needed refitting. She visored her eyes with her hand, watched Lucas and Maxwell stroll toward her.

"But it sucks 'cause the last two times I've played EDH decks, I've gotten mana-screwed," Maxwell was saying obscurely when they reached the bench.

"That does sound suctorial," Lucas said.

Five minutes later they drove into a parking lot near a whimsically painted candy-and-nut factory. They waited for the attendant to finish giving directions to a family whose numbers, to Karyn at the moment, suggested carelessness or fringe religiosity.

"Any nut allergies, Maxwell?" Lucas asked. "Maybe this candy place gives tours."

"I think nut allergies are fake," Maxwell said.

"What? They are not!" Karyn said, looking back at him.

He raised one eyebrow.

"Here comes the guy," Karyn said. The lot didn't take credit cards, and neither Karyn nor Lucas had any loonies yet. So far on the trip she had felt rather too much like the adult of the group, but now she felt as if they were all children.

"Oh, you can just park for free, then," the attendant said.

"I have US currency," Karyn offered.

"Sure, I'll take that."

As they pulled into a spot, Karyn whispered, "It's real-life Monopoly. Free Parking."

"Except you did pay," Lucas said, not whispering, "and there's no pile of money in the middle."

"That's actually a made-up baby rule," Maxwell said. "If you look at the real rules, Free Parking is just a free spot."

From the attendant they learned that the Winnipeg Goldeyes were about to play minor-league baseball in the large stadium Karyn had recently and obliviously driven by. They could go there. Lucas had at moments gotten on her nerves over the past few days, but she liked how amenable he was to the planlessness she favored on vacations and weekends. When Maxwell was little, she had passed whole Saturdays like this, by simply leaving the house, letting him stop at whatever safe-enough thing interested him, playing kicking games with orphaned nuggets of sidewalk, drifting from yard to yard like dandelion seeds.

She followed Lucas and Maxwell through the crowd toward the box office, watching their backs and listening to the organ music and pregame announcements. Lucas cocked his wallet to buy the tickets—a nice gesture—but was instead handed freebies as part of a father-son promotion sponsored by the fire department. "Is it meant for fathers and sons taking in the ballgame without their, like, wife-mothers?" he asked the woman in the booth. "Because his mom's right here."

Karyn smiled.

"Oh, I didn't know you were all together," the woman answered from the booth.

"We're not *together* together," Lucas said, "but we're here as a group."

"That's cool. I'll just pretend it's a father and two kids. And if you're ever in the market to buy a fire truck, you know who to call."

"Also I'm not the father," Lucas said.

"Such honesty! For that I'm giving you a bratwurst coupon."

The seats were in a front row. It happened that the Goldeyes were facing the Saint Paul Saints, whose third baseman ended the first inning by catching a foul and tossing Maxwell the ball. "Hey, thanks!" Tomorrow was forecast to be uncomfortably hot, but it was beautiful tonight. It wasn't her normal way of looking at the world, but Karyn felt as if she were being *spoken to.* Maybe none of it—the (briefly) free parking, the tickets, the coupon, the familiar opponent, the ball, the breeze—was singly so remarkable, but the run of encounters with good fortune and offhand generosity seemed charmed in the aggregate. She put her arm around Maxwell, then put her left hand on Lucas's bicep. "Everything's free in this town," she said to Lucas. The fixity of his expression made her look down at his hands, at a vein-crossing scar on his wrist, a subtle tan line from bike gloves. "It's like we've been given the keys to the city," she said. She looked up when he cupped her elbow, but whatever he was about to say or do was interrupted by an inter-inning sack race.

At game's end it was coming into focus that Archer's friends were implicitly rescinding the offer of their guest room. Lucas texted them once more on the drive back to the hotel, a rambling DJ now doing a theme show of songs about con artists and small-time criminals. "The radio's so good here," Karyn said. "It makes me ashamed to be an American." Lucas agreed, his voice perhaps showing some embarrassment and unease about his sleeping arrangements. "There's room at the inn," she said. "Don't worry about it."

Lucas waited in the hotel bar while Karyn redeemed the last of her points. She couldn't help feeling miffed when all the available rooms sounded better than the one she and Maxwell were sharing. They said their goodnights.

Ten minutes later there were three quick knocks on her door. She opened it.

"The pool's open till eleven," Lucas said from the hallway.

She waited. She didn't want to appear overeager or in a swimsuit in front of Lucas just yet.

"You up for a quick dip?" he finally said.

Maxwell: "I am!"

She looked at Lucas's cutoff Dickies. "Is that regulation swimwear?"

"You gonna rat on me?"

"I think I'm too tired to swim."

"I'll take Max," he said, and stepped inside. "Damn, my room's nicer than this."

"Is it?"

"We should totally switch. My bath's all, *Calgon, take me away.*"

"We're unpacked." (They weren't quite.) "It's no big deal."

Maxwell was already in his trunks and shirtless.

"Thanks," Lucas said. "I mean for everything." Some vibrato in his voice. "I . . . I don't think I'm a lifelong fuckup."

"I know."

"I had fun tonight."

"Me too."

"I have fun with you."

Maxwell, getting gooseflesh in the overconditioned room, followed the adults' conversation like a tennis spectator.

"Take him swimming before it closes," she said.

She listened to Maxwell's voice get quieter as he and Lucas made their way to the elevator. With the two of them gone, a quiet spread over the room and opened up a line of thinking that she'd repressed for the past few hours. She reached for her purse, took out the pregnancy test, and walked into the bathroom. She thought she had to urinate, but only a few drops would come. Maybe it was that false signal she used to get before performances.

She put the dry stick on the sink, drank a glass of cloudy water, and decided to use this unforeseen privacy to finally commit to an outfit for the wedding. Two weeks earlier, she'd gone shopping for a new dress, but everything in the stores had seemed ugly, expensive, or both. So she'd packed two older dresses, both purchased in what for her constituted a shopping spree in the postdivorce spring of '07. She pulled on her shapewear, then the front-running dress, black and effectively scoop-necked but marred by a silk tie that now seemed twee and an Empire waist that now seemed unflattering. There wasn't a full-length mirror in the room and the lighting was bad—the bathroom unforgivingly bright, the bedroom gloomy and jaundicing—so she stood on the lip of the bathtub to see her legs and shoes, then tried the dress several times with and without a cream shawl that was beginning to curdle, as it were, with age. Intended as a glamorizing agent, the shawl was working instead on behalf of dowdiness. There might be time to buy something tomorrow. She wanted to make a good impression on Archer and the other relatives, most of whom had never seen her grown up, and she wanted to look somewhat transformed for Lucas, who had never seen her completely made up. Weddings were always erotic for her, and though her own wedding night had been sexually uneventful, she and Jason had usually made love after other people's weddings, had even had hasty, bibulous sex in a reasonably isolated gazebo during a wedding party, a memory sometimes revisited years later when they needed to applaud themselves for bygone wildness. She looked over at the test, took a moment to gauge if she was ready, and glimpsed, with an odd laugh, the Norplant scar on her arm. No, not ready. She turned to the backup dress, a low-cut, studded thing in an indecisive color (perhaps a hybrid plum) that had earned her many spoken and unspoken compliments but now made her feel like the lopsided webmistress of an Emmylou Harris fan site. Not right for a wedding, anyway, and she wanted to blend in more than stand out, or blend in outstandingly.

She got into her nightie and took the test, her bladder now cooperative. Holding the stick, she walked slowly, as if the test were delicate, to the edge of her bed and sat down. The stick was supposed to rest for five minutes on a flat, dry surface, so she put it at her feet on her room's copy of *Winnipeg Vistas.* With Maxwell and the miscarried pregnancy before him, it had been impossible not to stare at the results window in a state of intensified Polaroid anticipation, but naturally this time was different, more like the feeling you have when the phone rings at three a.m. She stared straight ahead at the gray TV screen, not quite able to cry, trying not to think about the test, trying to resolve whether this thing with Lucas could be called courtship and, if so, whether her feelings could be called love. She turned on the TV, turned it off, looked down: a faint positive.

January 2011

Outside the Elmwood Villager, a man was shouting at something or someone invisible to Sara, spreading his arms in protest as if his fruit stand had just been disrupted during a climactic car chase. Sara looked back down at the proof sheets from *The Second Stranger* and took a bite of her pumpkin-cranberry bread. She was spending every morning in this café now, forcing herself to wake up by eight, shower, blow-dry her hair (most days), and put on something other than yesterday's outfit. The baristas knew her by name; she had watched the bulletin board take on fresh overlayers of business cards from handymen, guitar teachers, psychics, and dog walkers.

Shawn, the café's lanky, gray-haired owner, liked to spend some of his time performing routine tasks: cleaning the espresso machine, making folk-art changes to the chalkboard menu. Now he was wiping off one of the round wooden tables near Sara's. He nodded at her dictionary, papers, and red Pilot G-2s. "Whaddaya got going there?"

She answered with the mix of pride and humility she had adopted when proofreading was a full account of her work: a modest office, her tone said, but an important one not entrusted to fools. As for the full account of her work, it had been an unsettled half year. Her demand for retroactive parity had been followed by months of quiet from Archer, interrupted only by sporadic businesslike phone calls during which nothing was uttered about their earlier argument or Sara's fattened salary. There were no in-person interactions. Not sure if she was sincerely welcome at Archer and Gemma's engagement party, she had cited a prior family obligation. Meanwhile she carried on with her basic duties: communicating by e-mail with Archer's editor and agent, pitching and writing reviews, turning down a teaching opportunity, trying to stay more on top of his social-media presence. She still forwarded everything for his input, but after giving him a few days to respond, she would take his silence for ratification. She felt simultaneously like a lame duck and a regent, on her way out but more powerful than ever.

"Yours?" Shawn said.

"No, no, it's by this guy, Archer"—she pretended to check the name—"Bondarenko."

"Bonda . . . yeah, I read a cool essay of his a few years back, trying to think where."

She worried that he would want to talk about masturbation.

"About this blues singer, Arkansas Bob. You see that one?"

As if searching her memory: "No, I don't think so." She had often hoped for a chance meeting with an unwitting fan, getting to be both the fly on the wall and part of the conversation being overheard, or Viola disguised as Cesario discovering Olivia's love for Cesario via Malvolio, if Olivia's love was really directed at Cesario's selection from *Best American Essays 2008*. But Archer still didn't have many readers, and for a long time Sara hadn't taken steps, such as those leading out of her apartment, to bring about meetings of any kind.

He sat down across from her but at a neighboring table. "Oh, it's a great story," he said. He sniffed, pushed away his dishrag. "So a few years ago this old guy from the South Side of Chicago dies."

The West Side.

"His grandson's sorting through the old man's stuff and finds a small collection of classic blues 78s." Every Wednesday night at the café, Shawn hosted a songwriter's showcase that Sara never attended. "This guy—the granddad—had grown up somewhere in Arkansas—"

Helena.

"—then came to Chicago via Memphis in the forties. Played a bit o' resonator guitar but never recorded or performed in public. But he kept his 78s—there weren't more than nine of them—"

Exactly nine.

"—in pristine condition. So the grandson passes 'em on as a donation to a company that puts out compilations; I'm talkin' beautifully packaged comps of old blues, country, gospel—all type o' old-timey stuff. Come in boxes with, like, a repro train ticket inside, or some fuckin' actual dirt. Just a one-man operation run by a kid in Chicago."

A classmate of Archer's.

"The guy's records, the dead guy's, are cream—there's a Charley Patton, a Washboard Sam, a Blind Willie Johnson—all pretty familiar stuff, 'least to aficionados. 'Cept there's one record, 'One-Sided Love' by Arkansas Bob, kid's never heard of. Seems to come from one of the operations where you paid a quarter to have an acetate disc cut on the spot for your own personal enjoyment. Used to be a bunch of those. Chicago address on the label; kid dates it circa '51, '52, but more in an early thirties style, if you can even nail it down. Flip side's just so-so, but 'One-Sided Love,' Jesus H.: solo performance, but there's like all these polyrhythms, whacked-out guitar figures and little paradiddles or some shit tapped out on the body o' the guitar; guy singing with a low, razor kind o' sound, then talking, then going way up high—it's immensely raw and complex and, like, you know, where's he going? And heartbreaking! He's just leaving it all on the table like this ammonia-funk rag, though I'm not gonna leave the rag here. Buddy of mine, used to work at Jazz Town before they closed, sent me a link. You listen, you think the guy's gonna deliver his twenty-five-cent record to his old lady, then go off and shoot himself." Shawn held his index finger to his temple and made a sibilant gun noise.

"Jeez."

"One of the most riveting country-blues records ever made. And no one's even heard of Arkansas Bob! Before, I mean. The kid, record-label kid, asks around. Nothing. A complete unknown. They think maybe it's one of the major cats recording under a different name, 'cause that happened for contract reasons 'n' that. But who? Sound like Patton? No. Sound like Broonzy? No. Guy's one of a kind. So the label kid makes 'One-Sided Love' the leadoff cut on his next comp, and a thousand, whatever it is, two thousand blues junkies like Wade used to work at Jazz Town go nuts for it. I call him up, I say, 'Man, I gotta get my hands on more o' this Arkansas Bob shit.' Yeah, well, good luck."

"Just that one record?"

"Naw, it's better. A blues professor from down South somewhere—"

Alabama.

"—hears something hinky about the record. The hisses and pops seem to be—what's the word?—looped. It's like the outer groove on a bunch o' old records was digitally fused together, but then they start to repeat. So he asks, the scholar asks, to examine the record itself. Finds more anomalies."

"Okay."

"Turns out Arkansas Bob's really Tyler Russell—"

Russell Taylor.

"—the grandson who donated the collection."

"Wow."

"Yeah, Russell's been making this throwback stuff for years, in private, though, and never to his satisfaction. Born at the wrong time. No matter how good he is, it always sounds to him kind of, I don't know . . ."

"Ersatz."

"*Ersatz* is exactly the word Bondarenko uses! You gotta read this thing. I'll find it for you. What happened was Russell heard about a pressing plant in Germany that still made 78s. Vinyl's back, right? So he cooks up his scheme, prints the labels himself. He told Bondarenko he just wanted people to really *hear* the shit, you know? Without baggage, without, whatever, *Is it authentic?*"

"Right. It seems, though," Sara said, "that before the hoax was revealed, people would be listening with lots of historical baggage. Maybe Arkansas Bob's record sounded rawer, more nakedly emotive, because that's what people look for in blues records from that period. Or it sounded especially impressive because it had gone so long undiscovered."

Shawn wasn't visibly swayed. "Yeah, maybe," he said. He stood up, picked up his rag. "Bondarenko didn't get into any o' that."

Of course he did!

"I should help with lunch. To me, the important thing is—the who, what, why, when, how, none o' that matters when you listen."

"Yeah."

"It's a beautiful record."

"I see what you mean."

"It just is. 'One-Sided Love.' Google it."

July 2011

In the otherwise empty pool, Lucas and Maxwell competed in a series of races, beginning with freestyle, proceeding to a hybrid form that Maxwell incorrectly dubbed the crawl, finally to hopping, running, and various so-called rematches in which Lucas was saddled with an insurmountable handicap. They were both unlessoned swimmers, flailing around with their heads above water, their splashes reverberating in the high-ceilinged, half-glass room. Lucas's cutoffs exerted a strong drag on his swimming and didn't decently cover his ass. Breathless at the edge of the pool, he looked through the partially steamed window-wall at the Friday night traffic, the hotel sign, the silhouette of an evergreen, trying to remember the Kool G Rap couplet that rhymed "silhouette" with "pillow wet." The water was warmer than the air, and he bent his knees to submerge his shoulders while Maxwell dived for a penny.

There was a moment of relative peace as Maxwell searched underwater, bubbles popping around his legs, his hair sticking up like those troll doll pencil toppers. A nineties MOR hit with religious overtones played on wall-mounted speakers, taking on a layer of pathos that Lucas figured was mainly situational. The industrial sadness of piped-in music was most pronounced in uncrowded places built for fun, he thought, the fast songs like empty seats at a kid's birthday party, the ballads like wrinkled balloons dropping from the ceiling a week later. This particular ballad was one Lucas's mother liked. He remembered her humming along with it in the second truck, the glove box held shut with duct tape. Hearing it with Maxwell, he felt homesick for the home he couldn't return to in Thomas Wolfe's terms and the one he hadn't jointly established in any. The water lapped his chin. Maxwell breached during the song's go-for-broke key change, a penny between his thumb and middle finger. Lucas had brought the penny for that purpose and was happy to see his instincts affirmed. "You got a lot of lung power," he said.

"In Cancun once I held my breath for five minutes."

"Come on."

"It was thousand-one time 'cause my dad lost his watch." Maxwell cupped his hands and poured water on his forearms.

"What's his name again," Lucas asked, "your dad's?"

"Jason. What's yours's?"

"His name was Gary."

"Oh." He looked at Lucas. "Is he dead?"

"Yeah."

"Sorry."

Some of Lucas's friends had children—mostly babies, toddlers, and preschoolers—and he tried to tousle their hair, take an interest in their rumored talents, remember their names. If nothing else he tried to hide his irritation over the screaming, shrieking, and whining, the interruptions and distractions that obliged him to take three shifts to finish a thought whose resumption was never solicited by the parents. He hoped to sustain relations with his procreative friends just enough to permit a renaissance when the kids were old enough to be off in their rooms quietly sexting. Maxwell, though, was older than the other kids on the fringes of Lucas's life and easy to warm to: kindhearted, quick to laugh, somewhat precocious but not smug or dweeby, except maybe about the Free Parking kitty. It was a relief, too, to be around someone who didn't care that Lucas wasn't currently in possession of health insurance, a working car, or respectable swim trunks, though Karyn didn't seem put off by those absences either.

Maxwell butterflied, in a way, to the other side of the pool and back. He was rapping the chorus to "Flava in Ya Ear."

"You can have that mix from the car if you want," Lucas said. He felt bad for the kid, having to endure the Insufferable String Band and the rest of his mother's Ren Fest music.

"Really?"

"Sure."

"It's cool with no one else here," Maxwell said. "Like having our own pool."

"Or our own hotel chain."

"Can you do the penny thing again?"

When the pool was about to close, Lucas taught Maxwell how to air-dry by flapping one's towel, touching it only with one's fingers and thus eliminating the need to launder it more than annually. Then he escorted him back to Karyn's room. It seemed overdone to say goodnight to Karyn at close range, so he lingered by an ice machine till she opened the door. When she poked her head out, he gave her the Air Force One wave while walking backwards to the elevator. She smiled. "See you tomorrow."

Back in his room, the prospect of the Adult Adventures channel birthed some tiny wingbeats of excitement, but of course he couldn't make such charges as Karyn's guest, and he was trying to cut down on porn. Particularly in these time-teeming years of his joblessness, it was important to manage the habit, not to impose unrealistic Lents of abstinence, but to stick to the liberated DVDs available for rent at the local woman-owned sex shop, or to the campy Jessica Rabbit site on which he was a leading pen-named commenter. When he was troubled by his porn consumption, he couldn't determine whether his concerns were mainly feminist and ethical (which concerns he wanted to take seriously) or mainly puritanical (which concerns he wanted to overcome). Maybe what bothered him most was the idea that something as seemingly personal as sexual proclivity—personal beyond the biologically determined or influenced fundamentals, that is—might be so lacking in autonomy, so historically shaped (a gay male friend's reaction to this theory: "Gee, you think?"), and what's more that some of his primary sexual influences were depraved misogynists. (Although hadn't he learned to kiss, in part, from Hollywood? The search for autonomy and independence in these matters was in two senses vain.) At any rate, he was trying to watch in moderation, often as a carrot for finishing an arduous task, or an easy one.

Because it seemed appropriate to reward his forbearance with another sensual thing, he started running water for a bath. It wasn't much of a treat; he found baths dull and uncomfortable unless he was sick or chilled, usually stayed in for less time than it had taken to fill the tub. Tonight he got in when the water was just a few inches deep, easing his back against the cold, suctioning fiberglass, and as the water crept up his legs he started thinking again about Karyn. A year ago he would have said that he'd only been in love twice: with his first girlfriend, who was also the first girl he'd kissed (confirmation retreat, fishing dock), and with Gemma. But that reckoning, he now believed, was too conservative. There'd been an unrequited love from high school that was short-lived at full strength but that still lingered, and an only briefly requited love from college, and a love he suspected was requited but unspoken on both sides, and maybe one other that he wouldn't admit to because it ended so badly. And he knew he loved Karyn. There was something mysterious and pheromonal about her that had hit him from the start and was getting to him more and more, along with things easier to identify: her quarter-smile wit, her variegated hair, her steely intelligence, her easy manner with Maxwell, her ass in those bike shorts. He expanded on that last thought for a few minutes, and before long the bathwater seemed poorly constituted for a lingering soak.

He dried off in the regular manner, moved to the bed, and picked up the galley of *The Second Stranger.* He had started the book mostly on Karyn's account and to confirm his revived suspicion that Archer was a soulless charlatan. So far, unfortunately, he hadn't found much evidence in that line, save for a few irritating word choices and an interloping passage comparing clitoral with vaginal orgasms. All in all the book was pretty well done. Not to say that he liked it any more than the black-and-white photos that paddingly illustrated it; it was slow, meandering, sometimes primpingly belletristic, the sort of book he used to admire and abandon back when he took on and abandoned admirable books. But it was the work of someone who more or less knew what he was doing. Archer's competence never failed to infuriate Lucas, no matter how many times he discovered it. He set the book down on the unoccupied side of his enormous bed and tried to fall asleep, but after an alert forty minutes, part of which he spent draping sheets and other ad hoc shrouds over the room's static light show of digital clocks, TVs, phones, smoke detectors, and DVD players, he returned to the book, mostly with hopes of sleep inducement.

The next section—there were no proper chapters but many breaths of white space—was a long flashback about an epistolary romance between two kids separated by seventy miles of Idaho interstate and county road. The section confused Lucas, both because it wasn't clearly germane to, or as good as, the rest of the book, and because it seemed familiar. His first thought, illogical but typical, was that he had dreamed the events depicted in the flashback. Déjà vu for him was always the feeling of experiencing something previously dreamed, which mostly made him regret that he never dreamed anything prophetic or psychologically instructive.

As he read on, he came to the less paranormal conclusion that he had read the chapter before—under a different author's name. Not just a run-of-the-mill charlatan, then, a plagiarist! A dumb one at that, since if Archer was stealing from texts familiar to Lucas, he couldn't be digging into the deepest stratum of esoterica. Lucas tried to step back from these accusations, thinking he'd skimmed the excerpt in that "20 Under 40" circle jerk and had later suffered some sort of literary amnesia, which wouldn't be unusual, considering that—

Then he laughed out loud, not sure if he was laughing with or at Sara and her lazy brilliance.

Part Two

Postnuptial

July 2011

Appazato was said to be the oldest and most luxurious country club in Manitoba, though Sara didn't imagine that to be the grandest of distinctions, and she had overheard one of Archer's uncles admit that Niakwa had the better course. It was a hot, humid afternoon, and as she walked uphill from the well-kept but nonluxuriously concrete tennis courts, she felt as if she were walking through a cloud of her own sweat. When she reached the top of the hill, she saw that Gemma was standing on the brick porch of the club's Georgian command post and inn.

"Did you drum up a match?" Gemma asked.

"With a somewhat temperamental ball machine," Sara said. "I lost."

"I used to muck about with that, but now it aggravates my injury." She touched her shoulder.

A few windows were open despite the air-conditioning, and Sara could make out a guest playing watercolor piano in what might have been called the club's drawing room. "Are you waiting for someone?" Sara asked.

"Not expressly. I stand on porches sometimes in bouts of nostalgie de la fumée." She took a deep breath as if she were trying to cure hiccups. "Mostly I'm putting off getting ready for dinner. It's dangerous for me to stand at prolonged length before mirrors, so I pursue these dilatory stratagems."

"Oh, but you're beautiful," Sara said. "I'm sure you'll look beautiful." Maybe that sounded too sadly envious. A long sedan purred by senescently.

Gemma thanked her, then looked behind her as Archer stepped out of the black double doors. "Oh! Here I said I wasn't waiting for anyone," Gemma said, "but I see now that I was waiting for you."

Archer smiled. His plaid shirt was 43 percent unbuttoned.

"But I can't stay—'Hello, I must be going.' Will you be wearing the blue?"

"The blue?" Archer said.

"It doesn't matter. We needn't complement each other in dress. We're to remain individuals, after all. We won't begin speaking at all times in the first person plural, will we?"

They would, he said, "but satirically."

"Aren't you clever," she said, and left.

"Thanks for the racket," Sara said, arriving by chance at a double meaning. She brushed some of its flaking grip off her palm. "Or is now a bad time for you to take it back? I can hang on to it if you want."

"Now's fine," he said. He waved at another passing motorist. "Is your room okay?"

"It's great," she said quietly. All over again she was nervous around him, obsequious in a way that seemed completely unlike her and completely beyond her control. Over the past few months, as the book's August pub date approached, Archer had returned as overseer, sending considered replies to her e-mails, texting her half-formed ideas and bits of news, calling or Skyping when he felt the need for a more detailed conference, proceeding as if things should return smoothly, without comment, to normal. It was as if they were staying together for the sake of the children. And things did more or less return to normal, except now it was all friendly formality in place of teasing rapport, and where Sara was previously determined to change or sabotage her employment, now she was comparably eager to preserve it. She was never as tenacious about staying put, however, as she was about breaking free.

"I need to give a toast tonight," Archer said. "Maybe you could help."

"Sure, of course." Perhaps this was just the thing to relax their starchy rapprochement toward their old near-intimacy. "D'ya think I need to, though?" Better not to leap in. "It's a toast, not an address."

"But I feel I have a certain reputation for wordsmithery to uphold. I know you'd punch things up, smooth things out, whatever's needed."

"Maybe just deliver it extemporaneously. You're very eloquent off the cuff."

"You think so?"

"Yes." Now she regretted her demurral. "Don't get me wrong," she said, "I'm definitely up for helping. I guess we'd have to do it now."

"No, you're right," he said. "I'll be okay."

She smiled.

"You doing good here?" he asked.

"Doing good deeds? No, I never do those."

"Doing well?"

"Yes. Very well, actually."

"I thought I'd see you at lunch."

"I went to see those Kertészes I love at the WAG," she said, "and then I was busy writing. I've been writing *a lot.* I meant to tell you this earlier, but last month a novel came to me, came to me practically in full."

"Like in a dream?"

"More like an epiphany. It was just, presto, there—or for the most part there; I'm still contemplating the ending. But I'm working so quickly. I feel like Stendhal or Kerouac or Trollope or someone like that."

"Or those novel-in-a-month people."

"Well, no, not like that," she said. "I'll show it to you soon."

"You don't need to."

"I'm writing it partly on the clock. So it's yours, really."

"Not so loud!" he whispered. "Jesus."

"Sorry. I didn't mean to," she said. "I wasn't thinking. I'm—"

But now he was chuckling, and she berated herself for being too apologetic.

By the time the groom's dinner rolled around, she felt ill-equipped for society and was relieved to be placed next to an absentee grand-aunt and an eight-year-old model-airplane enthusiast who didn't want to talk about it.

Two short speeches preceded Archer's. "As many of you probably know," he was saying now, having tripped through his introductory remarks, "I have a book coming out in just over a week. Thank you, and thank you in advance for your multiple purchases. Feel free to whip out your phones right now and place your preorder." He looked around the room. "I'm serious. The title is *The Second Stranger,* and Bondarenko is b-o-n-d . . ." He had one hand on the back of his chair; in the other he was holding a glass of red wine at an angle that couldn't have been popular with the cleaning staff. "But, uh, writers often say their books are like their children, right? And I think that's true. You spend all this time with them, try to do right by them, as my parents did right by me." He nodded to his mother and stepfather, then to his father. "And you love them despite their imperfections—ditto—and then you send them out into the world, where they take on their own unpredictable lives. If you're lucky, they never call you at two a.m. asking for bail money." Laughter. "So it's an apt metaphor—which must make this a shotgun wedding." He tipped his head. "I hope I'm not showing, eh? But"—he consulted his notes—"without, let's see, I'd be remiss if I didn't acknowledge that I couldn't . . ." He glanced in Sara's direction; he seemed unusually nervous. "Sorry, I can't claim to be the Seneca of modern Manitoban oratory. Who I meant was Cicero."

"You got this, bro!"

"I'd be remiss if I didn't acknowledge that I didn't make this baby alone."

Sara's heart rate accelerated. She thought, He's going to reveal me right now to everyone.

He went on, "This is a book—spoiler alert—about a love that doesn't work out. And there's no way I could have written and revised and revised . . . and revised"—this final *revised* he huffed with little-engine-that-could perseverance—"and gone through the whole obsessive ballet that gets a book from acorn to Amazon, as it were—I couldn't have done that if I didn't know about a love that did. And is. And will. Work out, I mean to say. Was that trackable? And this woman"—he stepped to his right, put his hand on Gemma's shoulder—"is . . . I don't know how to put it."

But he tried, and acquitted himself reasonably well. His fumbling enhanced his sincerity. Sara would have made things too clever.

Feeling foolish and sick to her stomach, Sara left the dinner at the first opportunity. For an hour or so she sat in bed hunched over her laptop, listening to the din and then hum of the more lingering guests. Her room seemed moneyed precisely in its cramped, outdated modesty. There were dowdy floral drapes, two ornithological prints, a diamond-patterned carpet, and a green club chair with an icicle of stuffing hanging from its black cambric bottom. After the party broke up, she started to hear the younger relatives walking, talking, and laughing in the halls. Sara was one of only three non-relations staying at the club, and though that was a kind of honor, she also felt out of place and conspicuously lonely. She tried composing a handful of tweets to be parsed out on Archer's account over the next week, including a few demonstrative options to post during the wedding party, but her stomach discomfort forced rest. She lay on the nubby white bedspread, trying to quell her nausea through stillness and denial without letting that denial keep her from making it in time to the toilet.

She spent much of the night lying on the bathroom floor, partly on a moplike bath mat, partly on cold hexagonal tiles that felt dusty but weren't. Around two o'clock she had occasion to remember that Archer's high school rock band had been called the Dry Heaves, and she thought of how thin the walls were, how to a few of the guests she would now be known not as the strange, friendless woman who worked in some enigmatic capacity for Archer, but as the strange, friendless, pukey and diarrheal woman who worked in some enigmatic capacity for him. By three she was taking cold comfort in the idea that her embarrassment was only her vanity; that, after all, no one cared, no one was listening, no one knew who she was or which room she was in. She wished someone would come to take care of her, stroke her hair, ease her back into bed, so that in the morning she would be inexplicably dressed in a fresh, oversized T-shirt, her rinsed pajamas drying on the shower rod, and on the bedside table there would be a tray of fruit and toast and those little sealed bottles of uncommonly flavored jams.

But of course she woke up to none of that.

John sat cross-legged on the dewy grass, rotating the sleeve around his coffee cup while uncomprehendingly watching a cricket match. He took a photo of the bowler (was it?), posted it, and lay down with his knees up. Maybe he would stay on for a week or two in Winnipeg. After a half hour or so, he strolled over to the zoo, where blue peafowl roamed free. He was kneeling to inspect a male when he noticed a thinner Lucas Pope walking toward him with an unknown woman, north of forty it looked, and a boy of eleven or twelve. John held out his hand so they wouldn't disturb the bird. "Amazing creature," he whispered. It walked away, and John stood up. "Quite a coincidence."

"Well, your Instagram inspired our trip," Lucas said.

"You should've texted. We could have met up."

"We did meet up."

"Looks like you've lost weight."

"Yeah, but I found some of it—that's my joke. So this is my friend Karyn Bondarenko, Archer's cousin, and her son, Maxwell."

John reached out his hand. "Pleased. Archer and I go way back."

"You're already dressed for the wedding," the woman said.

"I might go straight there."

"But this guy's known for his gear," Lucas said. "He's always, you know, to the nines."

John leaned down slightly toward the boy. "What do you know?" It was a question he'd picked up from George. He liked its open-endedness.

"About what?"

"These critters, if you like."

"Zoos are kind of sad."

They parted ways at the musk oxen.

John drove on to the Exchange District, where the paving stones looked like imbricated dog bones, the buildings looked like Chicago, and the photograms at an Archer-endorsed gallery looked like the grease-stained interiors of oven windows. "It looks," John started to say to the gallerist, then stopped, fearing he would sound naïve. "Like a." He had hit on the idea of feigning some sort of speech impairment. "Window."

"Yes." The gallerist's arms were folded.

"From," he said.

She turned her head toward him.

"A stove."

"I see that," she said. "I do."

And then it was time to drive to the ceremony.

At the wedding dinner Lucas was seated between Maxwell, now clinking at the smears and crumbs of his cake, and Alan Motrinec, a shinily balding sexagenarian with rows of dancing elephants on his light-blue tie. Alan and his wife didn't fit in with the relatively young and artistic table, and Lucas guessed that they'd been set aside like tricky monochrome puzzle pieces during the seating debates, then dumped here as a last resort. During dinner they had mostly murmured to each other, though they did exchange scattered banalities with the photographer Jessica Kim and her new boyfriend, and with Lucas when he wasn't talking football with Maxwell or listening to Karyn discuss politics with a young authority on Inuit sculpture. "So I didn't catch your connection to the happy couple," Lucas said to Alan as the waiter poured decaf. "Happy couple" seemed like an expression Alan would like.

"We're old friends of Cole and Pamela." It took Lucas a moment to remember that Cole and Pamela were Archer's parents. Alan took his last bite of cake with what seemed to be compromised dexterity. Advanced stage of stroke rehab, Lucas guessed.

"But it's complicated, as they say these days," Alan's wife, Francine, added.

"I'm not judgmental," Lucas said.

"Complicated, not sordid," Alan said with a chesty laugh. "Well, maybe a mite sordid. Let's see, Cole is Pamela's *third* husband, you know."

"Yes."

"My older brother, Charles"—he pronounced it in the French way—"was her first."

Of course, Motrinec's!

"Their separation was less than amicable," Alan continued, "but we managed to stay on good terms with Pam."

"Well, *I* did," Francine said. "At first it was me who kept the friendship alive."

"That's true," Alan granted. His wedding band chimed his wineglass when he took a clumsy sip.

"You'll need a baby bib, Alan."

"I've been eating with my left hand," Alan explained. "Neuroplasticity."

"I think I read about that."

Alan tapped his head. "Start eating with your nondominant hand and you'll *know* whether you read something or not. So are you part of the literati with Archer and his gang?"

"No, not really."

"Not my bag either. I like to read history when I have time, though I did read—what was the name of that novel I stayed up to finish the other day?"

"*Loaded for Bear,*" Francine said.

"*Loaded for Bear.* Outdoorsman from Little Rock. I couldn't turn the damn pages fast enough."

"I'll look for it."

"Don't try to finish it on a school night. But yes, Frannie kept things alive with Pam, and Cole and I have done some business together over the years."

The table broke to watch Gemma and her father inaugurate the dance floor.

"What kind of business?" Lucas said after a dutifully sentimental minute.

"Just a few stray dogs with Cole," Alan said. "Mostly I'm in the grocery biz. My family ran a small chain of supermarkets for many years, eventually sold to a competitor. But after the noncompete expired, I got sucked back in."

"On an even smaller scale," Francine said.

"Right, sucked into a Dustbuster more than an upright Dyson."

"Isn't he impossible?" Francine said.

"We just have the one store, Select Table," Alan said, "but we do all right."

"So I have to ask, are a lot of your customers bringing in their own bags?" Lucas said.

"Oh sure, we're seeing more of that."

"We were selling some for a while at the registers," Francine said, "branded and the whole shebang, but we found—maybe this was just me, but I didn't think they washed well: got peely, took an eternity to dry."

Lucas sat up straighter. "Exactly," he said. "I bring this up, see, 'cause I have a line of reusable grocery bags, kind of a back-burner operation for me, but they're great bags, sturdy vinyl ones available in all sorts of—an array, really, of collectible colors and designs." He pointed to Alan's tie. "We don't have elephants yet, but we have one with tigers, another with llamas. Eminently washable, in cold."

"We have our girl do most of the laundry in cold now," Francine said, "not just the darks. Although some detergents, I understand, aren't activated in cold water."

"And these bags dry—what is it, in a twice?" Lucas said.

"Trice, I think."

"Wham: dry," Lucas said.

"Wham, I like that," Alan said. He nodded a few times, sucking in his lips. "Wham. What's the name of your outfit?"

Lucas swallowed. He had learned to downplay the name. "Brand Nubagian."

"Come again?"

"Brand Nubagian."

"Brand Nubagian!"

"Yes."

"Now that's . . ." He trailed off contemplatively. "You say this bag outfit isn't your principal employment?"

"A sideline. I've been in banking and footwear, but I'm getting into air dryers."

"Hair dryers?"

"Hot-air electric hand dryers."

"Ah."

"Like you see in restrooms."

"No need for further explanations," Alan said. "The technology has reached us." He pulled his card from his breast pocket, laid it on the heavy white tablecloth, stood up, and took Francine's hand. "Send me a few samples, the llamas for sure." Lucas wondered if Alan was pursuing counterinstinctual business opportunities in support of neuroplasticity. "Now if you'll excuse us," Alan said, "I think we'll get in a dance or two while they're still playing the geriatric music."

"You do that," Lucas said. He tucked the card into his wallet and looked over at Karyn. She raised her eyebrows. He looked from side to side at the two-hundred-odd guests, the chocolate fountain, the buttery wallpaper, the swelling dance floor. He hoped to dance with Karyn when the music got less geriatric, though maybe for Maxwell's sake they would have to leave early. He stood up. "Need anything?" he said to Karyn, tipping his hand to his mouth. "I'd better not," she said, moving her hands in a steering motion.

As he made his way to the bar, he felt a druggy combination of secret relaxation and heightened awareness, saw the room with mellow clarity, as if he'd just put on new sunglasses in a strengthened prescription. John Anderson's hand startled his shoulder.

"Oh! Sorry 'bout that," John said.

"No, my fault," Lucas said.

"Y'all stay much longer at the zoo?"

"Another half hour maybe."

They talked briefly about bikes, but John didn't seem excited by the topic, and a silence fell between them too soon and too sadly for Lucas to use it to excuse himself. Some raspberry sauce had found its way to John's lapel. "So—I didn't ask you earlier—are you still in Chicago?"

John took a sip of his drink. "Outside Chicago? No. To be straight up with you, I'm living in my car just now."

"Oh."

"It's a full-size car so it's not so bad." If he wasn't drunk, he was at least tipsy. "And I'm at the Sheraton for a few nights."

Lucas nodded.

"Hey, I got a mint Wilson T2000 for sale if you're interested. With the case."

"I'm not really in the market for that stuff these days."

Hilarity broke out by the photo booth.

"Archer seems happy, huh?" John said.

"Well, you'd hope."

"Just finished the new book," John said. When he gestured with his drink hand, an ice cube dropped to the floor. "He let me borrow an advance so long as I promised to buy the real thing. 'Course I would've anyway."

"And?"

"Amazing." He let the adjective stand on its own awhile, then said, "It's not the kind of book I read, but he sucks you in, you know?"

"I do."

"It makes me wish Sara had stuck with it more," John said. He seemed to be looking around the banquet hall for her. Leaning into Lucas: "I think sometimes smart people just can't stop questioning themselves, you know, all the time analyzing and second-guessing, and then in the end they don't finish anything." He leaned away. "Archer, he just does it. In school he had no confidence in his writing. None. Goes to show."

"Goes to show what?"

"That sometimes the thing you're most afraid of is the thing you most need to do."

"The thing I'm most afraid of is burning to death."

"Sara would never show me her stuff. Which, to level with you, kind of hurt. I always knew she must be great, though—well, you went school with her and all, so you know."

Lucas wasn't sure if he ought to let this pass, or if Sara had planted the truth for him to find and disclose. "I should"—he hesitated—"I should send you one of her old stories."

John seemed to snap into focus. "You kept that stuff?"

"You don't know the half; I keep everything. It's on my laptop, PDF."

"You think she'd mind?" John said.

"Well . . ."

"You know, I'd love to see something. I don't have a computer at the moment, but my phone might work, or I could stop at a library. You reckon that would work in a Canadian library?"

"Not sure, man," Lucas said. He reached up to put his hand on John's shoulder. "But I'll send it tonight."

John liked some of these old Motown or whatever songs, but so far only people near the poles of the age continuum were dancing, and he was starting to feel kind of Weeble-like on his feet. He put down his whiskey sour on a highboy table and walked over to the coffee station. At this juncture in his life it didn't matter *when* he slept, and he would want to be alert if Lucas remembered to send Sara's story tonight. Most of the people back at John's table were still finishing dessert, so he returned to the same highboy, took a last swig of the whiskey, then a tongue-burning sip of coffee.

Archer and Gemma were independently visiting each table, Archer struggling to be at his most hail-fellow-well-met. His tuxedo fit nicely but was incorrect in three or four respects. A tux, for one, should never have a notch collar, only a peak or, if you must, a shawl. A redheaded boy was circling around the back of the ballroom, leaning to his left and holding up a model airplane, making engine sounds with his lips puffed out. When the boy got closer, John called out, "Northrop P-61 Black Widow." The boy ignored him.

John's most accomplished model had made the trip with him to college. His parents had driven him from Idaho Falls to Cambridge.

A tarp secured over the truck bed covered three or four boxes, one of which included a basically flawless Stearman PT-17 biplane. About a month later, Archer and John were awaiting guests, women, at their suite, when Archer picked up the plane from John's shelf. "But when I became a man," Archer said, "I put away childish things." Handing the model to John, he added, "You have nothing to lose but your planes." John put the model in a bag and stashed it under his bed, but by the next morning that seemed like a half measure, and he found himself dropping the bag in a trash bin outside Santander just after sunrise. It felt like a step toward manhood at the time, but he remembered it differently now. He walked over to the boy.

"That's a really nice Black Widow."

"Thanks."

"Hang on to it."

"'Kay."

"Don't let anyone convince you that it doesn't have value."

The boy moved away, sputtering at a higher volume.

By the time Archer made it to Karyn's remotely situated table, she and Maxwell were the only ones sitting at it. He took the chair to the right of hers. "I'm so glad you could come," he said.

"I wouldn't have missed it. This is Maxwell."

"Hey, Maxwell."

"Hi."

"You can keep playing," Archer said, and Maxwell returned to his tablet.

"I loved your book," Karyn said. "*Both* books, I mean, but Gemma sent me a galley of the new one. Transporting, really. It reminded me of Jean Rhys—not that it seemed at all derivative."

"Wow, thank you. I did feel that something, I don't know, clicked with that one." He paused as if waiting for an elaboration of her compliments, then said, "Any shows coming up? My dad said he got to see you in *The Cherry Orchard*."

"*Three Sisters,* yeah. He and I were just reminiscing about that. But no, I haven't acted in years."

"No?"

"No."

"So what *are* you up to?"

"I'm in HR," she said.

"The House of Representatives?"

"That's right. I legislate during the day and hit the stage at night, pining for Moscow."

"My dad said you were the best part of the show."

"It was an uneven production."

"Well, you might come back to it. I've been working with this guy who studied painting in his twenties, then gave it up to work in infrastructural consulting. Now he's having his first solo show at age sixty-five."

"I like stories like that." Feeling expansive, she said, "I have been fooling around with something. You know, acting is funny because"—she nodded at him—"unlike writing or music or painting, you don't as a rule do it alone for your own amusement. But I found that you can."

"Like you're talking to yourself?"

"Putting together a play, I guess, something I've been performing at home. Improv-based but, you know, composed."

"That's cool."

She hoped she didn't sound like some crazy aspirant. "You think it's all about crowd energy, but working without an audience can be invigorating."

"What kind of thing is it?"

"You should get to that last table."

"They can wait. I'm curious."

"In a way it's nothing; that's what I like about it. But it's a period piece, I guess you'd say, set in the late sixties, early seventies. A sort of hippie bildungsroman about a woman who's dating the coleader of a psychedelic folk group."

"Really?"

"And then she starts playing in the group, and—how do the summaries go?—trouble ensues."

"Funny, I love psych-folk from that era."

"You do? I wouldn't think someone your—I was about to say 'someone your age,' but it's not my era either. My play's based on this group hardly anyone knows, the Incredible String Band, though my protagonist is an American."

"You're kidding."

"Well, I knew it'd be hard enough making the guys sound Scottish, and I figured—"

"No, I mean, they're my favorite band!"

"Seriously?"

"So your heroine's like a Rose- or Licorice-type figure?"

"Yes! I was thinking of Licorice in particular."

"Christina McKechnie."

"My God, you know her real name."

"I told you, they're my favorite band. I followed them around the UK on one of their reunion tours a few years back—Licorice wasn't with them, of course—then did the same thing last year when Mike Heron was out doing some shows with his daughter. His voice is a bit worse for wear but still great."

"But his voice has always been rough, right?" she said. "That's what's so affecting about it; he's always stretching to make the best of things."

"Oh my God, *Smiling Men with Bad Reputations*?"

"So fucking good."

"A lost classic."

"I can't listen to 'Flowers of the Forest' without crying," she said.

"Me, I know you like I know the song in my soul," he sang off-key, closing his eyes.

"It's gonna be all right," she sang.

They sat for a moment without talking, as if they were hearing the song over the noise of the crowd and the Adele song that was actually playing. He pulled out his phone, scrolled for a half minute, and held up a photo to her face.

"What's that, a gimbri?" she said.

"Ding ding ding! You're hardcore, eh?"

"I guess."

"Sharpied by Robin himself." He waved at Gemma. "Well, I have to get to that table you mentioned." He touched the veiny back of her hand. "I need to read your play."

"Oh, like I said, it's hobby work."

"Dude, I *need* to read your play."

Dude?

"You can't be at brunch?" he confirmed.

"I'm afraid not."

"Remember that joke? I'm a frayed knot."

"No."

"It's about a rope in a bar." He stood up. "I'll call."

"Are you feeling quite all right?" Gemma asked. She was the third person to express concern over Sara's intestinal health.

"Yes, fine," Sara said, watching the swing of Gemma's gold drop earrings.

"I understand you had a rather trying night."

"But I'm fine now."

"I suffer horridly from motion sickness so I can empathize—oh!"—Gemma's unmistakably American-accented sister was pulling her by the arm to dance. "Feel better!" Gemma called out.

"I do!"

John replaced Gemma from his nearby lurking station. His linen suit was the color of milky coffee and wrinkled in a way suggestive of a transoceanic flight spent restlessly in coach; his knit tie was partly undone, and his normally shaven upper cheeks were stubbled. She couldn't tell if he seemed refreshingly loosened up or scarily unhinged. He hadn't been given a role in the wedding, and though he was normally forgiving to a fault, during the service—she had sat one pew behind him—she detected a bitter profile when Seth, the best man, pulled out the ring. "I'm sorry you were so sick last night," he said.

"Could we talk about something else?"

"Sure." They stood for a moment. Sara watched two little girls spin each other on the hem of the dance floor. "You look great," he said.

"Thanks." She was wearing a floral-print dress of, for her, unusual bravado. John didn't seem as laid-back as usual, but still Sara felt the calming, room-changing effect he could have, like when you turn on the vacuum and all the lights dim.

"Since we're here, should we dance?" he said.

"Ahm."

"One song."

There are times when the mere knowledge of being loved and desired is pleasure and comfort enough, and times when you're more susceptible than that.

He held up his index finger. "Just one."

Maxwell stepped shyly onto the floor when the DJ honored his request for Jay-Z, and Karyn wondered if this was the last time until his own wedding that he'd be willing to dance in such proximity to his mother. Lucas had taken off his oversized suit jacket and was sometimes mouthing the words with Maxwell, sometimes looking at Karyn, sometimes bobbing slowly and sexily toward her, then backing off at the same rate. He danced almost imperceptibly, like a buoy on a calm lake.

Karyn had allowed herself one more drink after all, and she wondered with a blink of paranoia if she ought to be observing a just-in-case teetotalism. Over the past twenty-four hours, the idea of a second kid had drifted sporadically into her realm of consideration, which was also the realm of miscarriages and complications and four a.m. feedings redolent of supposedly pain-relieving menthol gel. How could she lift a child anymore; how could she rest a crying three-year-old on her hip while opening the door to an overpriced day care with one hand? The kid would be touch deprived, would grow up to slaughter a farm family for thirty-seven dollars and a bag of Doritos. It was good, at least, to be alone with the decision. Were Jason and she still together, he would want the baby (he never bought her argument that having more than one child was environmentally immoral, and in fact he took the opposite line, that population decline would eventually become macroeconomically disastrous, that people should stop being so selfish and churn out more kids). He would defer to her in theory, but with a sulkiness pointing to enduring resentment from one party or another. The DJ millimetered up the volume. Archer's thickset friend from the zoo, moving in small but zealous circles with Archer's unfriendly yeoman or proofreader, bumped into Karyn and apologized in a deep, blunted twang. "No worries," she said, and smiled at Lucas. Still, if she wasn't ready to say that no aspect of her life had been as fulfilling as motherhood—too soppy to say that, too self-denying—she was willing to say that no aspect had been *more* fulfilling, and as she looked at Maxwell, growing up to be so kind and funny and smart and handsome, and at Lucas, whom, she admitted it now, she was falling for, she wondered if a baby, an expanded family, was the unknown she needed, one that had announced itself in this strangely fortunate city, in the winter of her fertility, one that would enrich rather than negate her plans for middle age.

Sensing that her intoxication would soon give way to exhaustion, she moved closer to Lucas: "We should go."

During her second dance, Sara held her phone at her hip, thumbed out a quick one:

> Archer Bondarenko @archerbondarenko · 13s
> Cue "Crazy in Love." #justmarried

Lucas crouched in front of his room's minibar. "Is Maxwell asleep?"

"Probably not quite," Karyn said. "I told him we were having a drink together." She thought that would sound straightforward enough without getting too explicit.

"*Are* we having a drink?"

"Nothing for me."

He broke the seal on a rectangle of almonds, took a beer, and sat down on the room's desk chair. When he held out the almonds, she stood up partway and cupped her palm for a small handful.

"Archer wants to read my play," she said.

"Oh? You're not gonna let him, are you?"

"Turns out he's an Incredible String Band fanatic."

"You think it's hereditary with you people?"

"Ha." She looked out at the window's black nothing, wondered if they should close the curtains. "Ever do the thing, 'If Bush wins'—or whoever—'I'm moving to Canada'?"

"Nah. I was always prepared to stick around and not really fight. I used to think the left benefited from a conservative administration, and maybe it does, but I'm not sure it's worth it."

"I should have moved when I was young," she said.

"You still could, right?"

"We're settled here—or there. It wouldn't be fair to Maxwell. I'm not moving."

"No," he said. "I'm glad."

"You could not move with me."

He stood up and held out his hands for her to stand up too. "Okay, I will," he said. His kiss smelled pleasantly of beer, and she moaned kind of purrily when he massaged her scalp behind her ears. A love kiss—the first in a long time. Five or ten minutes later he was kneeling over her on the bed, his knee pressed between her legs. They were still dressed but becoming undone, and she was lightly scratching his lower back underneath the band of his underwear. "Not that we need it this second," he said, "but I'm afraid I don't have a jimmy hat."

She started to laugh. "You're still saying 'jimmy hat'?"

"I'm reviving it."

"I thought you were buying condoms at the gas station. I was all excited in the car, thinking about you in there buying them."

"You were?"

"Yes."

"I just stopped for a Diet Pepsi like I said. I didn't want to seem, like, presumptuously or promiscuously prepared."

She shook her head. "That's . . ."

He moved off of her, reached for his boatlike dress shoes. "I'll go back."

"No, you know, I—to tell you the truth I don't think we need one. Maybe we do, I don't know, but not for birth control."

"You're on the pill."

Just say yes, go on it when you're back home, and avoid sex for a while. "No," she said.

"Is this a guessing game?"

If she decided to have the baby, could she pass it off as his? He was presumably familiar with the standard human gestation period. "I'm pregnant," she said.

A period of nonplussation.

"I only took the test last night. I haven't seen a doctor. But I'm late and it was positive. Faintly positive, but . . ."

"Huh."

"I don't have a boyfriend. It was a work thing—that sounds weird, 'a work thing.' It was a consultant from Chicago, just in town for a few days. So, um. If both of us are disease free, we could skip the condom. I've always hated them."

"Yeah, sure, I—"

"Sorry," she said. "I killed the mood."

But she hadn't.

Standing in front of a spectral figure in a late-sixties Richter, Archer talked to a circle of Sunday brunchers about his latest project, *The Hangman's Daughter,* "a drama à clef," he said, "about music, love, countercultures"—he pretended to zip his lips—"but I shouldn't say more." Archer sometimes sprang ideas on Sara in this way, though the ideas rarely came with names or other claims to specificity. He hadn't been this animated in years.

"A play?" Sara said. She tried to smile.

"I'll leave the taxonomy to the critics."

Sara said, "You'll have to categorize—"

"Slow down, bro," Seth interrupted. "Your new novel's not even out yet, and you're already plugging the next thing."

"I know. This crazy restlessness. I start disowning my work before the ink dries."

"But I think Seth has a point," Sara said. She knew her face looked anxious.

Archer's mother turned to Sara. "He was always like this," she said confidentially. "So hard on himself, never satisfied."

"Yes," Sara said. She looked down a wide hallway in which many hockey pucks were encased in glass.

Archer's mother shook her head proudly. "But that's the price."

Parsimoniously, incautiously, they decided not to fill up in Winnipeg and later found themselves coasting a good distance west of the highway to Hamilton, North Dakota (no filling station), then to Cavalier. For twenty miles the fuel gauge warned that they had enough gas left in the tank to travel less than one mile, and Karyn joked that they were living out Zeno's paradox, which she had never found interesting or intelligible. When they made it to town, they learned that it was the last day of the Pembina County Fair. It seemed wrong not to use their detour as an excuse to attend.

They parked in a patch of dirt not far from the carnie camp and made their way to a white clapboard ticket stand. The outdated rides and games looked photogenic against the azure backcloth, but Karyn thought they would look trite if actually photographed. One of the rides, Hit Parade, featured elongating mirrors and airbrushed portraits of pop stars who were either unrecognizable or dead. She expected the fair's prices to cater to small-town thrift, but, if anything, her sheet of tickets paid for fewer sick-making rides in Cavalier than it would have in Saint Paul. Most of the carnies sounded Southern, she noticed.

While Maxwell built up speed in one of the Spider cars, Lucas gently pulled Karyn a few more feet away from the small crowd of onlookers. "I liked this ride when I was a kid," he said.

It didn't seem like what he had wanted to say.

"I know this is too soon," he said after a breath, "but I want you to know that I can be there for you, if you want me."

"I'm not following."

He turned his gaze back to the ride. "Whatever you decide with the pregnancy. Like, if you need someone to go to the clinic with you. Or."

It was an odd place to broach the subject, but perhaps as private as anywhere. "I might want to have a medical rather than a surgical abortion," she said, trying to keep her intentions uncertain.

He inclined his head thoughtfully.

"They have pills now."

"Oh, right."

"Though I'd still need to go to a clinic," she said, "and it would still be hard. Like a miscarriage, at least physically. I don't know, maybe I'll have it done surgically. Either way it'd be nice to have support."

"Okay," Lucas said. He nodded toward Maxwell. "He doesn't seem to be having much fun."

"No, he really doesn't. I think it's just disappointment, though, not nausea."

"Yeah."

"But I'm not always the most perceptive parent. I was never one of those moms who could recognize the cry of her baby coming from an unseen room full of dozens of potentially crying babies."

"Something you had an opportunity to test?"

"Once in church."

"I think bat moms can do that kind of thing, in caves with billions of bats."

She laughed. "Not billions."

"But a lot."

"Last year I was watching Maxwell's first game of the season. I didn't know his jersey number yet. So I studied the players, thinking that of course I knew the contours of his body, the quirks of his gait. Plus I was pretty sure what position he'd be playing. I watched the wrong kid till halftime."

"Yeah," Lucas said. "But all that padding." They followed the ride's spin. "Or even—again, I know this is weird—but even if you wanted to *have* the baby," he said. "I just want you to think of me as someone who could be around."

"I am thinking of you that way."

The ride slowed to a stop. Maxwell stumbled out, trotted behind a bush, and threw up.

August 2011

Karyn's room overlooked the playground in Union Square, where kids were embroiled in a game of king of the hill on what looked like a giant overturned mixing bowl. Archer had paid for her hotel and airfare, and with those expenses covered, she had sprung for Lucas's ticket. She bit into one of the room's complimentary Granny Smiths as Lucas emerged from the bathroom, a towel wrapped under his belly. His walk was almost his dance. Before they left for New York, he had received a small order from Alan Motrinec, and he had just now had sex. "When do we need to leave?" he asked.

"Half hour?"

He zipped up his cargo shorts. It was hot outside, but she wished he would wear pants. On the wall was a photograph of a miniskirted

woman diving into the sunroof of a vintage European subcompact.
"You okay?" Lucas said.

"Yeah." She sipped her slightly oleaginous bottled water, also complimentary, and let it pool for a few seconds in her lips. "I don't want to make the wrong decision."

"About," he prompted.

She had only told him that Archer might talk to a producer. "The play."

"Are there decisions to make?"

She paused to consider Lucas's status in relation to the nondisclosure, whether, contractually or otherwise, he should know everything or just what he already knew. "There's no harm in hearing me out," Archer had said less than five minutes after she got to his apartment, "and I can't say anything until you sign this." She was confused, she signed. He asked her again if Lucas was the only other person who had read the play. She said yes. He told her he was suffering from writer's block—"severe," he said, though Karyn didn't see how severity could enter the picture on the dawn of his latest novel's publication. The last book had depleted him, he explained, if not for good at least for a long time to come, and until reading *The Hangman's Daughter*—he kept calling her untitled play by this new name—he had thought about quitting. *The Hangman's Daughter,* he said, was what he'd always wanted to write; reading it was like coming across something he'd done long ago and put away, where everything and nothing seemed familiar. She was trying to make out the meaning of this preamble when he offered her what sounded like three hundred thousand dollars. He repeated himself: three hundred thousand for the play, plus another three hundred thousand if—and he was optimistic—it were produced at any professional level. "Three hundred thousand dollars for the rights to the play," she said, not quite as a question. "For the right," he answered, "to present the play, or the film, or whatever it becomes, as my work." The money could be wired as soon as tomorrow. Lucas would have to sign a confidentiality agreement too and would be offered a much smaller figure. She promised to get back to Archer soon. Glory, she thought as Archer saw her to the elevator, was an even baser motivation for art than greed; therefore, handsomely compensated anonymity would be a step closer to purity. She pictured writing on weekday mornings, the mortgage paid off, a year in Africa working on clean water or something like that, something that would do some good for the world while boosting Maxwell's appeal to an upper-tier college, from which he would graduate like a debtless blue blood. Silly to pass that up to avoid a sellout that few people would decry and only three people would know about. Who even used the word *sellout* anymore?

"I guess not," she told Lucas while watching a boy raise his arms in triumph atop the mixing bowl. "It's just, I worry I'll screw it up. I worry this is my last chance to get it right, that doors are closing." Not ready to lay out the present dilemma, she settled for this reiteration of how she'd felt on and off for years.

"Torschlusspanik?" Lucas said, or a word recognizably close. He finished buttoning his shirt and stood behind her at the window.

"I don't want to be this old and still not know what I want to do with my life."

"Maybe if you knew what you wanted to do with your life," he said, rubbing the knobbiest vertebra leading up to her neck, "it wouldn't be your life. You said before how you like uncertainty and all that." He pushed both palms up the sides of her nape. "Like I've been thinking, all my regrets, all the stuff I wish I'd done differently, it's really just me wishing I'd been someone else."

"Mmm, a little higher, please." Massages like this were best because they were always ending; all you could do was concentrate on each last instant of pleasure. During a long, hired massage, she would get caught up in cost-benefit analyses, worrying that she would fall asleep or that too much time would be given over to chakra rituals or the flipping of pan-flute cassettes.

"But I'm not going to do that anymore."

"That's smart," she murmured, not remembering what he was going to stop. Then she thought, Probably Archer would be willing to pay more.

Sara walked down to the bookstore's basement and found a seat in the fourth row. The reading was scheduled to start three minutes ago, and the crowd still wasn't one. It was the book's second and less spectacular New York event; at the first, there were projections of Jessica Kim's photographs as well as alcohol, a pensive rock band, and more attendees, including an honest-to-God movie star. Here she recognized a few seminotables: Archer's agent, a midlist novelist, and the lit blogger and podcaster Joshua Kehr. Gemma turned from the front row to see how things were filling in, waved at Sara, then at someone in the back. Sara waited a few seconds to turn her own head. She groaned internally when she spotted John, unexpected and unwelcome, looking like he'd woken up on the wrong side of the park bench. He didn't seem to take in her fiercest look of admonition. She had told him she was sorry, that their reunion wouldn't extend beyond the wedding party. This past week had provided a respite from his calls and texts, but maybe he'd only wanted to quiet the stage for his entrance as stalker.

A bookseller tapped the microphone, began announcements.

Karyn had made up her mind by the time she and Lucas got to the bookstore twenty-five minutes before the reading. Perhaps she had made up her mind in Archer's apartment and had just needed an afternoon to reconcile her decision with her ideals. She wanted to whisper her answer in Archer's ear, but she couldn't find him and figured that would be imprudent anyway. She told Lucas she needed to call Maxwell, stepped outside to the narrow sidewalk, and spent a minute or so watching passersby. It was a good spot to feel bad about the decisions you'd made regarding sunglasses. She'd wait till spring to buy a new pair and enjoy for now the fruits of this afternoon's splurge: the unconscionably expensive Jason Wu purse, the dominatrix-like zippered boots she'd kept on that afternoon in the many-mirrored hotel room. Archer answered on the first ring. "Where are you?" he said.

"At the bookstore. Outside it."

"I'm two blocks away."

"Have a sec?" she said.

A stretched-out yes.

"I talked to my friend about that painting she wants to sell," she said. The code had occurred to her only a minute ago; she hadn't quite worked it out. "She really appreciates your advice, but she says that since the painting has, you know, such sentimental value for her, she'd only want to let it go for five up front and another five in the event of an intermediary sale."

A few heartbeats of silence.

"Archer?" She looked at the phone to see if the call had been dropped. "You still there?"

". . . could work out," he was saying. "Maybe if you don't mind carrying on as your friend's representative, we could meet over breakfast tomorrow, hash out a few last things."

"Sure, that would be—"

He hung up, but only because he was standing next to her. "Nine o'clock at my place too early?"

"No."

"I'm afraid you'll have to bring Lucas."

"It'll be early for him," she said, then felt bad for falling into step with Archer's dismissals.

"Okay, cuz, I'm gonna load up on water and tea." He raised his hand to his face. "Cottonmouth before readings."

Throughout the reading John stared at Archer with a knowing, mirror-tested smile—less a smile than a fractional upward curl restricted to the left side of his mouth. After a while it seemed to frazzle Archer; he shifted more, looked up less, and when he pretended to make engaging, Toastmasters eye contact, he was obviously looking over everyone's head. When the floor was opened for questions, John straightened Sara's manuscript by tapping it on his new *Second Stranger* hardcover. He looked around. He didn't want to be the first to speak.

The question-and-answer period opened with a repose during which Karyn was conscious of her own whiffling inhalations. "I could have read longer," Archer joked. A titter, a cleared throat. Finally an arm near the front rose in an indecisive *L*: a general question about Archer's "process," fielded warmly. Next a maundering speech whose interrogative component was thrown in at the end like a hungrily mumbled amen. Then a hand went up in the back. "John!" Archer said, and there was that weird, drawly bass—Karyn turned around—of Archer's thickly bearded former roommate.

"I guess I'm curious about process too," John said, "but more about the editorial process." It was the sort of voice, Karyn thought, that might have been salable in the era of radio suspense serials. "I see that you thank a mess of people in the acknowledgments, editors and readers and what all, and I'm wondering how much influence those people wind up havin' on the end product."

Archer looked at John with what seemed like confusion. "Probably not enough," he said, gesturing toward humility. "I can be, oh, intractable, you might say. But, that said, I've benefited immeasurably from the sage advice and quiet corrections of all those people thanked in the acknowledgments. And many more who aren't. Thanked, I mean; the list could easily become infinite, influence coming as it will from all corners. I see that Josh Kehr is here—you're all familiar with *Dog-Eared*?" Archer nodded at a man across the aisle from Karyn. "For my money it's the best literary podcast in the English-speaking world. Josh and I were talking on the show about—what?—character and agency, Burke's pentad and all this, and I've no doubt that our talk will affect my writing, however slightly. So it's all, you know."

"Well, it's interesting," John said, "because one of the folks thanked in the acknowledgments is a mutual friend of ours, Sara Crennel, who's here tonight, and I recently had a chance to read one of her unpublished early stories—"

Sara, the assistant from the wedding, turned around. "What?"

"And it's kind of crazy how close the story is to a part of *The Second Stranger*," John continued.

Sara: "How'd you get your hands on—"

"I'd love to just read a chunk of it, and maybe get your take, Archer, on the similarities."

"No one cares about my juvenilia," Sara said with an actorly laugh.

Josh Kehr said, "Let's hear it."

"Those with a copy of the book handy might want to turn to page 112," John said. He stood up, started to read:

> For seven years we lived in a small city in southeastern Idaho. The singer Carole King lived on an estate a few hours from us,

> and supposedly there was a white-supremacist compound in the nearby countryside as well. Much later I came to feel restive and unprotected in cars, like a just-bottled grasshopper, so it's hard for me now to see the fun in the Sunday drives we used to take, but I enjoyed them then, despite the backseat clamor, so loud with the windows rolled down that I couldn't hear the AM radio or my parents' conversation. My brother, in the backseat with me, listened to hair metal on his Walkman if he hadn't successfully lobbied—

"I really don't see what this is proving," Sara said.

"It seems to be proving quite a lot," said Kehr, holding open Archer's book. Karyn was following along too. The words were nearly identical.

"Yeah, I'm not sure this is really the place for whatever's going on here," Archer said. "Comp lit."

John loudly cleared his throat:

> —lobbied to stay home.
>
> One windy Sunday morning in midsummer we went looking for King's place, but our directions were speculative, our map illegible from Thermos rings.

In the book, the map was simply "out of date." Karyn missed a sentence while noting that change and a few others. Sara tried unsuccessfully to interrupt John.

> —leaking with now louder tinniness from his earphones, their foam covers mismatched because he'd lost one, stolen mine. I watched my father's face reveal more frustration as he put on a show of hiding it. I don't know how sincere our quest was in the first place—I was only eleven and couldn't always tell when

my parents were joking—but I know we were sincerely lost. We tried to retrace our route but only got farther off course. We pulled over, my brother turned off his music, and my mother joked that, "knowing our luck" (but I've been very lucky), we would fatally drive our rickety imported car and its peeling NO NUKES bumper sticker into the white-supremacist compound. But the compound, my gravel-kicking brother pointed out, would have a daunting gate. He was humorless, my brother, and perhaps honestly afraid for his safety (he was adopted and less Aryan than the rest of us). My father tapped the bone behind his ear while my mother and I pinned the map's corners to the car's sloping hood. Without trying to, I got the heel of my palm to indent the hood and make a noise when the indentation popped out. Trying to, I did that two more times. "Stop!" my father said.

"What do you think you're doing?" Sara said, more loudly this time. She stood up and walked toward John. Josh Kehr was taking notes. Another man was holding up a phone, recording the scene.

"This is absurd," Archer said. "A crazy man types up variations on part of a book, and we have to listen to him read it?"

"The date of this manuscript can be authenticated in the wink of an eye," John said, shaking the pages.

"You need help, John. I'm sorry this is happening."

"I'm as sane as houses."

"That's *safe* as houses," Sara said.

"Would you mind putting down your phone?" Archer said to the sudden documentarian, then looked behind him at the engrossedly noninterventionist bookseller. The audience seemed much more attentive to John's reading than they had been to Archer's. Now Sara was trying to tear the manuscript from John's hands. He held it above his head, stood on his chair.

We were about to get back in the car [he read] when a couple-colored pickup emerged on the horizon. We stood under a cloud-shadow on the side of the dirt road, watching the truck get closer. It slowed, stopped. A boy about my age, tanned to the shade of a baseball glove, stared blankly at us through the passenger window. The driver urged us to join him for lunch at the "best café in Idaho." The café was just off the highway we needed anyway, he said.

The boy's name was Kevin. He was the first Kevin I'd met, though later it seemed you couldn't get away from them. He didn't talk much, but everything he said was in earnest. By the time we got to the pudding course, he had asked me to "go with him," and for five years we carried on a correspondence, the unusual candor and exhaustiveness of which only became clear to me years later, when I was living on the island and began to write letters to myself from an imagined adult Kevin, letters I would post at the—

Sara had managed to push John off the chair and confiscate a page of the manuscript. Another page, after floating in loops and dodges, landed not far from Karyn. It seemed to include a great deal of marginalia. Sara turned to Lucas. "You fuck!" she said.

He spread his arms. "I thought you wanted to get caught."

"What's going on?" Karyn said under her breath to Lucas, who shook his head.

Gemma was casting distraught looks around the room, one hand on the back of her chair.

"So what does this mean?" Kehr asked Archer, who seemed frozen at the lectern.

"What *does* it mean?" Archer said.

"Are you returning the question rhetorically, or . . . ?"

"I think," Archer started hesitantly, "I think the whole notion of authorship is evolving, becoming fluider. I've always been interested in collage, sampling, appropriation art."

"Passing off someone's unpublished story as your own work is appropriation art? Seems more like plagiarism."

"It wasn't that," Archer said.

"Is it ghosting?" Kehr said.

"Everything changes in context," Sara broke in from the floor. She was still standing up. "Look at 'Pierre Menard, Author of the *Quixote*.'"

"*Reality Hunger*," someone else offered.

"Listen," Sara said, "I was doing some proofreading on *The Second Stranger*, and I happened to mention to Archer that his novel reminded me, in mood mainly, of a piece I'd written years ago. So I sent him a copy of the story, and we just kept coming back to it. Finally we thought, you know—"

"Let's put it in," Archer said.

"Let's put it in," Sara parroted.

"Your story seems to be evolving at a faster pace than our notion of authorship," Kehr said.

"We could have done better at laying out that section's provenance," Archer said.

"But it's a different piece now," Sara said. "You can't step twice into the same stream."

"Bullshit," John said. "She wrote the whole book. She writes all his stuff. She's actually a genius."

"I'm not your damsel in distress, John," Sara said.

John pointed at Archer. "And he's not true," he said. His "not" came out like "nawt."

Gemma got out of her seat and started to walk down the aisle to leave. She was looking at her sandals, but you could tell she was crying.

Archer called to her without vociferation, stepped away from the lectern without urgency.

Gemma held an arm up behind her. "Don't follow me."

The bookseller delicately reclaimed the lectern. "Thank you all for coming," she said. "If you'd like to have books signed, I believe that can happen at a table upstairs." Kehr asked who would sign them.

Strangely, Archer, as instructed, didn't follow Gemma.

But Lucas did. Later, Karyn couldn't remember him getting out of his seat. She just remembered sitting there, watching his back as he trotted after Gemma, watching the croupier sweep away her jackpot. Karyn waited outside the bookstore for ten minutes—not long, but she was already furious and devastated by the end of two. She felt like one of those scarves that overflow lost-and-found boxes on the first springlike afternoon.

Lucas's first text chimed in as she was coming out of the subway, his first call as she was having their room's keycard changed. She turned away from the desk, stared at the cucumber water and the Granny Smith tube, and let the call go to voice mail.

In her room that night she cried for maybe twenty minutes and then started to feel a calm indifference to her life that she hadn't felt before, a sort of nothingness. It wasn't a break from thanatophobia; she rarely worried about death and found death-obsessed people tiresome and self-important. Nor was it suicidality; such thoughts made her acutely aware of the pain she would cause Maxwell and others. It was more that the rest of her life didn't matter—*to her.* She didn't dread the future; she just didn't need to experience it.

Lucas wasn't invited to the meeting with Archer the next morning, which of course was canceled anyway, and his seat on the plane that next afternoon was occupied only by Karyn's now regrettable new purse. A week later she listened to half of his first message—"Hey, I don't know what I was thinking; I guess I thought she needed support, but, you know, it was jerky of me to"—but she never picked up his calls or answered his texts. He backed off with insulting haste.

September 2011

A bell rang as John walked into the UPS store. He looked awhile at the bubble wrap, envelopes, and packing tape, then walked to the counter. He pushed the Wilson toward a parcel servant with brown hair that hung jaggedly over his right eye. "I want to send this to New Avenues Senior Living, in Barrington, Illinois," John said. "I don't have the street address."

"We can look it up."

While the clerk did that, John stepped over to a spinning rack of photographic greeting cards. He had just under twenty-four hundred dollars left. "Do you only have funny cards?"

"Most of those cards aren't funny to me," the clerk said.

He picked one featuring a pigtailed baby on which eye black and a football jersey had been photoshopped. Inside, the card read TACKLE IT ONE DAY AT A TIME. "You been living in Harrisburg your whole life?" John asked.

The clerk measured the racket. "Most of it. I was born in Middletown."

"Nice place?"

"Middletown?"

"Harrisburg."

"It's all right."

"Can I use a pen without buying it?"

"Have at it."

"I'm sorry I stole your tennis racket," John wrote. "You were a good friend to me, and I hope you're happy in your new ~~abode~~ home. I soon begin my teacher's training in Harrisburg, Pennsylvania. It's all right. Please thank Chick for the hotel room. The wedding was a success but it looks like the marriage won't be. All the best, John Anderson."

The players were starting to arrive when Lucas got to the North Side park at quarter to six. He straddled his bike and chewed a taffy-like energy bar, trying to subdue any hint of predation by affecting weary, contemplative pride, as if he'd been riding for sixty miles instead of the six it took him to get here from work. Less than ten minutes of internet research had determined that Maxwell would be practicing in one of two parks. It wouldn't be hard to bike to both in the two-hour window he had to work with.

The temperature was falling, but he squeezed a few drops of water into his helmet vents, then walked in his concrete-clicking bike shoes to refill his bottles at the rec center's drinking fountain. In the basin there were bright wads of chewing gum and a drain-clogging pulp of sunflower shells. No sign of Karyn's car. The kids strapped on their pads, scattered their straw-topped water bottles on the edge of the field, praised their own catches. At six sharp, they were whistled into line. Lucas doubted that Maxwell would be among those compelled to run laps for tardiness, but he waited till twenty past just in case. He reexamined the circuitous, highway-skirting route to his next stop, reached into his bike shorts to disengage some pubic hairs from his foreskin, and started riding south.

He didn't quite know what he would do or say if he found Karyn. Only when he got within a mile of the second park did he realize that a posture of nonchalance wouldn't fly. He would start with an apology. He had chased after Gemma stupidly, impulsively—but he wouldn't say that—partly because no one else was stepping forward to comfort her, partly, he admitted, because he wanted to witness more of her ekphra . . . no, her peri . . . Karyn would know Aristotle's word . . . her sudden change, her discovery of who Archer really was, though of course she wasn't at all grateful to Lucas for setting this discovery in motion. (Lucas had looked forward to seeing Archer exposed in the papers, pilloried on Facebook, dissected in slapdash essays by self-advancing pundits; but his schadenfreude was used up in minutes.)

It would be better, Lucas realized as he tried to shake away a tingle in his forearm, to strip his apology of all explanations, to simply tell Karyn he was sorry, sorry he'd hurt her, and from there move quickly to a declaration, something bold and earnest.

He rode past the park, then slowly toured its neighborhood, his rear wheel's pawls and ratchets chirring as he coasted in the center of the streets. He tried to clear his head by imagining he was walking through an enormous warehouse filled with fast-spinning fans that he was turning off one by one. The warehouse was really a version of his apartment duplicated over and again like your arm in a mirrored elevator. There was no air-conditioning in his apartment—in his actual apartment—so he relied on fans, box fans with thick layers of brown dust on their blades. Whenever it got mild enough to turn them off, he would be equally struck by two sudden things: the apartment's sudden peacefulness, and the suddenly strange fact that he had endured days, even weeks, of steady, unmusical noise. With each fan in his mental warehouse, he would pinch the plastic switch for a moment before turning, then gradually power it down: three, two, one. The last fan was whirring to a stop when he returned to the park. He locked his bike to a parking sign and started wending his way through the practice field. It was dusk, but he thought he could make out Karyn sitting in a lawn chair near the sidelines of one of the scrimmages. White helmets were facing off against helmets wrapped in yellow fishnets. He pictured the three of them in the kitchen, making dinner, listening to Karyn's terrible music, asking about the details of their dumb days. He could feel the blood in his veins. He slowed his pace, his shoes sometimes sinking into the ground, and she came more clearly into view.

Dear Ms. Crennel,

I've just finished reading your *God's Good Side,* and my partner can attest that its choicer passages often cried out for recitation. Eventually he moved to another room. Let's not be discouraged over that. I'm glad you came across Mr. Miller's mostly kind profile of me in *Poets & Writers.* You weren't the first to contact me in its wake, but you were the first to do so by traditional post. Perhaps you were pandering to my reported fustiness. I'm sure the young man meant only flattery by calling me "the last of a dying breed," but still and all, it was an impolite memento mori. I've had a sore throat ever since.

Though I'm not beslobbered just yet from the jaws of Death, I am old, born long enough before your Janice that we wouldn't have overlapped at Palmerville High, had I been fated to attend. She and I are contemporaneous enough, however, for me to feel that I knew her and her milieux. Such an outstanding, easeful job your book does of evoking that period, without once exuding a malodor of mildew, unwashed army jackets, and whatever else might be redolent these days of libraries. Parts brought me back to *Memoirs of an Ex-Prom Queen, Kinflicks,* and some of those, though nothing feels loudly derivative. The HoJo's scene sings. I'm applauding you now with my frail, parkinsonian hands.

About the ending:maybealittlerushed. A captivating urgency there but something short of the encircling reality that pervades the preceding chapters. I hope we'll have cause to discuss.

I appreciate your candor concerning the Archer Bondarenko business. Tawdry, but it seems you were guilty only of a certain want of circumspection. Ah, but you were careful to save your truly exceptional, your truly original, work for yourself. So, onward! In defeat, defiance! If you are indeed still seeking representation, we should talk. Normally my signature line excludes my telephone number, but I've made an exception for you, as I did for Menachem Begin. A good time to call would be tomorrow morning between nine and ten. Or suggest another.

Regards,
Richard Parlett
Parlett Whelpdale Kachru

▬▬▬▬▬▬▬▬

New York, NY 10011

▬▬▬▬▬

Karyn sat in her saggy lawn chair reading an Italian novel that, by being both genuinely lyrical and deeply boring, was conducive to reflection, to looking up frequently at the sunset, which from top to bottom was deep blue, light blue, pink, and orange. It was beautiful to the cusp of oversweetness. It might have crossed that point had it not been darkened by dragonflies, finches, and blackbirds, maybe some starlings and bats, all black in the early twilight and mingled so that you couldn't always tell if you were seeing a fairly close dragonfly or a distant finch. Maxwell's team, one of four practicing in different territories in the park, was scrimmaging, white helmets versus netted yellow ones.

The wind blew harder. Karyn buttoned up her raincoat with one hand while turning a page with the other, glad she hadn't brought her e-reader this time and could enjoy the dexterity of her fingers as she held the verso in place with her forefinger, turned the recto with her thumb, and quickly moved her finger to the next page, the operation more interesting than the book, though without the book's model she might not have noticed the operation.

There were a few weeks of the football season when sitting in the park during practice was the thing of all things she most wanted to do; when she only had to click on her insect-luring book light for the last half hour of the practice; when it wasn't chilly enough yet to nudge her into the car or to the characterless coffee shop down the road; when the coaches, having made their bracing first and second impressions (her favorite shouted command: "You've got to relax!"), were bending toward lower-volume motivation. She moved her chair from under one of the shade trees around the park's periphery to a spot closer to the scrimmage, wondering as she did if the new vantage would ruin the scene, ruin the moment, if it wasn't already ruined by her awareness that a moment was there to be ruined. But the new spot was fine, maybe better. Her phone vibrated with a note from a friend from her theater days. Yes, the friend said, she would love to work on *The Hangman's Daughter* for next year's Fringe Festival. That made three interested actors and a director. A production like that, Karyn had decided, wouldn't tarnish the play's "purity." It could be fun.

Voices sounded all around her, of the birds and the variously aged players, of the lulling Italian novelist, the other parents talking to one another or on their phones, teenagers swearing and flirting in and around the skate park, laughing as they leaned against the chain-link fence surrounding the paint-chipped wading pool. Added to all that were sounds of shoulder pads hitting chest protectors, feet and bodies falling on grass, occasional whistles. It was noisy, but in a rounded, ambient way, the park imbued with the solitude and silence that somewhere Austen says only numbers can give, the peace that somewhere Auden says no bird can contradict.

She read a sentence, looked up, reread the sentence, looked up. A running play ended fruitlessly for the offense, and a mom yelled, "You gotta block! You *got* to block!" Some of the parents grew so inflamed, even during these scrimmages. During games, they didn't always stop short of hectoring the volunteer coaches. Ridiculous, but at times Karyn felt guilty about her comparatively tempered responses, her single claps and pipping cheers, sometimes delayed or misdirected. She probably didn't care as much about the games as some of the other parents did, but she didn't want it thought that she cared less about her son. She didn't want Maxwell to think that, at least. One of her tenderest maternal moments had been holding him after his team lost its big game the previous year, lost it badly on a cold, wet night, the rain abetting fumbles and defeating cleats. He had held back his tears for two hours. They burst forth as he stood under the archway between their living and dining rooms. She could hear the belt of his football pants banging around the dryer in the basement. "I really wanted to win," he said, "I really wanted to." His head still tucked easily under her chin then.

Right up to the moment when the first pill was still floating in her mouth at the clinic, she felt a bit less than certain, but she knew that in a month or so it would be okay, that she had always wanted just one, that she wouldn't be lonely forever. Something about the sadness and indifference she'd felt in the hotel that night had given her clarity, an ability, for now, to know what she wanted day to day. She was figuring out how to cut her play to an hour if they were accepted into the Fringe; she was serving meals once a week at a downtown shelter; she and Maxwell were making experimental smoothies. When she needed to, she put on headphones, and Mike Heron sang, "*Me, I know you like I know the song in my soul / It's gonna be all right.*"

She looked down to resume reading, but a twitch of her leg unclipped the book light from the paperback, and when the light hit the ground, she closed the novel without marking her place. A mannish figure walking awkwardly in what seemed to be cycling clothes was scouring the park in the distance. Maxwell was lined up now as wide receiver, all spring-loaded and serious, his fingers drumming the air. The snap was high, but this time the erratic quarterback responded smoothly, caught the ball in front of his face, surveyed the field, saw a yellow helmet advancing, and threw a spiral nicely attuned to Maxwell's route. Karyn hadn't learned the names of the routes, but she could follow this one's hairlike curve as Maxwell accelerated, his gait somewhat splayed, toward the arcing ball. He readied his hands as he'd been taught to, thumb touching thumb, forefinger touching forefinger, a position that, Karyn had noticed before, formed an interior shape somehow more like a Russian cathedral's onion dome than a mere onion. Right before making the catch, whether he needed to or not, he leapt.

LITERATURE
is not the same thing as
PUBLISHING

Funder Acknowledgments

Coffee House Press is an internationally renowned independent book publisher and arts nonprofit based in Minneapolis, MN; through its literary publications and *Books in Action* program, Coffee House acts as a catalyst and connector—between authors and readers, ideas and resources, creativity and community, inspiration and action.

Coffee House Press books are made possible through the generous support of grants and donations from corporate giving programs, state and federal support, family foundations, and the many individuals who believe in the transformational power of literature. This activity is made possible by the voters of Minnesota through a Minnesota State Arts Board Operating Support grant, thanks to the legislative appropriation from the arts and cultural heritage fund and a grant from the Wells Fargo Foundation Minnesota. Coffee House also receives major operating support from the Amazon Literary Partnership, the Bush Foundation, the McKnight Foundation, Target, and the National Endowment for the Arts (NEA). To find out more about how NEA grants impact individuals and communities, visit www.arts.gov. Special project support for this title was received from the Jerome Foundation.

Coffee House Press receives additional support from many anonymous donors; the Alexander Family Foundation; the Archer Bondarenko Munificence Fund; the Elmer L. & Eleanor J. Andersen Foundation; the David & Mary Anderson Family Foundation; the Buuck Family Foundation; the Carolyn Foundation; the Dorsey & Whitney Foundation; Dorsey & Whitney LLP; the Knight Foundation; the Matching Grant Program of the Minneapolis Foundation; the Rehael Fund of the Minneapolis Foundation; the Schwab Charitable Fund; Schwegman, Lundberg & Woessner, P.A.; the Scott Family Foundation; the US Bank Foundation; VSA Minnesota for the Metropolitan Regional Arts Council; the Archie D. & Bertha H. Walker Foundation; and the Woessner Freeman Family Foundation.

The Publisher's Circle of Coffee House Press

Publisher's Circle members make significant contributions to Coffee House Press's annual giving campaign. Understanding that a strong financial base is necessary for the press to meet the challenges and opportunities that arise each year, this group plays a crucial part in the success of Coffee House's mission.

Recent Publisher's Circle members include many anonymous donors, Mr. & Mrs. Rand L. Alexander, Suzanne Allen, Patricia A. Beithon, Bill Berkson & Connie Lewallen, the E. Thomas Binger & Rebecca Rand Fund of the Minneapolis Foundation, Robert & Gail Buuck, Claire Casey, Louise Copeland, Jane Dalrymple-Hollo, Mary Ebert & Paul Stembler, Chris Fischbach & Katie Dublinski, Kaywin Feldman & Jim Lutz, Katharine Freeman, Sally French, Jocelyn Hale & Glenn Miller, Roger Hale & Nor Hall, Randy Hartten & Ron Lotz, Jeffrey Hom, Carl & Heidi Horsch, Kenneth Kahn & Susan Dicker, Stephen & Isabel Keating, Kenneth Koch Literary Estate, Jennifer Komar & Enrique Olivarez, Allan & Cinda Kornblum, Leslie Larson Maheras, Jim & Susan Lenfestey, Sarah Lutman & Rob Rudolph, the Carol & Aaron Mack Charitable Fund of the Minneapolis Foundation, George & Olga Mack, Joshua Mack, Gillian McCain, Mary & Malcolm McDermid, Sjur Midness & Briar Andresen, Peter Nelson & Jennifer Swenson, Marc Porter & James Hennessy, Jeffrey Scherer, Jeffrey Sugerman & Sarah Schultz, Nan G. & Stephen C. Swid, Patricia Tilton, Stu Wilson & Melissa Barker, Warren D. Woessner & Iris C. Freeman, Margaret Wurtele, and Joanne Von Blon.

For more information about the Publisher's Circle and other ways to support Coffee House Press books, authors, and activities, please visit www.coffeehousepress.org/support or contact us at info@coffeehousepress.org.

Coffee House Press began as a small letterpress operation in 1972 and has grown into an internationally renowned nonprofit publisher of literary fiction, essay, poetry, and other work that doesn't fit neatly into genre categories.

Coffee House is both a publisher and an arts organization. Through our *Books in Action* program and publications, we've become interdisciplinary collaborators and incubators for new work and audience experiences. Our vision for the future is one where a publisher is a catalyst and connector.

Dylan Hicks Recommends

The Play and Other Stories
by Stephen Dixon

Selected Poems
by Mark Ford

Miniatures
by Norah Labiner

The Pink Institution
by Selah Saterstrom

The Moon in Its Flight
by Gilbert Sorrentino

Dylan Hicks is a writer and musician. His first novel, *Boarded Windows,* was published in 2012, along with a companion album of original songs, *Dylan Hicks Sings Bolling Greene.* His journalism has appeared in the *Village Voice,* the *New York Times,* the *Guardian,* the *Star Tribune, City Pages, Rain Taxi,* and elsewhere. He lives in Minneapolis with his wife, Nina Hale, and their son, Jackson.

Amateurs was designed by Bookmobile
Design & Digital Publisher Services.
Text is set in Arno Pro, a face designed by Robert Slimbach
and named after the river that runs through Florence.